MW00943134

Current Affairs
A Tiara Investigations Mystery

by

Lane Stone

Cover Designer: Karen A. Phillips

All rights reserved

Names, characters and incidents depicted in this book are products of the author's imagination or are used fictitiously. Any resemblance to actual events, organizations, or persons, living or dead, is entirely coincidental and beyond the intent of the author or the publisher.

No part of this book may be reproduced or transmitted in any form or by any means, electronic or mechanical, including photocopying, recording, or by any information storage and retrieval system, without permission in writing from the publisher.

Copyright © 2011 by Lane Stone

Published in the United States of America

2011

First Published in the United States by Mainly Murder Press
PO Box 290586
Wethersfield, CT 06129-0586

To Pat and Sue Stone

~

Acknowledgments

It's been said that a good friend will bail you out of jail at three in the morning, but a true friend will be sitting next to you in the cell saying, "Damn, that was fun." Since this is primarily a book about women's friendship and support, I have to thank my own BFFs for making my world a happy place: Keeley Carter, Ellen Pollack, Terrie Simpson, Patrice Wilde, and Theresa Wood.

Next, a big cheer for all the members of Sisters in Crime, both writers and readers, for all you do for women writers. I particularly want to thank Marcia Talley, author of the Hannah Ives mystery series, for her help with the sailing section; and Susan Schreyer, author of the Thea Campbell mystery series, for helping me with the equestrian section. Then there's Jacqueline Corcoran, my amazing critique partner. Our books are so different, but you never once said, "What the ...?"

Thanks and love to my husband, Larry Korb. Over twenty years ago I told him, "We may not be married forever, but I'll bet I can make it seem like it." How am I doing?

And to you, reader. I hope this book makes you laugh and say, "Damn, that was fun."

Stay in touch.

Lane

One

Statement by Leigh Reed. The FBI Special Agent told me to start writing and to begin from the beginning. The subject of this statement is the late Mr. Taylor. Not late as in tardy, late as in taking a dirt nap, which he has been doing since last Friday night.

At the time it seemed the bullet that had killed our client's husband might have done the same to Tiara Investigations. Now I'll tell you how three former beauty queens, living in a sunny Atlanta suburb, created a successful detective agency and saved the world. You can thank us later. I'm Leigh Reed.

I'd have to say that as far as we're concerned, the real beginning of the David Taylor case was when a certain police detective's wife hired us. She stayed with him, and he has stayed on us like a bad rash, like white on rice, like trouble to a fool. You get the idea.

Tara, Victoria and I met at our usual table at the Cracker Barrel in Suwanee after the breakfast rush Monday, two weeks ago, the first week of October, and waited for our client. I arrived first, and Victoria came in about five minutes later followed by Tara. They did exactly what I do every time I come in. They took a long sniff, inhaling the aroma of the best cooking in the world.

Gina Kent arrived ten minutes late. I held out my hand to her. "I'm Leigh. We spoke on the phone."

She looked at us one by one, checking us out. "Why did you pick this place? I thought I would never find it."

As a greeting this was a tad short of the mark, and I was
pleased to see the waitress walk up with her order pad. "I'll
have the Country Morning Breakfast, eggs sunny side up, no
meat, and a breakfast dessert of fried apples." Tara and
Victoria ordered the Smokehouse Breakfast, and our client
chose the aptly named Breakfast Sampler Special. That's the
one with six meat choices.

"You said you had trouble getting here? I'm so sorry." If
anyone other than Tara had answered her, it would have
sounded sarcastic. I kept my mouth shut because I know my
own limitations.

"We can just about see Interstate 85 from where we're
sitting." Victoria sounded almost not-Southern with that last
comment. She's sweet and direct at the same time. And
brainy as hell but usually patient with those of us who aren't.

"I didn't come on I-85. You didn't say to."

"I said, 'It's right off I-85 at exit 111, in Suwanee'." So far
this was not a typical first interview.

"I didn't know that's what you meant." Surprisingly
enough, she wasn't embarrassed about it. "I tend to get lost a
lot. My husband calls it unintentional kidnapping when I
have anyone else in the car."

Quoting something funny he said? Not a good sign. The
clients we like best want to go to divorce court with hard
evidence. Believe it or not, "Who are you going to believe, me
or your lying eyes?" is alive and well.

"Would you tell us why you suspect your husband?" It
might have sounded cryptic, but we both knew exactly what I
was talking about. Then I sat back and observed her. Mrs.
Kent had blonde, chin-length hair and a square jaw. She wore
khaki shorts, a black polo shirt and leather sandals. I guessed
she was in her mid-thirties. We had ten years, give or take, on
her. She addressed me, and Tara and Victoria leaned in to
listen to what she had to say. It was all pretty standard:

unaccounted-for periods of time and money, phone calls he wouldn't take in front of her, wearing his music player earphones during lovemaking. Okay, I made that last one up.

We said we would take the case and told her to call us when she suspected something was up, and we would follow him. She left, and we stayed to pay the bill.

"Guess what today is?" Then Victoria answered her own question. "It's the one year anniversary of our first case." I looked, I mean really looked, at her when she said this. She's five feet six inches with dark brown hair and looks like the T.V. heroine who throws off her glasses and shakes out her hair to make the leading man forget his own name. I saw something different. She was happy, but she definitely had something on her mind.

~

Gina Kent called the Wednesday after our initial meeting to say her husband planned to take a long lunch, verbally italicizing the words. We scrambled into action. Victoria picked up Tara, then me, and we got to the police station just before noon. We hadn't been sitting there five minutes when he came out and got in a shiny red Ford Escort rather than one of the three Crown Victorias lined up in front.

Victoria followed him west on Highway 20, keeping back just far enough for comfort. "Look what he's driving. A real player, right?"

Tara kept her eyes on the Ford while she spoke. "Obviously not compensating for anything."

I had been typing notes on my laptop and looked up. "Something doesn't feel right. There's no tentativeness, no looking around, no overly cautious driving."

Victoria passed another car, then returned to the right lane where she could innocently turn off at a moment's notice. "I know what you mean. People sneaking around are usually guarded. Why does a plumber or an exterminator think he is so fascinating that someone might recognize him and call the six o'clock news team? Really, the only person who cares is at home."

I put my computer away before I got carsick. "I think Detective Jerome Kent is so arrogant he cannot imagine anyone would have the gall to follow him. Or maybe he just feels he belongs everywhere. Did you notice that when he walked to his car, he never so much as looked around?"

We followed him into the city of Hartfield Hills, where I live. While we're only seventeen thousand souls, the town is anything but sleepy. There's a steady flow of traffic all day long. On Suwanee Dam Road I pointed out a brand new assisted living facility across from the golf course. "I may never have to leave this town again." Then we passed my subdivision. A couple of miles later Suwanee Dam Road ends at Buford Dam Road. He turned left. We turned left. We drove over the dam, on our left a grassy slope dropping to the Chattahoochee River and to our right rocks leading down to Lake Lanier.

The Ford Escort pulled off at West Bank Park, just past the dam. We followed and photographed. Victoria even slowed down for Tara to take one of the sign at the entrance. In the 1950s the U.S. Army Corps of Engineers built Buford Dam to hold the Chattahoochee and Chestatee Rivers, creating the lake.

There were all kinds of parking spaces available, but he pulled in next to a late model Corvette. A twenty-something girl jumped out. Literally.

"If you can afford a Corvette, you can afford a decent bra," Tara said.

Victoria left the engine running to cover the sound of the three cameras. "Are we still in Gwinnett County? I thought I saw the Forsyth County line."

I summoned memories from my Park Ranger days. "A small portion of Lake Lanier is included in the Gwinnett County Police North Precinct, but it's not this part."

Tara was getting her camera ready to go again. "I imagine he doesn't want to be seen by other officers, but he can't be too far out of his jurisdiction."

The fool around-ee ran up to Detective Kent and laid a big, juicy one on him. She was definitely braless, but no one was hurt. The disposable cameras went click. She took a picnic basket out of the car and handed it to him to carry. Natch, she had to thank him for that, so she kissed him again. With arms around waists they headed to a walking trail.

"Real nature lovers, I see." Victoria said this tongue in cheek, but nearly seven hundred miles of the lake's shoreline is wooded to this day.

We decided we could do with a walk ourselves and changed shoes. Good thing the dogs weren't with us that day, because they're not allowed in this particular park. We don't usually bring them on daytime stakeouts anyway, because it can get too warm in the car.

I double-tied my shoelaces and started toward the path. "Can you smell that cologne? Why did his wife hire us? She could have just driven around town until she smelled him."

"Yeah, but that odor would still be around an hour after he'd left," was Tara's comeback.

The cheating, lying, sneaking lovers covered a concrete table with a vinyl cloth and then they did something really bad. They took out enough food to feed an army. They ate chicken that was fried, not grilled. Add to that deviled eggs, baked beans and potato salad. Then the cornbread. Good

Lord. It was almost more than we could take, but we kept our
professionalism.

"How many carbs do you think are in cornbread?"
Victoria was staring at the table.

"I don't know, but I bet it has bad fats." We had to get out
of there. None of us photographed them eating. There was
something about it that was so intimate we would not have
wanted to show those to the wife.

As we hiked back to the parking lot and were out of
earshot, I brought up an item of Tiara business. "I'm not wild
about our signal to get out of the house. I know it's Three Dog
Night because of our three dogs, but I've never been a fan of
seventies music. And it's so obviously code for something.
Who goes around saying 'three dog night'? I'm telling you,
it's a struggle to work it into a conversation."

Tara stopped walking. "How about, 'On my signal
prepare to unleash hell'?"

"Oh, that's subtle."

"I have a suggestion. How about, 'Do you know Eve
Wood?'" We waited for Vic to tell us more. Instead, she
looked back down the trail, lost in thought.

"Hon?" Tara touched her arm. Victoria smiled and
started walking again. She slid behind the wheel of her Lexus
SUV.

"My husband has become a man of small appetites."

I pictured Shorty's wiry body and stiff limbs and
understood that by appetite Vic meant passions or desires.
Tara and I looked at each other and got in the car. We didn't
speak. She hadn't asked us to fix it for her, and she didn't
need us to tell her if it was or was not a problem.

"Or maybe Frank's always been that way, and I'm just
now noticing," Victoria added.

"Frank? Not Shorty?" I asked.

"He doesn't deserve a nickname."

Both Victoria Blair's children are grown. After running the regional office of a dot com for years, she was sick of the hours, the politics and having to prove herself every time upper management in Oregon rotated mid-level managers through the Atlanta region. She wanted out. Victoria was married to Frank "Shorty" Gale, Medical Director for Cardiac Services at Gwinnett County General Hospital, so relocation was not an option for her. She and Shorty introduced Tara to Paul, an OB-GYN who's crazy about her and with whom she was having hot sex, if you happen to run into her ex. It should be noted here that Paul's not like us. He's from the *North*. Enough said? But the fact that Tara Brown has a body made for sin takes care of most communications problems.

As for me, I left the Park Service and started moving every few years for my husband, The General's, career. He is, well, let's say he's away on business. If I've learned one thing, it's that the danger in being gently reared is a life that looks good on paper only. In 1980 I was Miss Georgia. I might as well tell you that, because you would learn it from my mother sooner or later. That's all my mother seems to know about me. I have always felt that entering the county pageant, which started the ball rolling, was the biggest mistake of my life, because I have spent the rest of said life trying to avoid being a cliché.

I met Victoria and Tara at the pageant, and when I moved back to Georgia, we reconnected. I've never been happier. My husband says I still have a face that can start a fight, which makes me smile, but it's not enough. It never has been and it never will be. And I hate to say it, but I take material blessings for granted. Tiara Investigations has given me what I was looking for—a good reason to get up in the morning.

~

At the time we were indeed using yellow disposable cameras, and you might be wondering why. On our first stakeout Tara got in the car with a K-Mart shopping bag. Yes, K-Mart. She had been charged with getting camera equipment, and I was anxious to lay my hands on some real high tech, professional private eye gear. When we parked at the end of our client's street, Tara reached into the bag and brought out three yellow disposable cameras and handed us each one.

"What are these?" I turned mine over and over in my hand.

"You know how I'm always losing things? I don't have to worry with these. And you know how sometimes pictures don't turn out the way you thought they would? Well, this way we can all take photographs, you know, increasing our odds."

"Right." That was so Tara, standing at five feet four inches, add two or three if she's wearing heels, and tossing her auburn-streaked brown hair. I'm tallest at five feet eight inches, and I have brown hair with blond highlights and hazel eyes. These are not the hair colors we were born with; they're the ones we chose.

~

I called Gina Kent that afternoon after the photographs were developed. "Where would you like us to meet? Should come to your house?"

"No," she answered almost before I got the question out. "I don't know what time he's coming home from work."

"You want to wait until tomorrow morning to meet?"

"Yes. Can we meet at the same place? I sort of remember where it is."

"Sure. We don't need to go in. We can sit in my car and talk." Showing a wife these photos in the restaurant? No, thank you, we do not want to be banned from Cracker Barrel.

So the next morning there we were, sitting and waiting for the Mrs. Then we sat and waited some more.

"Uh, Leigh?"

"Yeah, Victoria?"

"Can we discuss your bumper sticker?"

"I ALREADY OPPOSE THE NEXT WAR. It's new. Do you like it?"

"Well, we're supposed to be undercover. That makes your car identifiable."

"Oh, okay, I'll take it off." I'm not a namby-pamby person, she was just right.

Tara was in the back seat. "My dad always said you should learn something new every day. Now you can take the rest of the day off."

"Is that her? There she goes!" Victoria pointed at a Mazda just like the one Gina Kent drives.

"And there she went. It was her. Good, she's turning around." I got out of the car, hoping she would see me.

Tara got out and stood with me. "She's passing us again." With the next pass she saw us and made an illegal U-turn.

Once we got her inside my car, we showed her the photographs. It was odd. Sure, she was mad, that's to be expected, but she seemed to be doing a triumphant victory lap in her head. I imagined her getting lost doing it and had to get hold of myself quickly.

Tara reached over and rubbed little circles on Mrs. Kent's back. We hate this part of the job with a passion. Sure, she came to us, but it still hurts to be the bearer of wounding news. And my friend knew what it was like on the receiving end all too well.

Gina gripped the photographs and then slid them into her canvas handbag. "Where's the binder?"

Victoria spoke up. "We don't do binders."

"And the write-up from the background check?"

"We don't do background checks." I was still twisted in my seat to address her. "We stick to who's, I mean what's, happening today. And, Mrs. Kent, with your husband being on the police force, he might find out a background check had been run on him."

She took this into consideration, but still gave a *hrmph*.

Tara continued to pat our client. "We help people."

Gina glanced at her handbag containing the photos as if to say, "Oh, yeah, you help people all right." She shrugged Tara off and huffed out of the car. "I hope I can find my way home from here." She looked around.

"Are you going to be all right? We can drive to your house, and you can follow us, just to be sure you get home okay. " That's Tara, nice to the end. I had started the car, and Vic was texting someone.

"No, I'm fine."

We watched her pull out of the parking lot and turn in the opposite direction of her house.

Tara banged her head a couple of times on the headrest. "Arghhh! We really did start Tiara Investigations to help women who can't afford big-time detective agencies."

She paused for confirmation and I gave it right away. "Yeah! When your marriage was all over but the shouting, you paid an ungodly sum to the one you used. A lot of women can't afford that."

I would like to write that achieving a money-making detective agency with a one hundred percent success rate, if I do say so myself, is due to brilliance, courage, and skill. Our little detective agency has all that—well, to some degree—but truth be told, much of our business growth is due to our pricing structure. When we first started, we were cheap. Not value priced. I mean blue light, final clearance cheap. Our billing plan is simple. We charge by the hour, not the day. The client calls us, and we leave immediately for the restaurant, hotel, bar, whatever. This seems to be empowering for her, usually a her, and she saves money. This manner of doing business has also made it possible for us to keep up our double lives as wives, or in Tara's case girlfriend, and private detectives.

Victoria turned to face Tara in the back seat. "To be fair, we had another motive for starting our own detective agency. We're going to be fifty pretty soon, and we knew if we didn't make some changes we would never have the lives we wanted."

Tara reached between the seats to our shoulders. "If I'm honest about it, revenge played a teensy part for me. Infidelity comes with a side order of gas lighting. That's what hurt the most. If we could spare some woman, somewhere, that torment, we had to go for it."

I pulled onto Lawrenceville-Suwanee Road. "Did you see her slip the photos in her bag?"

"Should we have told her we always give the client the photos?" Victoria looked up from her phone. "And how did she know about binders and background checks?"

"She's not new at this." It was such a nice crisp and clear day that I opened the sunroof.

"Something tells me, neither is he," Tara said.

We left without eating, which is not like us, but giving that kind of news ruins one's appetite. Anyway, we needed spa therapy in the worst way. With our first few cases we realized we had to do something to let the case go emotionally. High Hill Day Spa fits the bill nicely. I feel myself relax when the hostess parts the ornate walnut double doors. Once inside, where new age music seems to have turned all the walls lavender, you're escorted to a dressing room and handed your beverage of choice. All the estheticians are friendly. In Hartfield Hills no points (or big tips) are given for pretentiousness.

We developed a post-case routine of Tara calling her boyfriend and Victoria calling her husband. I e-mail The General. We tell them we love them and hear them say the same. The facials make us look really good, and two of the three of us have sex that night. After Victoria's comment the day before, I wouldn't swear on a stack of Bibles that she had continued that part. At the time of this case we drank heavily at the spa. This particular day, Tara's breakfast had been coffee. You see where I'm going.

Ronald, our favorite masseur, came in for my deep tissue massage and closed the door. "I can't believe you three are private detectives. I had no idea."

If our own husbands don't know, how would our rubdown-divine-being pick up that little fact? No one knows but our clients and the jurors in the two cases that went to court. I jerked up, forgetting about my current state, which was naked.

"Tara just told me about the case with the police detective. Good for you!"

"Ronald, she should not have told you about that. Please promise me you won't tell anyone." He gave me his word, and that was good enough for me. If you can't trust a masseur, who can you trust?

From the massage table to the manicurist I went, following in Tara's wake. The manicurist congratulated me on the case, as did Sherry when I got my pedicure. I didn't call Tara's cell phone because I was tipsy myself. In the limousine ride home, I talked to Tara about the need for confidentiality.

Victoria was scrubbing some kind of exotic oil off her glasses. "You would think it's okay to drink at a spa but not a tattoo parlor. Anywho, I think our rule should be, no more drinking on spa days."

"Ooooh, it wasn't the drinks, it was the massage. Or maybe the combination. After the first half hour I just started chattering."

The combination was lethal and not consistent with real P.I. behavior, besides being inconsiderate to our clients. We agreed to hold each other to our no-drinking-while spa-ing rule.

The headband the facialist used had left Tara's bangs sticking straight up, and she started working on calming them down. "No binders, no background checks, no bullets, and now no booze. Got it!"

We were feeling pretty good about our new, more professional way of doing business. Until we saw the Ford Escort sitting in my driveway, that is.

Victoria pointed to her gold wristwatch and arched her right eyebrow.

Tara shook her head, no. There hadn't been time for him to learn about us from the spa and get over here.

I tapped my wedding band. They both gave one nod, yes. It hadn't taken much detective work to figure out that his wife had confronted him, and when he demanded she tell him how she knew, she had sung like a canary.

We got out of the limo, and I tipped the driver a fifty. Detective Kent walked towards us. He looked mad as hell. "So you three are private investigators?" There was a beat between each word, never a good sign.

At Buford Dam I had noted his looks well enough to match him up with our photograph. My attention was focused on who he was with. Now I took a closer look. The detective was taller than average, slim build, and every blond hair in place. I would guess mid-forties. He enunciated each syllable, wreaking havoc on his Southern accent. The wind was blowing, and as he spoke he had to keep turning to protect his hair. We three circled to keep up with the pivoting of this human weather vane.

"I'd like to see your license." We invited him to come inside and wait while I got the folder with our documentation. Abby was barking and jumping in her excitement to see me, as well as Tara and Victoria. The detective, not so much.

He started to climb the stairs after me, and Tara stopped him, "We can wait down here while Leigh goes up to get what you want." The look he gave her and then Victoria would have done Clint Eastwood proud. He was loaded for bear, but so was Tara. He did wait downstairs. When I looked down the staircase from the top he was staring up at me. I loosened the death grip I had on the mahogany banister, went into my home office and closed the door. I leaned back against it and almost fainted. I'm not the kind of person that has to be liked by everyone I meet. Because I don't talk about myself very much and I don't walk around smiling like a jackass chewing briars, I put up with a certain amount of being misunderstood. I wasn't afraid, but I felt dread when I thought about his expression. It fell short of hate but hurt just as much. He was dismissive of Tiara Investigations. Something else occurred to me. If he was mad at what we had learned about him, what if he found out that half of the city's beauty industry knew it also?

Holding the folders of test results, certificates and letters, I really wished I had photocopies. I put my ear up to the door and listened. All was quiet in the foyer so I sent the documents through the copier as quick as they would go. I took a deep breath and hurried back downstairs to my friends.

Detective Kent went through the folder, tossing each sheet over as he scanned. His manner and the looks he shot us said that as much as we disgusted him, everything was in order.

"I could have told you it would be. Everything this woman owns is alphabetized. She's the only person I know that has a rental car washed before she returns it." Though I couldn't really see the relevance of Tara's last flattering remark, I started to relax a little because of her confidence in me.

On his way out he turned to me. "Your problem is you know nothing about romance."

I never expected such a personal comment from him. Maybe it's contagious, because I never expected a personal comment out of my own mouth either. "The three of us have forgotten more about love than you will ever know."

"So what case are you working on now?"

"Oh, we're looking for Jimmy Hoffa's baby. Wish us luck."

He squinted at me. "Wouldn't that be the Lindbergh …?" Better late than never, he realized it was a joke and stalked out, leaving the front door open like he was raised in a barn.

We watched through the living room window, and Victoria spoke first. "A regular fashionisto." He was wearing stovepipe jeans and a short leather jacket, not a good look for someone so short-waisted.

Tara walked away from the window. "He thinks he has a nice butt."

I led them to the kitchen and got the tea pitcher out of the refrigerator. "So we've learned a second lesson for the day. Number one was, do not get drunk in a tattoo parlor or a day spa. Number two, never trust a scared person."

"Scared? I didn't get the impression she was abused, did you?" Victoria reached for a packet of stevia.

I handed her an ice tea spoon. "No, afraid of losing him."

Tara pointed at me with Vic's spoon. "If you ask me, it was Stockholm syndrome that made her tell him about us. He's supposed to be the bad guy, and she sided with him."

Since then, either he's following us, or it's just a coincidence that we run into him almost daily.

~

That afternoon we played golf and started three new cases. One concerned the subject of this statement, the very dead Mr. Taylor.

Most Thursday afternoons you can find us on the golf course. We don't know if we are any good at golf or not because we don't usually keep score past the first hole. If I had to guess I'd say we're probably not that good. According to our rules you can pick up your ball if you have to go to the bathroom, if you make a bad shot, if the snack cart comes by, if you're too hot and you wish the snack cart would come by, if you either get or remember you need to make a phone call and you have to sneak your cell phone out of your bag, if you forget how many strokes you've taken, if you have taken too many strokes, if you thought you had taken your turn and you hadn't, if you just then notice another player is wearing a new outfit, if a famous actress dies, or if the stock market dips. Anyway, it helps us finish nine holes in a reasonable amount of time.

Kelly Taylor's call to our business line was transferred to my cell phone as we drove our carts to the third hole. These calls have a distinctive ring that Victoria downloaded onto our phones, so the others knew to, first, hide me from any pesky marshal that might be driving around trying to enforce course rules, and second, only have professional sounding noises in the background. We agreed to meet her at Cracker

Barrel at five o'clock. I was wrapping up the conversation, so Tara went to the red marker to tee off. Mrs. Taylor had one more question for me, "By the way, what is your hourly rate?"

"Fore!" Tara says this each time she tees off just in case.

"Four hundred an hour? That's fine. I'll see you this afternoon."

"Wait, I, I …," but she had hung up.

And just like that our fee went from one hundred an hour to four hundred.

Two

Continuation of statement by Leigh Reed. The three of us arrived at the Cracker Barrel before our client, Kelly Taylor. I found a parking space near the entrance to this little piece of heaven. The asphalt lot was surrounded by contrived landscaping. The trees were mathematically equidistant from each other, and the leaves were burgundy, orange, gold, and salmon. Along the front porch the world's most comfortable rocking chairs were lined up. I guess management's afraid they would be stolen, because they're bolted down. Mingled in with the plain rocking chairs were a few with the University of Georgia Bulldog insignia and two church pews.

When Kelly Taylor approached the table, I stood up and shook her hand. She was African-American, and I noticed she was about my height. She looked me in the eye, and her handshake was firm. She wasn't embarrassed to be there. No wife should be; the husband is the one who should be mortified. I liked her right away. Later, looking at her seated, she seemed, well, shorter and smaller. That day her hair was pulled back in a chignon, and she wore tiny pearl earrings. That's pretty much how the rest of the meeting went, my impression of her switching back and forth. Some of her mannerisms reinforced a demure façade, and some contradicted. One minute she was hard and tough as steel, and then with the next glance you thought she was going to cry. Who was the real Kelly Taylor?

I started the interview by asking her to tell us about her husband. "He's thirty-three years old, four years older than me. He's very intelligent. He owns his own consulting firm."

She said she loved him even though he was not romantic or demonstrative. When asked to give a more complete physical description, she had to think for a few seconds. Me, I can describe every hair on The General's head. Still, she claimed to be in love with him.

As I went about getting the information we needed to begin a case, I noticed she was pulling back into her chair. This made me wonder if I was coming across like I was grilling her. That was certainly not my intent. I stopped speaking, knowing that one of my colleagues would pick up on this.

Victoria took over. "What has made you suspect your husband of being up to no good?"

"Sometimes when I come into a room and he's on the telephone, he hangs up."

"Anything else?" I was glad Vic asked this because I hate wild goose chases.

"David used to work in his home office about half the time. In the last few months he's been spending more and more time at his office in Peachtree Corners. Lately he's been going there at night, or so he says. My husband has changed. That's all I know."

Most of her concern was due to a vague, but unmistakable, feeling that something was altered. We took the case based on that fact. She'd noticed this change a few months after they bought their new house in Duluth, Georgia. This was to be their dream house. We wrote down the license plate number of his car and all the addresses we might need. As we passed around the photo of the black, tall, slender man in glasses, I was pretty sure we were all thinking the same thing, "There is no type." Anybody can try their damndest to screw up their life, and there's no better way than infidelity.

Victoria continued on with the interview. "Might he have clients on the west coast that would necessitate him being at the office at night for teleconferences with them?"

"I know his biggest client is in Atlanta, that's why we moved here. But I don't know where the rest of his clients' offices are. This one is the only one I've heard him talk about."

Good, I thought. We try to throw in one easy out in the first meeting. It's a convenient way for clients to go into, or back into, denial. Kelly could have said or thought, 'Oh, yeah, clients on the west coast. That's probably it.' She didn't, meaning she was ready to hear whatever we would be telling her. I take that back, no wife or husband is ever ready to hear it. Kelly would be able to hear it.

Tara picked up a menu. "Want to order something? Tea or a dessert?"

I ordered apple pie, the no-sugar-added version, with ice cream. Victoria went with the chocolate cobbler, Tara the cobbler of the day, blueberry if I remember correctly, and then we looked at Kelly, waiting for her to say something.

She giggled, "I'll have the carrot cake."

"A seasonal choice, excellent." Tara gathered up the menus.

"And four sweet teas," the waitress said as she walked away. It wasn't a question. Like I said, we're regulars.

"Can I ask you something?" Kelly really did sound like a little girl when she spoke.

"Sure."

"Where are you from? You don't sound like you're from here."

"All three of us are native Atlantans. I was born in Crawford Long Hospital. I have an Atlanta accent instead of a Southern accent. Believe me, people up North say my accent is quite pronounced, and I lived outside the country for almost ten years."

"Outside the country." She was imitating me, like I had spoken in a foreign language and she wanted to be sure she got it right. "I've always wanted to travel. Are you sisters?"

"No," we said together, laughing.

"Then why do you dress alike?"

We were wearing jeans and white blouses. Yes, all three of us. The blouses were a little different but not enough to matter. Oh, and our shoes were different. Big whoop. I wore Donald J. Pliner thong sandals, and Tara and Victoria both wore boots, Tara in Stuart Weitzman suede boots laced up outside her jeans and Victoria in Calvin Klein riding boots.

"We didn't do it on purpose." Shit. I had hoped she wouldn't notice.

Three

Continuation of statement by Leigh Reed. On Friday morning I was at Publix buying groceries when I noticed a man following me with his cart. This annoyed me no end, so I turned around and headed his way. This might sound hypocritical, considering what I do for a living, but who did he think he was?

"Excuse me, ma'am. Is your name Leigh?" He was young and muscular with a buzz cut.

"Yes, it is."

"I served under your husband in both Gulf wars. I'm Roger Wilson. I met you at a reception a few years back."

I exhaled and felt my shoulders relax. I told him it was good to see him, and we rolled our carts down the aisles, collecting items. He seemed to want to tell me something. Twice he went as far as stopping his cart and facing me. He just needed time to get it out. I put three Granny Smith apples in my cart and smiled when he did the same. Then we headed to the soup aisle.

"We used to laugh about how little he socializes."

"I know. He's a man of few words." I had to laugh myself.

"One day we had gone into a village and wound up in a firefight before we knew what was happening. We were crawling on our bellies, and then I heard him say, 'Wilson,' in my earpiece. I was lying there thinking, wow, the General knows my name. He said, 'Head down,' and then I heard two quick shots. I looked up to see that he had shot an insurgent's hand off with a gun still in it and then shot the bas … him in the head."

I shivered, and he continued, "The next week I heard him in my earpiece again, telling me to halt. I did just before I would have detonated an IED. He had noticed the disturbed section of dirt they tell us to look for. That night I got up my nerve and approached him in the mess tent. I thanked him and said I would like to speak to him some time other than when he was saving my life. He looked up from the table and smiled." Here he did a pretty good imitation of The General's slow grin. "Then he said, 'Well, son, that's not a trade I'd make, but it's up to you.'"

"Thank you for telling me that," I said with difficulty.

"You're certainly welcome." It was hard for him to speak, too. "I'll be leaving for my third deployment this afternoon."

"Why are you buying groceries if you're about to leave?"

"My mom is pretty upset, and I don't want her to have to do it."

"How long have you been home?" My throat was narrowing fast.

"Two months."

"That's terrible. I think you all should have two years between deployments for retraining."

"Well, hopefully it'll be over soon," he said, avoiding agreeing with me, loyal to the end.

"I hope so, too." I had everything I had come for and more, so I went to get in the checkout line. For the millionth time I thought about how this war should never have started.

Back at home I checked my e-mails, natch, looking for one from my husband. There wasn't one, nor was he online. I have an overstuffed chair covered in velvet tapestry in my little home office, and I let it swallow me up when I sat down to read the newspaper. After starting the same article on North Korea's nuclear weapons tests over and over, I put it down. That was when I went into a funk I couldn't shake. I missed my husband. I was also saying and thinking *my* too much, as in my dog and my house. I felt that my whopper of a secret was hurting our closeness, and being surrounded by, even facilitating divorces for a living didn't help. He was far away, and as isolated as I felt, I still didn't want to tell him about Tiara Investigations.

I couldn't stand being inside any longer, and I realized it had been a while since Abby had been out, so I called her to go for a walk. "I'm taking a bag, just in case you are locked and loaded," using a military term because of where my thoughts had been wandering.

We walked around the block, including a killer hill. As soon as we walked through the door, Abby sprinted to her water bowl. After lapping for about a minute and getting more water in her beard than in her mouth, she returned to me and licked my hand once. She was hungry. I filled her bowl and went to my desk.

I spent a couple of hours working on the business aspect of Tiara Investigations, updating our spreadsheets, preparing a deposit and writing paychecks for Victoria and Tara. Before I knew it the day was about gone, and I had yet to exercise. An hour later Kelly Taylor telephoned and told me about her husband's plans for the evening. The call came in while I was mid-kickboxing video. Interruptions are the norm in doing business the way we do. As I walked upstairs I dialed Tara and then conferenced Victoria in. I told them about the call and asked who wanted to drive.

Victoria said, "I will. Who should I pick up first? Where are we going?"

"Duluth. Pick me up around seven-thirty. That'll give us time to get there and position ourselves."

I took a quick shower and then made myself a peanut butter and honey sandwich dinner.

It was literally and figuratively a three dog night when Tara and her Standard Schnauzer, Stephie joined us in

Victoria's Lexus SUV. "I hope he's not fooling around on his cute little wife."

"Well, he is." I gave Vic's dog, Mr. Benz, a good-to-see-you ear twirl.

"How do you know?" the ever-hopeful Victoria asked.

"He's going to his office for a 9:00 p.m. conference call. He doesn't have a phone at home?"

We let the navigation system lead us to the subdivision, and then we slowed down to read the carved wooden house numbers on the mail boxes. The neighborhood was established, upper middle class. For Duluth, Georgia, that's still not necessarily very old.

"This area was originally called Howell Crossing, but when the railroad connecting it with Duluth, Minnesota, was completed, the name was changed. Did you know Duluth elected Georgia's first woman mayor? Her name was Alice Harrell Strickland, and that was in 1922. She vowed to rid Duluth of that demon rum."

"Thank you, Miss Georgia." Victoria took her eyes off the road and looked at me.

"That's just one bit of Georgia history trivia left over from my years with the Forest Service."

"Are you sure you didn't learn it during your reign?" Tara leaned forward from the back seat.

For a second I couldn't breathe. "You know, you're right. That is where I got that from. I had completely blanked that out. Actually I've put most of that year, and the year before with the county pageant, out of my mind."

"Did you enjoy that year?" For a second there I was afraid Vic might release her ten o'clock, two o'clock hand position.

"Some of the expectations were hard for me."

Tara was still leaning forward, reading house numbers. "What was hard?"

"Talking to visitors about Georgia, for one. Now I know

why. It was because I was so close I couldn't really see. I had to get away and come back to be able to really know Atlanta."

Victoria slowed because we were getting close. "At least you didn't have to be kidded about being Miss Congeniality all year long."

"At least you didn't have to worry about Tara incapacitating you so she could complete your reign."

"Very funny. Why did you enter the pageant if you didn't want to win? I really wanted to win."

"My mother told me my father wanted me to."

"Did he?" Victoria wanted to know.

"He didn't even know about the pageant. Let's get to work."

By the time we parked two houses up from the Taylor's, the dogs had mercifully gone to sleep. We lowered the front and back windows on the driver's side by a few inches and settled in for some serious surveillance, the three of us looking through binoculars—okay, opera glasses. We liked to all be on duty at the same time. My way of turning a sentence into a novel had made the photographer lose her shot a few times on our first cases. Like, "I see him coming out of her condo wearing a yellow shirt, maybe it's a mustard yellow shirt, and actually that's a townhouse, and I am pretty sure the shirt is IZOD. Oh, yeah, and it was the third door down." Well, maybe more than a few times, more like several. Anyway you get the point.

Before long we went back to talking to pass the time. Victoria was filing her nails, short and almost straight across, known as squoval. "You think we might just have a happy ending this time?"

"I went to grammar school with a kid who said he had a friend who had been born out of his mother's butt. He would always add, 'but he's okay now.' That always gave the story, or at least the mother, a happy ending. Literally." Tara shared this touching story with us as she finger-combed Abby's beard. Abby is also a Standard Schnauzer. Picking up a pattern?

"That's gross!"

"That's not gross," Tara said. "I'll tell you what's gross, how much you learn about yourself when you wear black underwear. Now, that's gross."

"Eew," Victoria cringed but couldn't help laughing, and Tara laughed at that.

"You mean disgusting." I've known Tara for a long time, and I'm used to these comments.

"On a more ladylike topic, I'm going to be a grandmother. Twice. Twins." Victoria was smiling but looking befuddled.

"That's wonderful! Really, I am so happy for you," Tara exclaimed. "Is your daughter pregnant or your daughter-in-law?"

"My daughter-in-law."

"So what's that look for? What's the rest of the story?" I mean, I am a detective.

"Well, she's over four months pregnant, and she just told us today."

"Oh, wait. Here he comes. Smoke 'em if you got 'em, boys. We're goin' in." I knew it was David Taylor from the photograph Kelly gave us, and there was the fact that it was his house.

"Huh? Why isn't his garage door opening?" Victoria was whispering like we always do when we see the follow-ee.

"He came out a side door, must have been from the kitchen." During a chase I like to plan three or four moves ahead, and this guy was not helping. Mr. Taylor turned and headed away from the house.

"He's not going to his garage." Tara's voice had just a touch of panic. He walked purposefully down the long, straight driveway, which was flanked on both sides with yellow and purple pansies. At the end he stopped to look around. His one last glance back at the house was not in the usual cheaters' furtive manner. "Where does he think he's going?"

Victoria kept her eyes focused ahead. "We can't exactly ask him, so we need a plan. Just as soon as Leigh thinks of something, we'll have one. Leigh?"

"What do we do if he walks to wherever he's going?" I was thinking aloud, and as much as I would like to say I was shuffling through a deck of possibilities, I didn't have any idea how to follow a walker from a car in a quiet subdivision at night.

"Should we follow him on foot?" Victoria had her hand on the keys waiting for my answer.

Tara lifted up her left foot and put it on the console between the front seats. "In these, no way." She was wearing navy patent three-inch heels.

"Are those new?" Then I got hold of myself. "We can't let him see us sitting here. Let's pass him and then watch to see where he goes. He can't be going far."

"Maybe he's about to get neighborly with someone." Tara rotated her ankle, admiring her own shoes.

Victoria started the car and pulled away from the curb. We hadn't driven but just a few yards when we heard, or felt or sensed, a swish, and Mr. Taylor dropped to the ground. Victoria slammed on the brakes and cut the engine. In a matter of seconds the front of his shirt was soaked in blood.

We didn't duck. Nor did we look around, and that mistake came back to bite us. We left the car sitting in the road and got out. As we scurried to him, I reached for my cell phone and dialed 911.

Tara got there first and fell to her knees to begin administering first aid. She looked up and said, "He's dead." Then she leaned over him and prayed silently.

I couldn't speak, but Victoria had connected with her inner smart ass. "Well, I guess it's a good thing we're not in protective services."

She and I moved away from the body and sat down on the curb to wait for the police.

"We can't just sit here. One of us should go in and tell Kelly what happened. I'd rather it came from one of us instead of a police officer."

An ambulance, followed by a police cruiser with piercing sirens, came around the corner. Detective Kent swaggered up to us. "Muuuuch better," I said when I saw him.

"It just had to be him," Tara said.

"I'll go tell Kelly!" we all volunteered at the same time.

"All right, Victoria, you go tell her. Just hurry."

Unfortunately, she didn't get away in time. "So it's the ladies of Tiara Investigations. You found the body?"

"We saw him get plugged." Victoria turned toward the house.

Tara looked up at the detective. "She's actually very sensitive."

He did a double take at Victoria walking away. "Where does she think she's going?" Victoria stopped where she was. "All right," he continued, when he mistakenly thought he had regained control, "I would like you three to turn over your weapons to the crime scene investigators for analysis."

"The dogs?" Tara yelled out.

"For the love of Pete."

I put my arm around Tara's shoulder. "Sweetie, he means guns." Out of the corner of my eye I saw Victoria slip off to the house. Kelly was looking out a front window, but I didn't know how long she'd been there.

Tara turned to Kent and distracted his attention. "Actually, we feel our society has way too many guns, and we did not want to add to …."

"What's the deceased's name? Did you see who shot him?" This was through clenched teeth, clenched jaw and probably clenched butt, if I cared to look, which I didn't. The Dirty Harry routine had lost its power over me, owing to the fact that a real human had just died, leaving behind a wife and maybe grieving parents, maybe brothers and sisters.

"His name is David Taylor, and we saw him fall. That's all, I'm sorry to say." And I was.

"You didn't see anything else?"

"No." I drew the word out and glanced at Tara.

"How about you? Did you see anything?" he asked Tara.

"No." She had understood my look and was doing her part prolonging this until Victoria could get inside.

Then he looked back at me, "Did you hear anything?"

I just shook my head. "I think we heard the bullet swish by, but we didn't know that's what it was."

"How about you? Did you hear anything?" This to Tara. She also shook her head. I didn't catch his exact words, but by that time I could assume it was, "For the love of Pete."

We stared at him, both of us thinking the same thing. The entire staff of Tiara Investigations had witnessed a murder, but we could not give him one single clue. In our year in business we had helped so many women, ourselves included, and I had a foreboding that it was all slipping away.

Just then we heard a godawful racket coming from our car. "What the hell?" Both Tara and Detective Kent yelled this at the same time. She had almost jumped out of her skin. In any other circumstance, that would have cracked me up. All three dogs were scratching on the SUV window and yelping at the top of their lungs.

"Are those dogs?" Detective Kent was craning his neck to see. I noticed he had stepped in front of her. *What the hell, indeed. What am I chopped liver?*

Tara answered him, "We use our dogs for protection. With the type of cases we specialize in, it works out just fine. This close to menopause, gun toting just didn't seem like a good idea. And why the hell are we talking about menopause at a time like this? "

"We weren't, sweetheart. We were talking about guns." This time she wasn't faking it so Kent would forget about Victoria. She was really getting nervous. I felt she needed a break, and I was guessing the dogs were telling us they did, too, if we ever wanted to use that car again.

Tara put leashes on all three and got them out of the car. A second later they took off down the dark street at a breakneck speed.

Kent stared at the sight. "Is she going to be all right?"

"She'll be fine." *To do – train dogs.*

"No weapons in your vehicle?"

"No-o-o." Victoria joined me and stood by my side. *There would have been if she hadn't gotten those dogs out in time.*

"Has your vehicle been moved since the shooting?" I had read enough mysteries to know this would tell them the direction the bullet had been fired from.

I told him where we had stopped when the shot was fired.

"I'd like to get statements from the three of you. At the station. Tomorrow afternoon."

I said we would be happy to come, like it had been an invitation. Then I looked into the night at Tara and the three dogs.

"I work out of the North Precinct. The office is on Mall of Georgia Boulevard in Buford, next to the mall. Do you need to write that down?"

Me on the outside, "We're good." Me on the inside, *Oh, you mean that police station at the Mall of Georgia where we followed you on your way to have lunch with your girlfriend? That police station?*

I could only imagine how miserable the detective could have made our lives if we'd had guns at a murder scene. Maybe the dogs had provided the best protection after all. This little moment of reverie didn't last long. Kelly Taylor came out the front door with two female officers. She ran up to us at the end of the driveway and grabbed my arms and swung me around.

Tears streamed down her face. "You were here! How did this happen?" From the way Victoria took half a step back and from the surprised look on her face, I guessed this level of upset was different from what she had witnessed in the house for the few minutes she had been with her. Victoria walked around us and embraced her. Kelly let go of my arms and let herself be led away by a police officer.

When I told Detective Kent we would stay with her, he said no, or at least that's the construct I put on his laughing in my face. Tara returned with the dogs, and Victoria and I helped get them off their leashes and back in the Lexus. This added to the swarm of police activity and pretty much busted his give a damn, or so I thought until he swaggered up and stood right in front of me. "You three are untrained, ill equipped and incompetent." He had leaned over to get right in my face. One problem. I'm almost as tall as he is. He had to swoop back up. His comment stung, but I was still standing. Tara and Victoria saw I had the situation in hand and took this as the perfect opportunity to go the house.

"And you're not trying to undermine our credibility with our other clients, are you?" We stared at each other like ten-year-olds for longer than I care to admit. Finally, I walked around him and joined the others on the front porch. A female police officer passed us on her way out.

We three entered a large, sparsely furnished living room. Kelly Taylor was sitting on a citron chintz sofa, hugging her knees. The sofa and a coffee table were the only two pieces of furniture in the room. I looked down the entryway and saw a family room decorated with everything you'd expect. That room was contemporary and casual, but the living room seemed to be headed in a classic direction.

She seemed friendlier to us than she had been outside, so Tara sat down next to her and took her hand. Victoria and I stood near the wall. After expressing our sympathy, we asked a few questions. We wanted something to give Kent the next day. I guess we were just trying to save face—or prove him wrong when we were afraid to think he might be right in his characterization of the business we had built. Although we had not discussed what we would say, the three detectives of Tiara Investigations were singing from the same page of the hymnal.

Victoria went first. "What did your husband say when he told you he was going out?"

"He got a call on his cell phone. He said he had to go back to his office tonight for a nine o'clock conference call. That's when I called you."

"Is his office in walking distance?" I asked.

"No."

She had been through so much and would be going through more in the days and weeks to come. I would not have kept on if I didn't think it was important. "He was shot near the end of the driveway, not near the garage."

This was met with silence so Victoria picked up. "Could he have been meeting someone in the neighborhood?"

"I, I don't know," she stammered. "That's not what he said he was going to do."

Me on the inside, *hel-l-o-o-o, you do remember why you hired us, don't you?* Me on the outside, "Did the police give you David's cell phone?"

She shook her head no.

"I thought we could look at the call history."

"I'll check in the bedroom to see if it's there."

"Thank you." Tara gave her hand another squeeze.

She rose from the sofa, and every step made you tired just to watch. She returned shortly with a cell phone and handed it to me.

"He left it charging."

I gave it to Victoria to write down the phone numbers in the call history. Was the fact that he had left it behind further evidence that he wasn't going far or for long?

The front door opened, and a petite black woman with close cropped salt and pepper hair let herself in. Her lips were pressed into a straight line, and she looked, well, pissed. This was an emotion I didn't really understand given the circumstances. Anyway, she had First Baptist Church of Anywhere written all over her.

"Mom!" Kelly ran to her, and they embraced.

We looked at our shoes, then at one another. Kelly needed her mom, not us. They were doing what normal families do when tragedy comes calling. Tiara Investigations left, and on the way out we told her we would telephone the next day.

I stopped on the porch. "Where's Detective Kent?"

Victoria scanned the officers and vehicles that had sprouted all around. "I think he's gone."

"He forgot something." I led the way back to the car. We had to walk on the lawn because there was yellow tape wrapped around trees and the mail box, cutting off the driveway.

"He forgot to say goodbye." Tara stopped and put her hand on her hip.

"And he forgot to search Victoria's car."

We drove through the night back to our cul-de-sacs where we had houses that we hoped would keep us safe. Even when they did, *cul-de-sac* was still just a euphemism for dead end.

"Why do you think he left his cell phone at home?"

Victoria and Tara answered together, "He didn't want to be reached." One of the dogs barked in agreement. I was sure it was Abby, the smartest one. "We know he wasn't going where he said he was going, but we don't know where he was headed. Victoria, how did she take the news of her husband's murder?"

"It took a while for her to come to the door. She must have been in the back part of the house. She was shocked, but after about a minute she started processing it."

"Processing the reality of it?" Tara was rubbing her forehead.

"No, deciding whether or not it was a bad thing."

"Hm-m-m," we said in unison.

"We know she didn't shoot him." Tara threw this out, like it was common knowledge.

I turned around to face her. "How do we know that? Just because when she came outside she seemed to be blaming us for something?"

"I think the man the dogs were tracking shot him."

"Is that why you let the dogs drag you down the street? Are your shoes okay?"

She gave a little laugh at that. "Who said I let them drag me? But I was holding on to those leashes for dear life so I could get a look at him."

Victoria glanced at her in the rear view mirror. "So the person he was going to meet was out there?"

"Did you see anyone?" I asked.

"No, you know I don't see that well in the dark."

"Laser." I pointed to my eyes indicating a suggestion I had made before. "But you could tell it was a man?"

She pointed to her own eyes and replied to my laser suggestion with one of her own. "Night vision goggles, and yes, I could tell it was a he."

"How?" Victoria asked.

"Please." Tara rolled her eyes.

Victoria nodded and dropped it. By then we were back at my house, but we just sat in the car in the night air.

"So someone was coming to meet David Taylor or pick him up, since he didn't go to the garage," I summarized. Tara and I walked around to the driver's side and leaned on the side of the car.

"Since we didn't hear anything, does that mean the killer was using a silencer?" Victoria leaned out of the car. "I don't know what a gunshot sounds like. Do either of you?"

Tara shook her head.

"That sounds like something we should all know, doesn't it?"

Tara's eyes widened. "I hate to answer a question with a question, but why? Last time I checked we handled matrimonial cases."

"You're right, and besides, what are the chances we'll be at the scene of a murder ever again?" Here Victoria stopped speaking and reached her hand palm down out the window, the way we did it when we decided to start our agency. "But I don't want to just walk away from Kelly. I feel sorry for her, and I feel we have some responsibility here."

Tara looked at the outstretched hand. "I agree we owe Kelly more than we've given her, but that's not the kind of work we do." Then she looked first at me then at Victoria and exhaled. "Oh, what the hell." She covered Vic's hand with her own.

I put my hand on theirs. "Let's agree to sleep on it. We can talk about it in the morning, but I would like to point out that all three of us jumped out of the car when he got shot. We didn't consider our own hides for a second." We squeezed our hands together. When I raised mine, instead of lowering it, I brought it up and ran my fingers through my hair, over my ears.

"That's new," Victoria said.

"We now have a signature move. Let's practice," Tara added.

They each tried it a few times. We laughed the way people do when they're both tired and wired.

Were they thinking what I was thinking? I was hearing Kent's voice in my head calling us untrained, ill equipped and incompetent. It had been a long day, and we didn't need to go into it just then. We hugged each other before Tara and Stephie got in her car and followed Vic's up the hill out of the subdivision. I watched them and thought about our beginning.

~

Attorney Tara handled incorporating us. She had always wanted to use her law degree to help women and was finally getting her chance. Victoria drew up a business plan. I was a park ranger before my marriage, and in the state of Georgia that qualified me to apply for a private investigator's license. I handled getting us tested and certified. We studied hard, and we made it. When we felt prepared for our first case, we placed an ad in the *Gwinnett Daily News*.

In the first week after it ran, we got a call and met with a prospective client. She was a successful, savvy thirty-seven-year-old woman being courted by a man she desperately wanted to trust while every instinct was yelling at her to get away.

A day later she telephoned me. "He's here now. Can you come over? He says he can't stay long because he has to catch an afternoon flight. Coming up here is adding an extra forty miles to his drive to the airport and means he'll be driving through downtown Atlanta rush hour traffic." The whisper made *Atlanta rush hour traffic* come out as a hiss. Actually this is probably the way most of us talk about Atlanta traffic. "I offered to come to his place or meet in between, but he wouldn't hear of it. I feel terrible about being so suspicious but I have that feeling again, like maybe this means something or maybe it means nothing."

"Hon, from what you told us, the relationship became serious quickly. You're right not to want to buy a pig in a poke."

I hung up and called the others and told them it was time for our first stakeout. I loaded Abby into my Toyota Highlander Hybrid and picked up Victoria and Mr. Benz and then Tara and Stephie. We were to drive to the client's house and follow him when he left.

We drove north on Interstate 85 to Braselton, then north on Highway 211. The entrance to the Chateau Élan hotel and winery is just yards from the exit, but because of the dense cords of kudzu wrapped around the pine trees we didn't know we were close until we were right on it. A little farther up we saw the entrance to The Estates of Chateau Élan.

"Chateau Élan is the new Country Club of the South." Victoria was referring to metro Atlanta's ongoing expansion, which regularly changes the ranking of the most exclusive addresses.

"We're going all the way back to the other side of the golf course to the Legends section. The houses there go for a million and up."

I parked at the end of our client's street. "Look at us. We're on a stake out."

"That's her house there." Victoria pointed to a Tudor mansion on the left. The client had described her fiancé's car, and there it was, sitting in the driveway. Ten minutes later the groom-to-be drove his once silver, now gray, Porsche around the horseshoe driveway and passed us. I started the car and waited for him to get down the street.

"What's happening? Won't the car start?" Tara grabbed my arm and started shaking it, like it was connected to the engine.

"Don't worry, it's on. Hybrids are just very quiet."

We followed him back to the highway and south into Atlanta. Just past the Georgia Tech campus and Olympic Village he, and therefore we, exited. I'm not ashamed to admit I was getting a little nervous about keeping up with him in midtown when he pulled into the parking lot of a townhouse complex.

I exhaled in relief. "This isn't his address, is it?"

"Nope," Tara and Victoria answered at the same time. We parked and sat there for two and a half hours before he came out.

After a while we got bored and started yucking it up. "You know why divorces cost so much?"

"Pray tell."

"Because they're so much fun."

Just then the puppies in the back woke up, rediscovered each other, and started playing. Busy watching them, we didn't notice that their wrestling and jumping caused the car to sway until we heard a man's voice yell, "Hey, get a room." We looked around to see that it was our client's fiancé.

Ooops. He was wearing a woman's bathrobe with LAURA monogrammed on the pocket.

"Laura? Hmm. Not his." Victoria handed me a camera. "See this detective stuff isn't so hard."

He was putting a bag of trash in the garbage can. I lowered my window about an inch, clicking a photo with one hand while starting the car with the other. We drove down the street and turned around. Coming back we saw him kissing a woman, presumably Laura of bathrobe fame, as he re-entered the townhouse. I slowed down long enough for Victoria to snap a photo of this touching scene.

From the back seat Tara whispered, "You are about to be put on the curb yourself, mister."

We dreaded telling the client, and that part hasn't gotten any easier, but preventive work is a good thing. We also got crates for the puppies. Hard to believe, but that was a year ago, and with that first success we were off and running.

~

When Abby and I got in the house, I closed the door behind me and leaned back against it. I couldn't help but compare what I saw in my great room to Kelly Taylor's rooms with their few pieces of furniture. I had chosen soft buttercup and moss tones for the overstuffed chairs. The yellow- and vanilla -striped sofa had an S-shaped silhouette, and the moss-colored cushions were trimmed with a matching fringe. The tables and cabinetry were made of aged pine.

I filled Abby's water bowl and then checked for phone messages. The first was from my mother. "Leigh, this is Mom. Call me when you get home. There's a problem with Aunt Mary." I squeezed the telephone receiver against my lips. Aunt Mary was ninety-four years old. A broken hip? Worse? Without waiting for the rest of my messages, I took the phone to my balcony garden, speed dialing my mother as I walked.

"Mom, it's me. What happened to Aunt Mary?"

"Nothing happened to her. Do you know what she did? She cussed out Dr. Reeves this morning."

"Why? She's been seeing him for years. All of the aunts go to him. What did he do?" This was going to be good.

My mother settled in to tell the tale. "She has held a grudge for the last seven years about that little joke he made. Do you remember when he told her he thought she might be pregnant? What with her being a widow for the last thirty years, she didn't think it was one bit funny. Then after what happened this morning, well, do you know what she did? She hit the ceiling and gave him a piece of her mind."

"What happened this morning?"

"He told her to lie down on the examining table. You know how her osteoporosis is, she can't just lie down. She tried, but that old table was cold and hard. So she cussed him out."

"How is Doc Reeves?"

"He went into shock. He said he had never seen anything like it or been called such names."

"Did Aunt Mary apologize?"

"No, he did, but she's not accepting it, at least not till she's ready to. We do hope she will soon. He's a good doctor. Well, how are you, Dear?"

"Actually, I've wanted to tell you about something. My friends and I ..."

"Wait, there's another call. Look, I better get this. I'll talk to you later, dear. Bye bye."

"Bye, Mother. Please give Aunt Mary my affection." And Mom was gone, off, I was certain, to a call from one of my other aunts to receive a late-breaking bulletin on this escapade or another. "Lord, have mercy," I said to Abby.

She cocked her head from side to side.

"Let's go to bed, girl."

I activated the security system, grabbed the newspaper and climbed the stairs, Abby running ahead of me.

"Hey, I know you're a Schnauzer, but aren't you supposed to walk behind me?"

When she reached the upstairs landing, she turned around and gave me a look that said *I yam what I yam.*

"Good girl."

You may be wondering about the dogs. Here's the story behind that. We're not the gun-toting type, but we needed some way to defend ourselves, should the need arise. Victoria said she would figure it out. A week later she called a meeting at her house in Alpharetta. She had given my name to the security guard on duty at the entrance of the gated community, Chattahoochee River Close, and I drove through the streets of stately homes. Did I just say stately homes? What I mean is, Victoria and Shorty live high on the hog.

I had been with Victoria when she toured the model home. The red brick columns and black wrought iron gate at the entrance to the subdivision had been erected before a single house was sold. I was coming out of a bad time and wondering how they already knew women would try to escape.

As I walked up to her porch, I heard the yapping of puppies, but Victoria didn't have a dog. She opened the door, and Tara was with her, also grinning like a deacon holding four aces. Victoria stood aside and threw back her arm. "Ta-daaaaaa! Our protection."

Two skinny Standard Schnauzer puppies tottered across the marble floor on scrawny legs. Their faces looked round because they were too young to be groomed and didn't have beards. My husband gave me a Standard Schnauzer because he missed Christmas with me last year. These little guys reminded me of Abby at her puppy stage. Victoria explained the plan. The dogs would go out on cases with us.

"Right." I sat down on the Dover grey leather sofa.

"I've named mine Mr. Benz." Victoria beamed at the puppy.

"And mine is Stephen." Tara picked up her new baby and kissed the little salt and pepper head.

"Wait a minute. You named your puppy after your ex-husband?" I couldn't believe she would do that.

"Yeah, since he was a dog. Anyway, I'm going to call her Stephie."

That's the name of that tune. I have to say I love having Abby with me. My husband is about seven thousand miles away, and she's good company.

I performed my nighttime routine, scrubbing my face with a washcloth, massaging in PABA-free night cream, flossing, and holding my stomach in for a count of one hundred. Then I joined Abby in bed and opened the *New York Times*. She was already asleep, and I thought about her run down the street. "I really wish you could talk." I reached over and twirled one of her ears in my fingers. She opened her eyes and sighed. Then she showed her teeth and turned her head and took my hand in her mouth. I didn't bother to pull back. Then she licked my hand and went back to sleep. She could communicate, but she couldn't tell me who she and her pals were chasing away from David Taylor's house. "You did a good job tonight. Go to sleep because, as the good book says, tomorrow is another day."

Four

Continuation of statement by Leigh Reed. On Saturday morning at 7:30 we met at a parking lot along the Suwanee Creek Greenway for our weekly long run, despite what had happened the night before. For the ten miles we would need the smooth path and lush canopy of trees. Or should that be canopy of leaves? I was just wondering. Tara and I had parked at the Burnette Road parking lot, and Victoria picked us up to drive to the George F. Pierce Park at the north end of the trail, our starting point that day. Abby, Mr. Benz and Stephie were not with us because the mileage would have been too much for those short legs and twelve tiny feet.

We had been pounding pavement for almost a half hour when Victoria began, "I went back to the notes I made on my Internet search of David Taylor and his company, Flow Network Design. He was the sole proprietor, so Kelly may be a very rich widow."

Tara was ahead of her on the path and yelled back, "If he was sole proprietor, how can you tell how profitable it was? It's not listed, is it?"

"He had contracts with publicly held companies. Actually, company. I only found one, but that one was a real gravy train."

"Namely?" We were in my favorite part of the Greenway, the wooden boardwalk over Suwanee River wetlands.

"The Peachtree Group. They're a manufacturer of ..."

"Look!" I pointed at a Blue Heron on the wetland. I immediately started looking for a red-shouldered hawk I had seen around there before.

"Backpack UAVs."

"What's that?"

"Unmanned Aerial Vehicles." I was in the rear so I had to raise my voice. "NASA originally called theirs RPV's for Remotely Piloted Vehicles. The Department of Defense calls them UAVs, and they've taken to calling them drones more often. "

"Like the Predator?" Tara asked from the front of the line. "It was a Predator that tracked, what's-his-name, al-Zarqawi until the U.S. forces got him, right?"

"Yeah, that's right." I spit out between breaths. "The Predator is the most famous. It's about the size of a Cessna, but we're talking about Backpack UAVs, right?"

The path turned to asphalt and then a second raised walkway. Victoria took a bottle of water from the holder around her waist. "From what I've been able to find out so far, that's the only version using David Taylor's programming software."

That water looked good, so I got my bottle out, too. "The backpack-sized or over-the-hill UAV is the smallest version. They can be sent over a fence or around a corner. They can go behind enemy lines. They've even prevented infantry platoons from walking into an ambush."

Victoria poured a little water down her back. "He was a subcontractor writing computer programs for communications applications."

"Communications? For images to be sent to the ground?" The bank of Suwanee Creek was on our right. We crossed Martin Farm Road and headed to McGinnis Ferry Road.

"No, for interoperability."

I replaced my water bottle, trying not to break my stride. "Interoperability with what? Not only do they need to give what they learn to troops on the ground, sometimes the information is pieced together with intel from other UAVs. So which had he developed?"

"Both."

"Hmm, sort of vertically and horizontally?" Tara asked from the front of the line, but before I could answer we heard a familiar ring tone. Tara's phone was playing "Hey, Good Lookin'." She answered, agreed to something and hung up. "That was Detective Kent. He says we're to meet him at the police headquarters in Lawrenceville instead of the Mall of Georgia office. We'll have to allow more time to get there."

"I wonder why?"

"Duh. Because it's farther away."

"Very funny. Why did Detective Kent change our meeting place?"

"He didn't say."

I ran a little faster to catch up. "I'm guessing he's ashamed to be seen with us. He doesn't want to take a chance on anyone seeing us who knows what we do for a living."

Tara and Vic hmm'd at the same time, and I went on. "Did you find websites for Flow Network Design and The Peachtree Group?"

"Yeah, but there wasn't much more information." Victoria made eye contact with Tara, and then I had four eyes looking back at me. "Do you think you could find out more?" I knew she meant from my husband and that was suggesting a new turn for Tiara Investigations.

"Let's see if the investigation leads us down that road first." I pulled my arms out of my tee-shirt but left it around my neck. I don't have the nerve to run with only a jog bra, and the shirt sufficiently covered me up, plus giving me something to mop up the sweat with.

"We have an investigation? I thought we were just fact finding to help Detective Kent and try to make up for letting Kelly Taylor down." Tara called this over her shoulder.

Victoria skipped over her question and went on. "It already has led down that road. The call that Kelly says drew him out of the house was from a Peachtree Group phone number. I got that off of reverse lookup." The three of us stopped in our tracks. Granted, this is not much of a status change when you are already running an eleven minute mile. At the time we were under McGinnis Ferry Road.

"Did you dial it? I mean to get the name off of the voice mail?" Tara asked.

"No, I couldn't remember how to disable caller ID."

I stretched my arms out to the side. When I run I hold my elbows at a ninety degree angle, and they were some kind of stiff. "A menopause moment?"

"Yeah."

"It's star 59." Tara began running again. "I think we should attend the funeral. I'll call Kelly and ask about the arrangements."

"I think we should visit The Peachtree Group on Monday morning." Victoria lowered her voice because we were nearing a group of kids.

We passed the Buckeye Pavillion, where a group of Boy Scouts listened to a lecture.

"Wanna flash them?" In Tara's defense, we had been running quite a while and were getting loopy.

"You first." Despite my challenge there was no mooning of Boy Scouts, as least not that day. We're just big talkers.

The rest of our run was spent discussing other cases, a couple of new clients and those on hold waiting for a call. We made the loop at Suwanee Creek Park, which gave us four miles, and went into the ladies room. Then we ran out and back to our starting point. We turned around and ran back to Martin Farm Park and then retraced our steps to the cars. This gave us our ten miles. Victoria took Tara and me to our cars.

"See you around noon at my house," Tara called out the window as she drove off.

We didn't go straight to our respective homes because there was the little matter of Starbucks with their sweet tea calling to us. In a line we peeled off and into the drive-thru lane. Next it was home for showers, then to Tara's for lunch and to prepare mentally for our come-to-Jesus meeting with Detective Kent.

~

You can just imagine my surprise when I was met at the door by Dr. Armistead, or as we like to call him, Paul, Tara's boyfriend. Victoria was already there with a look of horror on her pretty face. He was supposed to be playing golf. I mean, when we're supposed to play golf, we play golf. He was making lunch for us, but still, I couldn't help but wonder if that was a northern thing. We followed him through the kitchen to the screened-in breakfast room where Tara was just placing a centerpiece of floating candles and the tops of Gerber daisies in a crystal bowl. The Lloyd Flanders white wicker dining table was covered with an ivory antique lace table cloth.

Wine glasses were on the table, but the three of us chose iced tea. What we knew that the good doctor didn't was that we had to be one hundred percent professional when we showed up at the police station. Nonetheless, I picked up the bottle and read the label.

"Very nice," I complimented him on his selection.

"Nothing but the best for the ladies." He smiled at each of us.

Tara leaned toward him and said, "Gimme sugar." She had puckered up, but Paul walked away and came back with the sugar bowl.

"What's that?" We cracked up laughing and settled into the chairs, realizing how good it felt to take a load off after that run.

"Have you ever noticed that when wine is bad, you drink a lot of it to make it taste good, but when food is bad you just push it away?" I asked the table. "The ladies" started nodding their heads, and *uh huh*-ing. Dr. Paul, however, tilted his head to one side and then the other, the way Abby does when she hears a noise for the first time. I've taken a lot of kidding from my husband and everyone else I know about my questions. Once I asked my husband why you say Home Deee-po, but it's Army de-po. And how about that expression, cusses like a sailor? Do soldiers have a broader vocabulary, since parents always say that's why people cuss? Natch, being a soldier, he agreed with that hypothesis. Or are sailors tougher? He didn't agree with that.

"Tara and I would like to get together with you and your husband when he's back in town. Right, Sweetie? I'd love to hear what he has to say about what's going on in the Middle East." This *non sequitur* was probably just because he couldn't think of a response to my bad wine versus bad food philosophical remark, but it made the hair on the back on my neck stand.

He went back to the kitchen and brought iced tea out to us. "So, how was your run?"

"Fine."

"Fine."

"Fine."

Paul decided to return to the kitchen and finish the salad. No sir-ree, no flies on Paul.

I leaned forward and whispered, "Did you notice the lack of furniture in the Taylors' living room last night?"

Victoria nodded. "Since she said the problems started when they moved into the new house, do you think they had money problems?"

Then Paul returned with the salad. "The leaves are spectacular this year, aren't they?"

"Oh, yes."

"Oh, yes,"

"Oh, yes." And back to the kitchen he went.

Tara waited until he was out of hearing. "I spoke with Kelly's mother. The service is on Monday at eleven o'clock with lunch at the house afterwards."

"That soon? They're performing an autopsy, right?" The tea was so good, I took more of a drag than a sip of it.

"It's just a memorial service," Tara answered quickly because Paul was coming back in with two bowls of homemade salad dressing. She patted the chair next to hers, and he sat down, beaming at her. We tied on the feedbags, as they say. In this case the feedbags contained garden salads with grilled shrimp.

I looked over at Paul. It was obvious he hadn't quite recovered his equilibrium. I felt bad because, let's face it, we are a lot to handle. "I think Dr. Paul wants to report us to Dr. Phil."

Just then Stephie ran in, and Tara leaned over to pat her head. "He could start with our unnatural devotion to our dogs."

"Easy now. You make it sound like we have sex with them." I looked over to Paul. "Which we don't, because they're girls."

Victoria threw her head back and laughed, and Tara snorted tea out her nose. I was cracking up at my own joke and dabbing my eyes with my napkin. Someone was missing. Oh, yeah, Paul wasn't laughing. "Get it? They're dogs!" He was trying, really trying. "We don't have sex with them because they are dogs!"

"Like they say, it only seems weird the first time." Tara patted his arm, and we went into hysterics again. Paul blushed.

The Tiara girls moved the conversation to safer ground, that of aging parents, a familiar topic. I recounted a piece of advice my mother had given me last week. She had looked at my watch and said, "Leigh, dear, only a party pooper wears a watch to a social function."

Tara said, "Up North, when you turn seventy, you move to Florida. That's the law up there, you know. Even if the person doesn't want to, their kin makes them move to Florida. This is one thing Yankees do right."

Victoria looked at her. "I'm only sorry I don't know of a group of Northern women who meet to talk about crazy things Southerners say about Northerners so I could tell them that one. Are Northerners really all that different from Southerners? I will admit it is a little funny when they say things like grocery cart instead of buggy. Speaking of which, it's almost always the Northerners that leave them in the middle of the parking lot at the grocery store. And our expressions are more, well, expressive. For instance, they say 'nothing to write home about' and we say 'nothing to run home and tell Mom about.' Other than that I'm sure we're really alike."

"Wait, let's go back to the part about sending your parents to Florida even if they don't want to go. You cannot send your parents to someplace where they don't even know what 'I swan' or 'I swaney' means!" I looked at Paul, "Isn't that right?"

"I have no idea what 'I swan' means."

"No, the part about Northerners sending their parents to Florida, whether they want to go or not."

"I don't think so. I mean, I don't know, I just ... I should check on something in the kitchen." We all shrugged our shoulders.

Tara stopped eating long enough to say, "I absolutely love your mother. Her funny expressions are etiquette advice. My mother would say things like, 'I'll slap you to sleep, then I'll slap you for sleeping.'"

A few minutes later Paul returned with slices of Coca-Cola cake and homemade vanilla ice cream.

"There's cake!" Victoria cried out.

"Now why did you do that?" I asked. "Why does cake surprise people? No one ever says, 'There's peas! But cake always seems to surprise people." Paul cocked his head again.

"Mmmm." Victoria had taken her first bite, and her head was swimming back and forth. "Y'all have got to taste this. It will make you take back things you never stole."

"It's just like going to church." Paul gave Tara a peck on the cheek when she said this and went to get more sweet tea.

I took a bite and froze mid-chew. "You mean it's just like going to Cracker Barrel!" I hissed with my mouth full. "He bought this cake there, didn't he?"

"So what if he did, Leigh? You look like that bite just gave you lockjaw," Victoria whispered.

"So what? We can't have him going to Cracker Barrel." Until then it was such a pleasant lunch, at least for the three of us. "Tara, handle it."

"Handle it? What do you want me to do, kill him?"

"Actually I think up North they whack them," Victoria corrected her.

I realized how we sounded and started to giggle, "No, just scare him." I got the note pad and golf pencil out of my pocket. I had brought them to use when we discussed our plan for meeting with the detective. I wrote something and slid it over to Tara: IF YOU KNOW WHAT'S GOOD FOR YOU, YOU'LL STAY AWAY FROM CRACKER BARREL. She passed it over to Victoria to read.

Paul returned and looked around the table at each of us. I could tell he didn't think he was up to asking what we were laughing about, and then his curiosity got the better of him. "What's so funny?"

"We were talking about how we say 'bless his heart.' You can say anything about anyone if you follow it with 'bless his heart.'" I was lying through my teeth. I mean, that is true, it's just not what we were laughing about.

"That's right!" Victoria exclaimed. "Her cooking is not fit to eat, bless her heart."

"Or he can't carry a tune in a bucket, so I don't know why he's in the choir, bless his heart." When Tara said we would clean up, he didn't argue. Like I said, no flies on Paul.

"Sweetie, it's our turn to take snacks to church for Fellowship Hour. If I put something in the oven will you take it out?" He kissed her, mumbling something to the affirmative and extracting a promise of recompense.

We gave him time to clear out of the kitchen before we got up from the table. The stiffness from the morning run made us moan and cuss. When we were able, we hobbled to the kitchen. Not real attractive.

When the decision to start Tiara Investigations had been made, we knew we had to get in shape. For us that means running three times a week and the services of a personal trainer, Julio (who you wouldn't kick out of bed for eating crackers, if you know what I mean) for strength training twice a week and working out to a kickboxing DVD Tara had purchased for us. "We'll be able to kick ass in, uh, the label says two weeks," had been her explanation for that.

We're stronger, and we walk taller. I, for one, am happy to report I no longer have to put talcum powder on my inner thighs just to make it down the hall.

Tara turned the cake mix box over to read the directions, "Look, we can make brownies out of this mix. Let's do that." And, yes, making brownies from a mix does take three of us. "They're called Better Than Almost Anything Brownies. Hmm, I guess they have to say *almost* anything because of sex. That's what we call a disclaimer."

I looked at Victoria, "She's an attorney, you know."

Victoria ran her hand along the granite counter top. "I don't think about sex as often as you two. At my age it's more fun to laugh about it than to do it. I mean, isn't that normal? The older women get, the less interest we have in it, right?"

"Listen, Hon, it's bad sex women aren't interested in." Tara was trying to see the tiny red marks on a measuring cup.

"I beg to differ. Teenagers have nothing but bad sex, and they're very interested in it." I can be quite the philosopher.

"Hmm. Have either of you ever faked an orgasm?"

Tara and I exchanged glances. "No," we answered together.

"Well, not in years," I qualified mine.

"Now, I may have embellished a few, but faked, never."

"And, Honey, remember I'm making up for lost time when my husband is home from deployment or here on TDY."

"TDY?"

"Temporary Duty."

Victoria looked at us from the sides of her narrowed eyes. "What is the wildest thing you've ever done in bed?" She looked at Tara first.

"I haven't done it yet."

"Let me preface this by saying some of my open mindedness is apathy. I don't judge what other people are doing," I answered, "with the exception of what we do for a living, that is. But once I made a man call me ma'am in bed."

"Do you like being called ma'am?" She was no longer squinting. Actually her eyes were round as saucers.

"Nope. I just wanted to see if he would do it."

"Did he?"

"Yes, ma'am. And there was the time I put a thong in my husband's popcorn at the movies."

"Did you take them off right there in the theatre?"

"Please. The seats. I brought a pair from home."

"Oh, that's right." Victoria remembered who she was talking to.

"What did he do?" Tara leaned over and put her elbows on the counter top.

"He said, 'What tha …?' Then he realized what he had and used it to eat his popcorn."

"That's so funny."

"Oh, it was a riot. The next week I reached into my bag of popcorn and there was a pair of his tighty whities in there. And his are big. Hmm, why do you think women's underwear is sexy, and men's underwear isn't? I was just wondering."

After a good laugh Tara turned to me. "Why did you tense up when Paul asked about us all getting together?"

"I just don't know how that would work out. My husband is not very sociable. As a matter of fact, he's an asshole to everyone but me."

"I don't believe that." Victoria sat down on a kitchen stool.

"Believe it. The Pentagon wants him to do some media work. A media specialist called him to talk about it. She said all he needed to do was show his personality. Want to know what he told her? He said, 'I don't have one, let's leave it at that.'" I know this is crazy, but even as I was saying it, my heart was absolutely swelling with pride and love. Pathetic, huh? And the Tiara girls could tell.

"But what about the political part of the job?" Victoria asked.

"He doesn't do it. He says you can't be a good general and political." I thought it was time I changed the subject. "Dr. Paul's very nice."

Tara nodded and smiled. "How's Shorty, Victoria?" Her husband is six feet, seven inches, so what else could his nickname be?

Her answer was a shoulder shrug. "What's this for anyway?" She ran her finger along the inside of the mixing bowl.

"Fellowship Hour at church. We serve refreshments after the eleven o'clock service. You can bring either a dessert or a heavy hors d'oeuvre."

Victoria retrieved a slip of paper from the side pocket of her handbag. "Heavy hors d'oeuvre? What's that, a fifty-pound cheese ball?" I cracked up, but Tara sighed because there's nothing about church that isn't serious to her.

While Tara finished the brownies, I dialed star 59 and the number Victoria read off to me. "Kerry Lee," I said when I hung up.

"Is that a man or a woman?" The buzzer on the oven told Tara it had preheated.

"It was an automated voice."

"So an affair is still a possibility," Victoria said. "You know, justifiable homicide."

"Yeah, an affair which may or may not be related to his murder. We can find out if Kerry Lee is a man or woman when we pay a visit to The Peachtree Group on Monday morning before the service."

Tara looked at me, then at Victoria, "Why?"

"Are we getting in over our heads?" Victoria asked.

"Probably. Maybe it's time to do more with the agency than just who-did-he-want-and-when-did-he-want-her, or in industry jargon, matrimonial work." I didn't want to get into a long discussion before we met with Detective Kent, and we were going to have to leave soon. So I asked, "Hey, what's the best thing ever to come out of a penis?"

Just then the air in the room changed. Shorty was standing in the doorway.

"Hi," Victoria walked over and stood in front of him.

"I'm picking Paul up to go play golf."

"I left a message for you by the kitchen telephone. Did you see it? It seemed important, at least the guy said he was impatient."

"He said he was an in-patient. He's a patient in the hospital and got my home phone number." I don't know which annoyed me more, his tone or that *my* phone number rather than *our* phone number.

"Sorry, I was on two phones at once." Here she glanced at Tara and me. That didn't sound like the kind of mistake Victoria would make. It had to be Freudian. "Did you call Aidan?" Aidan is their son and the soon-to-be father of twins.

One eye crinkled. "No, I'll do it later," but it was too late. The beat it took him to answer said it all. It said he had to think about who Aidan was, and it told me why the couple had waited until she was four months pregnant to tell Victoria and Shorty.

He grumbled, "They can't afford to have a baby, much less twins."

Victoria walked behind Tara and me to put a plate in the sink. "Oh, yes they caaaaan," she whispered.

In the nick of time Dr. Paul joined us. He walked over to Tara and kissed her goodbye.

"Ready to head out, Shorty?"

"Sure." Then to Victoria, "I accepted the Parkers'

invitation for Monday night."

"Okay, I'll have dinner with the girls."

"I accepted for both of us."

As they started toward the door, Paul froze. "I can't leave. I promised I would wait and take the brownies out of the oven for Tara."

"No, no, no, you go ahead. We'll wait for them." Tara shook her hand to shoo him out the door.

"Are you sure?"

"Yes, I'm sure."

He blew her a kiss, and before he got to the door he turned and took one last look back at her. Shorty just kept walking.

"The wrinkles," I said to the back of their heads.

"What?" Both men had turned around.

Victoria clarified it, "The best thing ever to come out of a penis is the wrinkles, Frank."

"That's hot," Tara said. "That is dashboard-hot."

Stephie heard the door open and scampered up, not wanting to be left at home if we were going out on a case.

"What're you doing here?" Shorty asked the dog.

"That's not your dog. That's Stephie, my dog."

"Hmm. We have one that looks just like it. Victoria, what's our dog's name?"

She hesitated. "Don't know." I jerked my head to look at her. She realized this was a tad shy of believable and recovered pretty nicely, "Donna. Our dog's name is Donna."

All of a sudden I appreciated Paul for being a wonderful boyfriend to my friend. "Paul? You were asking what my husband thinks about the situation in the Middle East. Well, he says that to understand the region you have to accept the fact that everything you ever heard about the Middle East is true."

"Oh, thanks." He did that head tilting thing again.

As soon as we heard the door click I turned to Victoria. "Hon, why didn't you want to tell him what you named your dog?"

"I know he thinks Mr. Benz is a dumb name for a dog. And all of a sudden I was scared we might lose Tiara."

Tara walked over to her. "We will not let that happen!"

"No, we won't."

"What are we going to say to Detective Kent?" Victoria asked.

Tara folded her dish towel. "My Daddy always said, 'Once you're explaining, you're losing.' So let's not say much."

"That'll work out fine since we don't know much." I turned to Tara, "Paul is so nice. Do you two ever fight?"

"Sure we do. Sometimes I'll pick a fight just for the make-up sex. When he gets exasperated his Northern accent really comes out. Like last night we had a few words, and I said, 'Stop talking like a Northerner.' He said, 'I am a Northerner!' Then I said, 'Well, I'm a Southerner, and you don't hear me talking with an accent.'" Tara turned off the oven. "What the hell?"

I looked around to see why she had said this last part. Victoria was crying. "Sorry. That is just so sweet."

Tara took her a tissue and started rubbing her back. "Menopause, Honey?"

"Yeah, menopause."

"I really like Paul. I don't usually like such nice people. They make me do things like spell cuss words." I said this to get us perked up again. "And mark my words we are going to kick a-s-s at that police station this afternoon. Now where is that note I wrote about staying out of Cracker Barrel?"

"I don't have it."

"I don't have it."

I checked the table, not there. "It was probably thrown

away. We can't worry about that now. Every time I think about talking to that detective, I get as nervous as a long-tailed cat in a room full of rocking chairs.

"Victoria, are you okay?"

"Yeah. I'm glad he got that straightened out about the in-patient. Once again he's overcome my mistake." Then to prove she had recovered from being spoken to like that, she said, "Let's get our meeting with Detective Kent over with. I'm as nervous as a whore in church."

"That never made me nervous," Tara answered.

Five

Continuation of statement by Leigh Reed. An hour later the Tiara detectives, heretofore described as untrained, ill-equipped and incompetent, walked into Detective Kent's office in Lawrenceville, the county seat. We wore pant suits. Mine was khaki, Victoria's was cream colored linen, and Tara's was dark brown silk.

"Ladies." He led us down the hall to a conference room. The chairs were aluminum with vinyl covered seats, the table was made of pressed wood, and the concrete block walls were painted beige. No waste of taxpayers' money here. They could not have made the room uglier if they had tried.

"I would remind you to be honest in answering my questions."

"Excuse me?" I raised my hand and interrupted, but I had a valid reason for doing so. "Do people ever forget to be honest?"

His lips moved, and I think he whispered, "For the love," but instead of finishing his sentence he cleared his throat. Next he explained he would be taping our statements, and we would be asked to return to sign them after they were transcribed.

Victoria asked if we were being observed, noting the mirror on the wall behind my head. Kent declined to answer; he just looked down and pretended to ignore her. Tara took this as an affirmative response. "That's hot. It's vinyl seat-hot."

I didn't get what was so hot about two-way mirrors, but then she explained herself. "Maybe for our cars?"

"Tara, you can't drive down the street with a mirror for a windshield," I said.

Detective Kent took a deep breath. "Can we proceed?"

He centered the microphone on the table. It was three sided and pretty hi tech compared to the rest of the room. Tara leaned over the table and tapped it twice. "Testing, test …"

"It's on. It's on for the love of pete!" He gave the current time and our location and then said each of our names. He should have known better.

"Leigh Reed."

"Present."

"Victoria Blair."

She gave the room a bow. "Thank you all for coming today."

"Tara Brown." She gave a beauty queen wave with fingers held together and wrist rotating. He ignored us the way you do when a child is acting silly and you don't want to encourage it, I mean, him.

He said that this statement concerned the death of David Taylor and then he gave the Taylors' address. We listened with what passes for rapt attention on our parts. Actually, when you hear something you already know, it's rarely what you'd call absorbing.

"Why were you sitting in front of the deceased's house last night?"

"Surveillance. His wife telephoned us, and we were going to follow him."

"So he was cheating on his wife?"

"She suspected he was."

"And that he was going to leave her for another woman?"

"Hold your horses. Aren't we getting a little ahead of ourselves? We never said that there *was* another woman." I was cool as a cucumber.

"Did Kelly Taylor suspect he might be planning on ending the marriage?"

"We never discussed that with her."

"That'd be nice to know, since his will leaves everything to her."

"To the other woman?" Tara shrieked, almost coming off her chair.

"I thought you said you didn't know if there was one." Detective Kent mistakenly thought he had us there.

"We don't." Then I turned to Tara, "He was saying everything would be left to Kelly Taylor."

Kent shook his head. "His business had recently become extremely lucrative. If he was about to end the marriage, he was worth more to Mrs. Taylor dead than alive. When you learn who …"

I interrupted him. "If."

He turned the volume all the way down on the recorder. "… if and who the third party is, I expect you to tell me. I'm still considering filing a complaint against Tiara Investigations with the state board."

"Sure, we'll let you know if we find a girlfriend," said my lips, but my brain was saying, *you're not going to file a complaint against us and tell the board how you learned about our agency.*

He turned the volume back up. "How did Mrs. Taylor seem last night when you spoke with her?"

Victoria took this one. "She seemed in control."

"What does that mean?"

"She didn't look like she was out of control?"

He looked at me. "Since you've had a few hours to think about it, did you all see anything to help us identify the perpetrator?"

My brain: *Thank you Lord for not letting him say perp.* Lips: "Nothing, we're sorry about that." And I was.

Turning to Victoria he asked the same question, but it was Tara who spoke up, "There may be something in the photos."

This time it was Kent jumping out of his chair. "You have photographs? With you?"

"They're being developed," I said.

"*Developed?*" he asked with disdain that he didn't have the decency to try to hide. "Does your little detective agency have any equipment at all?"

We didn't answer, and he assumed we had chosen not to dignify his remark with a reply. In fact, unless you count our wigs, the photocopier and some postage stamps, you'd have to say we don't have any equipment.

"How soon can I get them?"

Tara answered, "One hour or they're free."

"We'll pick them up and bring them to you," I told him.

"Don't make me get a warrant and confiscate them." That sounded familiar, and then I remembered, 'Don't make me pull this car over.' He gave us each a business card with his cell phone number underlined. We were to call him when we had anything to report.

"And another thing, I will need you three to stay available."

"Available?" Tara tilted her head. "They're both married. I'm the only one that's available."

"Tara, aren't you forgetting something?" I prompted her.

"Paul?"

"No, Sweetie. The person the dogs went after."

"You saw someone outside the Taylor house last night?"

"Actually, *saw* is a bit of an overstatement. There someone out there running away, but Tara didn't see the person. That's why the dogs were pulling her."

"Can you give a description?"

"I'm sorry, no," she answered.

"A man or a woman?"

"A man."

"You could tell that how?"

Tara stared at the ceiling. Victoria answered for her, "Let's just say it's a gift she has."

"For the love of Pete. I'll have the neighbors interviewed."

On the way out Victoria took one last look at the two-way mirror and then requested a copy of the DVD. His answer was his Dirty Harry glare, which we construed as a no.

~

We drove over to Target to pick up the developed photos. Tara was driving, and she started the debriefing, such as it was. "Didn't that seem a little, um, informal?"

"Was it?" I asked. "I'm usually reading by the time those police shows come on so I wouldn't know."

"Last night he should have separated us and then conducted interviews."

"Tara, I'm so glad you're an attorney." Vic was cleaning her eyeglasses. "Are there any other procedures he's easing up on? And why?"

I rummaged through my handbag for my cell phone and checked for missed calls. "Hmm. Maybe his opinion of us isn't as low as he would like us to think."

Tara laughed. "Or maybe he's just lazy."

"I hope you didn't drop off my camera for developing. I didn't take any pictures," Victoria said.

"Neither did I, but I turned in all three, because I couldn't tell which camera was mine."

I knew what was coming. "Wait, I didn't take any pictures either. So this means we have no photos at all? Nothing on any of the three cameras? I guess that shoots my

he-came-to-his-senses-and-realized-we're-brilliant theory all
to hell and back."

Tara pulled right back out of the parking lot. "For the
love of Pete," she mimicked.

"Why are we still using those stupid yellow cameras?"
Victoria winced and rolled her head back.

On a practice run, we had tried using the cameras on our
cell phones, but since so much of our surveillance takes place
after dark, this was a nonstarter. The cell phones worked well
enough, but we had to turn on the car's interior lights to use
them. Not good.

"That does it. Tomorrow I'm going shopping for a digital
camera." Then I called Kent and told him none of the photos
were able to be developed. It's what we like to call
constructive ambiguity. We drove back to Tara's house and
got in our own cars. On the way we hadn't said much; we
needed a break. Tara seemed especially quiet.

I unlocked the door to my house and went in. Sometimes
there's arrogance to a quiet house, like it's snubbing you.
That afternoon the house was a shelter, and that was a good
feeling. I checked for phone messages, and there were none.
Sometimes my husband can get a phone line, and sometimes
he can't.

The morning's long run had caught up with me, and the
events of the last twenty-four hours leaned on me, too. It felt
good to be alone except for Abby. Once upstairs I changed
into an ivory silk charmeuse nightgown and robe. At the time
I could not have told you why I was dressed like that to save
my life. I realized I didn't need a nap, I just needed some
down time. I headed back downstairs and went out to the
deck to my flower arranging table. I pulled on my gardener's
smock and went to work. I had saved flowers from my
summer cutting bed to dry for an arrangement. Most of them
were ready. I began by cutting a base of Styrofoam and

securing it to the planter. Next, I inserted stub wires into the roses. The pink roses symbolized love, grace, and beauty. Then I added lamb's ears for gentleness. I looked at my handiwork and found myself smiling. That was when I realized I was chilly. I went inside thinking how time had flown. I hung my smock on the hook and picked up the newspaper and took it to bed.

Abby was already on the end of the bed and snoring lightly. She whined and then kicked what my husband calls her rear driver's side leg twice. I gave her an air kiss, and she came out of her bad dream. It was time to lie down and read the *New York Times*, but not before the nighttime ritual I had resumed a year or so ago. I rubbed the excess night cream and eye cream onto the back of my hands instead of a towel and realized I was getting a kick out of doing all this. My pedicured feet sank into a soft rug with a pattern of cabbage roses. I don't know if it was caring about my looks again or spending time on myself or what, but I felt like I had been away and come back.

Finally in bed under damask bedcovers, I read Bob Herbert's column. A paragraph below the first column noted that "Thomas Friedman is off today." Wouldn't he have been off yesterday? And if he is really off today, are we going to have his column tomorrow? I was just wondering.

The phone rang, and I rolled over to the side of the bed to answer it.

"Leigh? Turn on your TV."

"What's up?"

"Turn to Channel 75. It's one of those shopping channels."

I did as she said, and then I heard a familiar voice. "Is that Tara talking?"

"Oh, yeah. The segment is on improving your retirement years. She's asking questions about a sound amplifier."

"So how big a room can you hear across? Can you, like, hear someone across the street?"

"Yes, m'am! Are you going to be ordering?"

"Just one more question. If you were sitting in a car outside someone's house, would you be able to hear what the couple, or whoever's inside the house, were saying?'

"We'll go on to our next caller, who has purchased the sound amplifier before. Hon, go ahead."

I turned off the TV.

"Leigh, are you there?"

"Yeah, but I just don't know what to say after that. Wait, I'm getting another call." I looked at the phone and saw it was Tara so I used three-way calling to include her.

"Hi! Guess what I just did for us!"

"You bought us old-people hearing gizmos so we can eavesdrop on people," Victoria answered.

"Uhh, I get how you know Internet everything, but …"

"Tara, we heard you on a shopping channel. Did you order three?"

"Of course. Don't you see? We'll no longer be ill equipped, or at least not so ill equipped. We should have them in ten days to two weeks. I feel just terrible about getting us those disposable cameras, and this is how I want to make up for it."

All of a sudden I was smiling, and I could feel them smiling, too. "Goodnight, Ladies."

Six

Continuation of statement by Leigh Reed. On Sunday morning I woke up early, and Abby and I were out the door. The day was perfect for my little black Jeep, top off. I belted Abby into her canine seat belt, then backed out. The CD from my last drive was Spanish neo-flamenco. I listened to "Ley de Gravedad," or law of gravity, by one of my favorite groups, Ojos De Brujo. The stable was a forty-minute drive north of home. I wore breeches, shirt, and a jacket, and I had thrown my open front shin boots in the back seat. I would wear those for jumping. In my bag I had my hunt cap and the rest of my paraphernalia. I called ahead, and General, my chestnut thoroughbred, was ready when I turned down the gravel drive. Sure, chestnut is one of the most common coat colors, but there are many shades. My guy is copper red. The first week I owned him I came to the stable every day and watched him walk, trot and canter. I memorized his gait. Then I rode him, and later I moved up to leading him.

I turned away the barn manager when he approached with a mounting block. Being a talented man, but of few words, he put it away with a smile. After petting Abby, who was outside the arena watching, he walked off. I slowly lowered my weight onto the saddle, thinking *ahhhh*. That's how right it felt.

We walked around for a few minutes just getting on the same wavelength. He talked to me all the time, and he was absorbing information from me, too. I had to be aware of what my movements were saying to him. I know the power of positive thinking in horseback riding. I didn't want to be inadvertently telling him what to do wrong. I sat in the deepest part of the saddle and imagined myself part of his movement. For flat work we practiced transitions, because if you can't do flat work, or don't want to, you can't jump. First, halt to walk to halt. Then walk to trot to walk. Next, walk to canter and then canter to trot. Canter to halt. Canter to walk with half-halts. Last walk to canter with half-halts. Then it was time for jumping.

I dismounted and placed a single pole on the ground. Then I raised my stirrups up a hole and mounted. I picked out a focal point in line with the center stripe on the rail. Always, I was looking where I wanted to go, keeping my technique simple. We crossed the pole with movements simple and efficient.

I dismounted again and put another pole two feet high between a couple of posts. Since horses look at jumps from the ground up, I left the first post for a ground line. Back on General, I had my heels under my butt and down. I pushed down on my knees. With noninterference we moved forward, sharing one center of gravity. We cantered to the railing, and suddenly I was flying. We landed, and I brought him back to a trot and repeated the jump. Later I added a second fence, and later still we rode the course as a figure eight. Finally it was time to cool down—or rather to come off our high.

Back in the car with my water bottle I sat and checked in with my emotions. The morning out here had cleared my head. I knew I was avoiding thinking about something, and I knew what it was. My work had added meaning to my life, but what was it doing to my relationship with my husband? Where was my center of gravity now? You have to know that in horseback riding, hell, in life. Was mine with Tiara Investigations or with my husband? And then the strangest thing happened. I felt at peace. Like it was okay. I could fly with the agency, but my marriage would be my focal point.

Sure, it was still an open question, but for now it was all good.

From there I went shopping for a digital camera. I accelerated onto Highway 20 in the direction of the Mall of Georgia. The road is lined with shops, and I swear, you can't throw a stick without hitting a restaurant.

After a while I noticed the same car had been behind me mile after slow mall-traffic mile. I told Abby, "He's following us." It was a rented white Ford Taurus. The driver was male, but with the glare from the sun that's all I could tell.

I found a parking space near the main entrance. I pulled the canvas top minus the window flaps onto the Jeep and locked Abby in. Since she was a Standard Schnauzer and not a mini, I felt okay leaving her by herself. Still, I didn't dally around in the mall.

When I came out with my new purchase, the white car was still there. Amateurs! What can I say? Do people no longer take pride in their work?

I walked to the Jeep and was careful to unlock the driver's side door only, just like they say in articles on self-defense for women. I pulled the top off and stowed it to give me an excuse to walk around for a better view of the license plate. I still couldn't make it out, nor did I have a better view of the driver, so I climbed in and drove off. The car followed me out of the parking lot.

"Shit," I said to Abby, "We really are being followed." I speed dialed Victoria and told her what was happening.

"Don't go home. Pick me up at the Cracker Barrel."

I drove slowly to give her time to get there and also because you have no choice on Highway 20 in front of the mall. I drove east to the entrance to I-85 and exited at Lawrenceville-Suwanee Road. When I got close my nerves got the upper hand, and I turned into the Cracker Barrel parking lot on two wheels. Victoria, Tara, Mr. Benz and

Stephie were waiting out front. They ran toward me, and I unlocked the doors to let them in. We didn't have crates for the dogs, and they seemed to understand how important it was for them to behave. Abby was still in the front seat and feeling superior. Victoria and Tara held their dogs in the back seat.

"I have a plan." I picked up my cell phone and hit the speed dial for the marina. "This is Leigh Reed. Could you have my boat out in about ten minutes? Thank you."

We drove north on Lawrenceville-Suwanee Road and cut over to Buford Highway. The Taurus stayed right with us.

I looked in the rearview mirror and saw Tara and Victoria with their arms wrapped around their dogs and holding their rather big and getting bigger hair down. "You two have been to church, haven't you?"

"Yes. This is how the Minister of Music likes it."

Victoria said, "I think your hair should always be as big as your head."

"Whaaat?" Tara had to raise her voice to be heard.

"That sounds like it should mean something, but what?" I yelled back to them.

"Oh, never mind. I just thought I would try a new look. Anyway, just forget it. We're here."

My thirty-foot sloop, Fourth Star, was in the first slip. I parked, and we jumped out and ran, Abby first and the other two dogs at our heels. She's such a little leader. We threw our handbags aboard, and then we tossed the dogs, who thought it was a fun new game. The sailboat had been backed in and, according to my hair and the masthead fly, was facing into the wind. I made that all-important, long step onto the boat and started the engine, giving my gauges and indicator lights a quick look-see. In the meantime Victoria and Tara had gotten to their knees and climbed aboard, then held their dogs close. I appreciated the caution they showed. Better safe than sorry, right? I cast off the stern line, then the spring lines, and last the bow line. Force of habit made me look at the rubber fenders, but I would pull them in later.

We motored away from the dock, looking back to see the man was out of his car and walking toward the water. He wore baggy jeans and a plaid flannel shirt stretched over his beer gut. He looked to be about sixty, or maybe he was forty-five and had been rode hard and put up wet. Then he started laughing, but we didn't get the joke.

It was a beautiful day still, just the right amount of sun, just the right amount of wind. We were well away from the marina, but I kept motoring longer than I ordinarily would. I'm a sailor, not a motor-er, but I had to put our safety above my pride.

"Will one of you hold the tiller?" Tara put Stephie down and scooted in.

"Just pick a spot straight ahead and keep us pointed that way."

"How about that mountain?"

"Perfect."

I unlocked and slid the main hatch open. "Abby, come." She jumped into my arms, and I lowered her down, then I did the same for Stephie and Mr. Benz, who had followed her. They'd have to stay below until I could tether them to lifelines. I got out my winch handles and headed back up top. The masthead fly told me the wind was coming from the north. I reached back to the tiller and turned the boat into the wind.

As I did, Tara patted me on the shoulder, letting me know she had confidence in me. "What's the name of that mountain, anyway?"

That was when the spray of water erupted, and we heard what sounded like someone spitting. Once, twice, three times. We were being shot at from the dock.

"Shit, shit, shit."

Call me a motor-er, call me a stinkpotter, call me anything but late for dinner, I left that damn engine on, and we got the hell out of there. I felt something on my hand and looked down behind me. There were three hands on the tiller, and we were out of danger.

Victoria went below to use her cell phone to call 911. The operator said she would send an officer out and for us to stay put. Stay put? In a sailboat? Ordinarily this would call for one of Victoria's zingers, but she left it alone.

Tara was squatting down but had kept her eyes on the dock. "He's leaving. Going back to whatever rock he crawled out from under, I guess." Then she took her strappy sandals off and went to the foredeck.

"Should I call them back and cancel? He could still be in the parking lot." We agreed that we would still like someone to come.

Vic and I freed the dogs one at a time, and Tara tethered each to bow railing. "Is there a snack boat?" she asked as she worked.

"A what?" I turned us into the wind and climbed on the cabin top where I raised the mainsail and tied off the halyard. The wind was light so I didn't need much tension. Next I raised the jib, the sail at the front of the ship, pulling in and cleating the lines, called sheets, which I'd use to control it. I returned to the tiller and steered us away from the wind enough for a relaxing sail.

Tara continued, "You know, at the golf course there's a snack cart. On a lake is there a snack boat that will come around with refreshments? Like a cold beer."

"No, but there may be a few in the fridge. I'm not sure how cold they'll be. And there might be chips and salsa somewhere down there."

Victoria found the tiny fridge and brought out three imported beers and the snacks. "None for me," I said and she put one back.

"Can I ask you something?" Tara shaded her eyes with a hand.

"If you're wondering who that guy is, I have no idea."

"Actually I was going to ask what kind of name 'Shit-shit-shit' is for a mountain, but yeah, who was that guy?"

I motioned for Vic to take the tiller and went below to change from my riding clothes into a pair of shorts and a tee-shirt. When I popped back out of the cockpit I said, "I didn't get a good look. When he was following us I saw that he had bushy gray hair. Did he look like any of the husbands we've followed recently?"

Victoria stretched out on a seat cushion. "I could tell he was on the heavy side. He didn't look familiar to me."

"He's short." Tara got up long enough to find her sunglasses and lay back down.

All of a sudden I realized how safe I felt with them around and how good that was. "Either of you ever been shot at before?"

"Nope."

"Nope."

We cruised silently for a while, just looking up at the sky.

"Leigh, can I ask you something?"

"Sure, Vic."

"Why did you come back to Georgia, uh, alone? I'm glad you did, but were you and your husband having problems?"

"We weren't having problems, I was. I felt like I had been cast out of the land of love, as they say. I didn't know if it was hormones, age, familiarity or being too busy to take care of myself. I just couldn't live in a world that revolved around him. Now my world revolves around me. And guess what?"

"What?" they said together.

"I think I'm a better wife for it."

Victoria nudged Tara with her foot. "Can I ask you a question?"

"Oh, why not."

"Would you ever cheat on Paul?"

"Maybe."

"Why? He's so nice."

"I've decided that when I'm married, I'll be married, and when I'm single, I'll be single."

"Well, then, can I ask something?" I said.

"Go ahead."

"If you do, will you tell us what it's like?" That got us laughing and took our minds off being shot at, sort of.

"Speaking of being single, you seem to have adjusted well." Tara and I raised our sunglasses to our foreheads. Why was Victoria bringing this up? I laid back down, wishing Tara all the luck in the world responding.

"I never for a second missed him, but it was scary at first. What I realized about myself is, I want to know everything but not *have* to know anything."

"Like what?" Vic was propped up on her arm.

"Oh, like how to rent a car in an airport you've never been to before, and being able to make connections when you fly. You probably take those things for granted with the business travel you had to do, but they scared me."

"But you're a lawyer. You didn't have business trips?"

"Nope. And my ex never wanted to go anywhere, at least not with me."

I smiled with love. Tara had neither encouraged nor discouraged Victoria from doing whatever she decided to do.

"What are you smiling about?" Victoria was sitting up by then.

"Mmm, we sure cuss a lot. I inherited the ability from my Aunt Mary and then I honed my cussing skills in stables growing up. What about you two?"

"With two kids, I couldn't cuss. I learned from you."

"Yup, I never cussed till I started hanging out with one Ms. Leigh Reed."

"Gosh, thanks guys. You two are so sweet, and it makes me feel so good."

"You're damn welcome."

"Hell, yeah."

I looked around to see if the Navy, actually I guess it would be the Coast Guard, had come for us. We were still alone. "You may not believe this, but cussing is frowned on in some circles."

"No-o-o." Tara shook her head back and forth.

"I've never heard that. Are you sure?" Victoria's church attire was a tan linen shirtdress and espadrilles.

"Don't you think there are much more irksome things people say in conversation than cussing? Like asking and then answering a rhetorical question, just to show they know something you don't." I paused to think of others.

Victoria smoothed her skirt. "Or when you do know something and they say, 'I knew that' when you know good and well they didn't."

"Or when someone says something so obvious, it goes without saying. I think it's irritating when people are surprised that it's hot in Atlanta and talk about it like they were the first to realize it. I wish I had a nickel for every Northerner that came for the Democratic Convention or the Olympics that said, 'It's sooo hot.'" This Tara said in a first-rate New Jersey accent.

My eyes were closed, and I had no intention of opening them for a while. "I hate it when people say curse instead of cuss. It seems like a curse word would have more than four letters in it, and I find myself racking my brain to think of one that does. That's why they call them four-letter words. Or when someone mispronounces a word and then says there are two ways to say it. Sure, you can say *pot pouree*."

"And there's always, 'good times, good times.'" After Victoria said this we all went into a sun stupor that a perfect-temperature day can bring on.

I thought about my friends. Good times, good times, indeed.

About a half hour later the Hall County police called Victoria's cell phone to tell us the shooter had taken off before they arrived, and there was no one in the parking lot now. She had him on speaker phone, and we heard the officer say, "The coast is clear."

"Pardon the pun?"

"Huh?"

"Never mind."

"Do you want to file a report?"

"Can we do that with the Gwinnett County police since that's where he started following us?"

"Sure."

On that note we headed back in. I dropped off the rest of Tiara Investigations, two and four legged, at the Cracker Barrel.

"Don't go straight to Tara's house," I warned Victoria as we pulled up behind her Lexus SUV.

"Good idea."

"Or better yet, I'll follow you as far as Peachtree Industrial."

"Very good idea." Tara was already looking around and chewing her bottom lip. "Good gosh a'mighty. I'm diet pill jumpy with no floors mopped at three a.m. to show for it."

Seven

Continuation of statement by Leigh Reed. So many emotions flowed through my body and brain, trying to get my attention. Some I could name, like sadness that the world had disappointed me, and some I couldn't. I even felt insulted, like, excuse me, did you just shoot that gun at *us*? If I didn't stop moving I could postpone dealing with the feelings, right? Made sense to me.

I had an apple with peanut butter for a late lunch, showered, threw on a pair of jeans and a sweater, tied a peace sign kerchief on Abby, and headed back out. Friends from different peace organizations were meeting up at Piedmont Park to hand out membership flyers. Sure, I wanted to do my bit for the cause, but I won't deny I also wanted to be out in public. After being followed and shot at, and not knowing how much the good-for-nothing piece of shit knew about me, I didn't care to be at home by myself.

I found Bobbi, the executive director of the women's peace group I'm a member of, and we headed to our assigned street corner. I handed out flyers--*Support the Troops , Oppose the War!* – and asked for signatures and email addresses. She gave out our signature bracelets, purple and yellow swirled, stamped with that message. Soon we were chatting. "I haven't seen you around much lately. Traveling?"

"No, just life." It was an answer that would have to suffice.

"Well, we're glad you're here today. We need all the help we can get."

"Glad to be here." The bracelets are always a big hit, and before we knew it a line had formed.

"By the way, do you think your husband would give us a briefing the next time he's home?" Her usual can-do tone carried just a hint of tentativeness.

I thought for a moment. "Yeah, I'll ask him, and I'm sure he will. That's not really his kind of thing, but I think it's important to hear what's really going on in Iraq and Afghanistan. I'll let you know when he's on leave again." I knew he wouldn't be wild about the idea, but he'd do it. It would be fun for us to do this together.

"I hesitated to ask because I didn't know how your husband felt about our organization. I thought generals' wives were supposed to be apolitical."

"I'm pretty sure a general came up with that little rule. I told my husband about my politics when we were dating. He's on the other end of the spectrum, but we make it work." As for not knowing I'm in this group, puh-leeze, like I would ever keep a secret from my husband. Perish the thought.

A couple of hours later Abby and I were back home. Everything looked normal from the driveway. I was happy my house sat just a friendly little distance from the road and vowed never again to whine for a larger front yard. I looked around at the mums, peonies and pansies. It's an orderly yard, and I don't mean that as praise. I was glad to see that nothing was crushed or stepped on or disturbed in any way. The security alarm hadn't gone off. Abby wasn't trying to tell me anything, except that she was tired and wanted to nap. I opened the garage and drove in.

On my way upstairs for a shower and change of clothes, I turned on my intercom music system, and the whole house was filled with Celso Fonseca singing from one of his earlier CDs, *Slow Motion Bossa Nova*.

I have two home offices. An upstairs bedroom is used for business files, and that door is closed when need be — read, when my husband is home. The furniture is white cottage style, and the chair is upholstered in a fabric of leaves and flowers.

My downstairs office is also a library and my husband's office. Needless to say, I was cautious about leaving files in there. "Let's go, girl," I said to Abby. Her response was somewhere between a huff and a sigh, but she followed me back downstairs.

That office was where my laptop was left to charge. The furniture and book shelves are a rich mahogany, and the chair is leather. I sat at the big, serious desk and installed the camera software and practiced taking pictures of my sleepy-eyed girl, downloading the photos off the camera and printing them. I enlarged a couple of them to eight by ten inches and propped them up against silver frames on the book case. Next I would try cropping a photo, but I stopped, my hands above the keyboard. I swiveled around and saw that I had covered up the photos of my husband. My mood deflated. I was so low I would have had to look up to see down. Just a few hours before when I was horseback riding, I had felt confident in myself and certain that everything was fine, but being shot at had cancelled that out. I wanted it all, and I didn't know how long I could have this bifurcated life.

I went online to check for e-mails. There was one from my husband saying good morning. Even though Iraq is eight hours ahead of Eastern Standard Time, we are always aware of each other's time zone. I keep Zulu Time in mind, too, mostly out of habit. Z Time is Greenwich Mean Time, not adjusted to daylight saving time. The US military synchronizes according to Z Time.

I started to respond to my husband's e-mail when the instant message box appeared. It was him, and my heart soared.

Are you waiting for anyone? This is our code so that I will know it's him. Those were the first words he ever spoke to me. That was ten years and three months ago, and I was waiting for someone, but I didn't know it.

I was sitting on the bleachers by the tennis courts waiting for a friend, I don't even remember who, when he walked up. Tennis whites were made for that tan. His sleeves strained over the muscles in his shoulders and upper arms. My eyes widened as I stared. Love at first sight.

He had to repeat himself, "Are you waiting for anyone? Would you like to hit a few balls?"

I managed a quick nod and followed him to a court, pulling my hair into the elastic band I kept around my wrist 24/7. He leaned over me as I opened a can of tennis balls. Pushing one ball into the pocket of my tennis undies and handing one to him, I walked to the base line. I tossed the ball and hit it over the net to him. With a one-handed backhand he sent the ball directly into the net.

He chuckled self-consciously, looking down and shaking his head. Then he took the ball out of his pocket and hit it to me. I ran to the midway point between the base line and service line and positioned myself with my shoulders perpendicular to the net. I hit the ball cross court, he returned it, and the rally lasted several minutes before I hit the ball wide. I reached for the other ball in my pocket and hit it long. He caught it after the bounce and froze. The ball must have been moist from my perspiration. He turned and tapped the ball over the net. I ran toward the net and returned it. With another light touch, he moved closer to the net. After my return I was at the net and in position to volley. We both knew this was a high-risk strategy in singles. I returned his volley, and he returned mine. I slid my hands around the grip for a backhand volley. Just then our eyes met. The ball hit the strings of my racket and startled me, and we laughed. Our friends appeared, and we played doubles, but it was too late to save either of us.

Just like that, we fell in love. This was the man I had waited thirty-seven years to meet. A beautiful woman in her twenties is the object of competition, each man peeing higher on the tree than the last. By some miracle I had avoided marriage until my thirties. This gave me time to realize I had been the tree, all along. The testosterone-fueled egos that led these future leaders of corporate America to court me made them inferior partners, preening, boastful and selfish. I had chosen to be alone and different. But I knew him when I saw him.

As luck would have it, I'm a peace activist married to a career soldier.

I'm here, Bellifortis. That's my code name for him. It means *he who is strong in war.* In these instant message conversations we have, I can't ask where he is or what he's doing in case some unfriendlies are eavesdropping; and we don't say we miss one another or want one another, because that just makes it worse.

Good to reach you at home.

Yes, I answered, not sure what that comment meant.

How are you? Is everything okay?

Yes, especially now that I've heard from you.

How is the weather there? He didn't mention Atlanta because he didn't want to make it easy for a terrorist hacking the computer network to find out where I live. Since I hadn't changed my name when I married, I felt anonymous and safe. Except for seeing a client murdered and being shot at, except for those things, I felt completely safe.

Beautiful fall day. Are you having breakfast now?

If you call it that. Not like your cook …

And he was gone. Oh, well, an e-mail and an instant message in one day was pretty good. Until last year my husband led night raids ferreting out insurgents. Now he gamed the missions but did not lead them himself. This is partly because of his age and partly to multiply his expertise exponentially. He had led these raids as he rose in rank even though it wasn't expected or commonly done. Of course, I slept better now. I just hate it when people take dangerous risks, don't you?

Several e-mail messages were jokes, one from a friend from my alma mater, the University of Georgia. *What do you call the useless piece of skin on the end of a man's penis? His body. Why does it take 100,000,000 sperm to fertilize one egg? Because not one will stop and ask directions. What's the best way to kill a man? Put a naked woman and a six-pack in front of him. Then tell him to pick one. Why did the man cross the road? He heard the chicken was a slut.*

I would take these to read at our next stakeout, and while I waited for the printer to hand over my pages, I looked around at my life. My eyes fell on the American folk art I collected, almost all with practical uses: weathervanes, decoys, tables, and bowls. I had shopped at flea markets and antique shops on Sunday afternoons. This was just after the house was constructed, and I was building a home, but I had not erected one so much as I had gathered it around me. This had been important to do after I took a stand with my husband that I was not moving again. Surprisingly, he loved having a real house and found it a comfortable place to come home to. Now Tiara was my home as much as that five-thousand-square-foot structure.

Next, I checked the Tiara Investigations e-mail account, and there was one message. Savannah Westmoreland wanted to hire us. Sure, there's a Contact Us button on the website

Victoria designed for us, but no one had ever used it. (And Mr. FBI, can I give a shout out to her for this? The website looks elegant in a sparse kind of way. She couldn't use our photos, addresses, real names, or complimentary letters from satisfied customers, and the website still looks good, and she deserves all the credit.) This was a first, to receive a request for services via e-mail. It felt peculiar. Maybe it seemed too easy. I telephoned Victoria and Tara to see if they were up to a meeting Monday morning before the trip to The Peachtree Group, and they were, so I responded to the e-mail with the location and time.

Later my mother called. "I am so mad I could just spit." I doubted my mother had ever spit in her life. Had hissy fits, sure, but spit, no. I would know it was a spat with one of her sisters if she referred to one of them as *your aunt*.

"What's the matter, Mother?"

"It's your Aunt Thelma. She received your thank you note for the birthday flowers. Do you know why she called? She called to tell me she thought your handwriting was atrocious. Do you know what she claimed? She claimed she could hardly read what you wrote. Do you know what I told her? I informed her that you happen to have excellent penmanship. Well, I was so exasperated. Do you know what I did?" There had been so many rhetorical questions that I did not expect to have to answer this one.

"Well, do you?"

"No, Mother. What did you do?"

"I called your Aunt Opal, that's what I did. And do you know what I found out? Your Aunt Thelma had already called her! Yes, that's right. Your Aunt Thelma called your Aunt Opal and complained about your handwriting! And then she called me! Oh, I tell you ... Oh, Leigh, I'm getting another call. It's probably one of your aunts. I should have known after I called your Aunt Opal she'd just turn around and call your Aunt Thelma. That is just something she would do. Are you doing all right? I'll talk to you later."

"Good-bye. Give them all my affection." When I was sure she had hung up, I added, "My two best friends and I were shot at today." As I live and breathe ...

I was glad my mother hadn't brought up the subject of my marriage. She's not overly fond of my husband and describes his family as the sort of people that buy their own silver. And there's something else. Even as she defends me, it's always more about her. But what else is new? Don't get me wrong, I love my mother, but I can see her clearly. I think.

My father died, and she became a widow on the very day I met my husband-to-be. At the time we didn't know either fact. During dinner at an outdoor café in the Virginia Highlands neighborhood the night following our meeting, I got the call from Mother. My father was missing in Antarctica. When my future husband learned I was going to join in the search, he surprised me by joining the team and staying with me. By the time his leave ended, he had told me much about his life but nothing more revealing than when he said, "I was so far gone I didn't think I had a soul anymore, but I guess I do because I've found my soul mate."

A few minutes later a Tiara call came in on my cell phone, and I ran to answer it. "Tiara Investigations," is how we answer the phone. Clever, right?

"This is Beatrice Englund," a woman said, and her tone indicated she expected me to recognize that name.

"And my name is Leigh."

"Uh, I'm Kelly Taylor's mother." A light went on. I thought, and I'm pretty sure I didn't say, "the First Baptist Church of Anywhere lady." I knew exactly who she was, helmet hair, tightly pursed lips and all.

"I would like to meet with you this evening, if possible."

Ordinarily I wouldn't be wild about working on a Sunday night, but I was in a good mood from my on-line conversation with my husband, despite the intervening call from my mother, so I agreed to the meeting. First I called Tara to ask if she wanted to come.

"I might as well. At least it'll keep me from getting kicked out of another book group."

"Now, Tara, how many book groups have asked you not to return?"

"Three, not counting tonight."

"What did you read for tonight's meeting?"

"That's just it. I don't exactly always read the book."

"I'm sure that happens to a lot of members from time to time." I was trying to be supportive but hoping she would blow it off and join me with Beatrice Englund.

"Tonight it was either *Jane Austen* by Jane Eyre, or *Jane Eyre* by Jane Austen."

"Hon, Charlotte Bronte wrote *Jane Eyre,* Jane Austen wrote several books, *Emma, Pride and Prejudice, Sense and Sensibility.*

"Then I guess one of you better pick me up."

I called Victoria, and she jumped at the invitation. "Do you want to get out of the house because Shorty's not home or because he is?"

"Yes." The cryptic answer told me he was there.

Victoria picked Tara up and then they came by for me. I told Abby she would be the man of the house until I returned. We drove the mile or so to Juanita and Juan's Mexican Restaurant, curious as hell to learn why Kelly's mom would want to meet with us.

"Tara told me she keeps getting cast out of book groups for not reading the books."

"They can kick you out for not reading the book?"

Tara was touching up her lipstick because we were almost there. "You're not technically thrown out. I'm just too embarrassed to go back. It's because I pretend I've read the book. Did you know *The Heart is a Lonely Hunter* isn't really about deer, rifles, camouflage and blinds? Well, if you're ever in a book group, you're going to want to know that. Next month is going to be even worse. They're reading something by Shakespeare, which is in a foreign language."

"It's English." Victoria turned off Suwanee Dam into the Publix parking lot, cutting through to the restaurant.

"Foreign English, the worse kind of foreign language. Have either of you read anything written by Shakespeare?"

"Almost everything."

I, however, put a feminist spin on it, "Just Juliet and Romeo. Don't give up reading. Some authors can make anything interesting."

"Who? Can I send one of them my husband?"

"I knew I could count on you two. I need a little humor. I just had one of those conversations with my mother. She had words with one of her sisters." I reached up between the seats and patted them on their shoulders.

"Is this the same sister she had words with a couple of months ago?" Tara blotted her lips.

"Yep, the one she accuses of sitting down to iron."

"Does your aunt sit down to iron?" Victoria asked.

"I have no idea. Maybe it was just the worst thing my mother could think of to say about her."

"What had the poor woman done to make your mother accuse her of such a heinous crime?" Tara asked.

"She told my mother that she was wrapping Christmas gifts."

"Wait." Victoria was laughing, "She was wrapping Christmas gifts in August? You're kidding."

"I don't know if she really was or not, but you have to admit, it does make you feel, well, inferior to think someone else is. Vic, what do you do when you're mad at someone?"

"Different things. For one, I use a regular postage stamp, instead of a Love stamp for their birthday card."

"That's gotta sting." Tara was looking out the window for Mrs. Englund.

"We're here. Let's get our game faces on." Victoria was looking out for a parking space.

"Now if I can just keep myself from referring to her as the First Baptist Church of Anywhere Lady, I'll be doing good." I had my brush out for a quick touch-up.

"What does that mean anyway?" Victoria looked back at me.

Tara tossed her makeup bag back in her oversize handbag. "It's like a male who says, 'I don't smoke and I don't chew …'"

At that point we finished in unison, "and I don't go with girls who do."

Beatrice Englund looked a little out of place. It wasn't the red vinyl booth with a sombrero on the wall over her head. It was due to the fact that she was eating salsa with a spoon. "Fewer carbs this way."

Tara looked for a waiter, "Can we have *queso* dip and some guacamole? Then, looking around at us, "Four margaritas?"

"Sure," Victoria and I answered together.

Tara instructed the waiter, "On the rocks, no salt."

I guess Bea's not much of a drinker, because by the time she finished that first margarita, her personality had undergone a transformation. Victoria had been waiting for that. "Did your daughter and son-in-law have a prenuptial agreement?"

"No."

Tara started her slow grin. "Prenups are for fat girls." Bea nodded and smiled that same smile. She leaned over the table and gave Tara five, and I thought, *is she a Tiara girl that has lost her way?*

Bea looked down at her lap and started to talk. "Since her marriage she's not been the same sweet girl I raised."

"Prison changes a woman." I shrugged my shoulders.

"She's been overwhelmed by that big house. I wanted to decorate it for her, but my son has been ill, and I've had to take care of him. Maybe Kelly will move in with me now this has happened." Here her voice trailed off like she was working out the details. "Do you three have children?" Tara and I shook our heads no.

"None that I know of." I smiled at my joke and at the fact. Tara was not because she had never gotten over not having a child. Victoria answered in the affirmative, so Beatrice addressed her.

"There are a handful of memories from your child's first years that tell their whole life's story, though you don't know it at the time. For Kelly it was when we left for a vacation when she was three years old. My sister and I took our kids to Florida every summer. Our husbands had loaded the luggage on the roof of the car, and we started backing out of the driveway. I'm not sure why, but I looked toward the bay window in the living room. Do you remember those big bay windows we used to have? Well, I am still shocked at what I saw. We had left Kelly! My baby! I mean, I could have described every bowel movement the child had had in the last month, and I had left her in the house. I guess I thought my sister had her, or there was just so much noise and confusion getting ready to leave. And you know what? She was standing at the window looking so sad and alone, but sort of resigned to being left. She just raised her little hand and waved at us."

Bea dabbed her eyes, as did Tara. "Trust me. It isn't funny the way it is in the movies."

"Dang." Quite frankly, even I was shocked by the story.

"I haven't really let go of her since then." Her voice was hoarse, throaty. "Did you wonder how I got to her so fast on Friday night?"

"Did you do it? Did you kill David?" Tara asked.

I stopped breathing, thinking we were about to have a *Murder, She Wrote* moment where the killer confessed everything at the end of the show. I was wrong. If you think about it, it was kind of a rude thing to ask, but Tara's way was so sweet. Sure, we're detectives, but still.

"For the last month or so Kelly has seemed distant when she talked to me."

Dagnabbit, I mentally noted that she had decided not to dignify Tara's question with a remark. "How so? Can you give us an example?"

"A mother just knows these things. I was concerned, so I made it my business to get to know a couple of her neighbors, and I asked them to keep an eye on her."

"Like you want us to do now?"

"Yes, I'm asking you to take care of my Kelly."

"We haven't done very well so far." I looked down and thought about how to sidestep her request, because for the life of me I couldn't see myself abetting in keeping Kelly Taylor a woman-child. "The reputation of our agency is in jeopardy, so we're very interested in learning who killed David Taylor."

"I'm just asking for an extra set of eyes. I haven't let go of her since she was three." Here she looked at each of us in turn. "And I'm not going to now."

Victoria waited while our empty chip basket was replaced with a nice full one. "Can you tell us what kind of person David was? What was he like?"

Beatrice took a beat to think before she answered. "He was very quiet, an intellectual. I think he was a good man but not the most exciting person on the planet."

"Where was he from?" Victoria asked.

"New York."

"Well, there you go," Tara answered. "How about you, where are you from?"

"Originally Athens. When I married we moved to Winder."

"Not much difference," I said because the towns are so close.

"My husband was a math professor at the University of Georgia. He passed four years ago. We didn't like living around everyone he worked with. It seemed like we couldn't have a private life."

"My father was a physics professor at Georgia Tech," I offered.

"Are you a Yellow Jacket or a Bulldog?"

"I went to Georgia, so I guess I'm more of a Bulldog than Yellow Jacket. Did you work outside the home?"

"I taught high school English. I retired seven years ago."

"How did Kelly and David meet?" Victoria noticed the *queso* bowl was empty and motioned for the waiter to return.

"David was getting his PhD at Georgia, and she was getting her Bachelors. They met at a fraternity party. They've been married six years."

"You said Kelly has seemed different. Are you referring to this remoteness, or is there something else?" I hated to belabor the point, but we were getting very little what I would call usable information.

"She's been moody and depressed. This weekend she has seemed to want to open up but then hasn't been able to tell me what she was thinking."

"She's had quite a shock." Victoria emptied her margarita glass.

"Maybe it's just being pregnant."

That comment shut my mouth. The story about Kelly being left home alone was definitely a buzz kill, but the conversation was brought to a screeching halt by this announcement.

Tara jumped into the breach. "Congratulations, Grandmother-to-be!" She raised her glass, and we toasted one beaming woman. "Victoria's about to be a grandmother, too."

"Well, congratulations to you."

"Thank you. My daughter-in-law is having twins."

They had a few more minutes of talk about babies while I took care of the check. Then we walked Beatrice to her car, a silver mid-sized Volvo. She got in but didn't close the door. "I turned sixty last week. Some birthday gift, huh? I've got my youngest back on my hands."

Victoria closed the door for her. "My mother used to say, a mother is only as happy as her unhappiest child."

"She wasn't lying."

She left, and the three of us loitered in the small parking lot to talk. Tara began, "I'll tell you what set me back on my heels, the way she told us her daughter is expecting. Maybe it's just being pregnant? Or it might just be that her husband was shot in cold blood in the driveway. Good Lord."

I watched Beatrice pull out onto Highway 20. "I know what you mean. I'm awed by her, and I'm intimidated, and I'm not ashamed to admit it."

"Did you notice the way she told us what she wanted to and not a word more?" Victoria clicked her key fob, and several lights on the Lexus came on. "Almost everything she told us led up to her appeal that we look out for Kelly."

"This is all new to us, but don't you think we should try to find out what kind of person David Taylor was?" Tara was biting her lower lip.

"I'm glad we're going to the memorial service." Then we were making the left turn into my subdivision and a right into my driveway. "Have either of you come up with any ideas, brilliant or otherwise, about the guy that shot at us?"

Both shook their heads no.

I was home by ten o'clock. I thought I should check for e-mails before taking the newspaper to bed to read. The first message was from my husband.

Remember a kid named Roger Wilson good kid loss talented

The cryptic tone and the lack of punctuation told me he had written this on his mobile.

Yes, I answered. A box popped up on my screen telling me he was on line. So my next message was written there. *Yes,* I wrote again. Then I realized I didn't need to write in shortened sentences. *I ran into him in the grocery store last week. I'm so sorry.*

Just returned. IED on road from airport. How r u

My mind went back to my husband saying, "You've got to find the IED before it finds you." I ran my fingers through my hair from my forehead to the nape of my neck and thought about how he would want me to respond. Then I started typing again. *I'm fine. I rode General this morning and went sailing this afternoon. Tonight I met Victoria and Tara for dinner at Juanita and Juan's. Another woman joined us and I found myself envious of her. She has such compassion for her daughter. I practically covet their relationship.*

Baby, your mother is who she is.

I know.

Good night I luv u

Good night. I love you.

I turned off the computer and pulled out a sheet of stationery. At that point I didn't know if I would correspond with a wife, now a widow. In the next few days that information would be forwarded to me. But Roger Wilson's mother, for whom he was buying groceries, I could write to right then.

I don't understand how any soldier ever dies. Isn't there a cord going from someone here to the soldier in Iraq or wherever? And they are all covered in a blanket of love and attention. Why can't that be enough?

Once more I would not write what was in my heart about my feelings on the war.

Eight

Continuation of statement by Leigh Reed. On Monday morning Tara and Victoria came over early for our standing appointment with Julio, our personal trainer. He specialized in strength training and Pilates for golf. It would seem we should be excused after all we had been through the last few days, seeing someone murdered, being chased and shot at, and last but not least having dinner with the Woman God Forgot. We couldn't tell him any of this, so we had to endure the full hour of torture.

I had set up bathrooms with guest towels and peach soap. After our showers we met in the kitchen. "We did it again," I noted. We were all wearing black suits. "I'll go change into pants."

Victoria lost the jacket.

Then we were off to the Cracker Barrel on Lawrenceville-Suwanee Road to meet with Savannah Westmoreland. We sat at our usual table and waited. Fifteen minutes later we got antsy.

"I'll walk around and see if I can find anyone that looks like they're waiting for someone." I was back in two shakes. "No luck."

"I wonder if she's coming." Tara looked out the window over her shoulder. "I say let's go ahead and order."

Victoria made eye contact with our waitress. "I'm with you. We don't know what her commitment level is since she contacted us by e-mail."

We placed our usual orders of the Country Morning Breakfast with no meat, but with fried apples for me, and two

Smokehouse breakfasts. Then I got out the e-mail jokes I had printed Sunday night. I read aloud while Victoria kept an eye out for Mrs. Westmoreland to prevent our being taken unawares, laughing our asses off. Women going through what our clients are going through don't want to see the professionals they are counting on being jovial. I don't blame them.

If the government is going to put health warning labels on beer, wine and liquor, let's at least have a little truthfulness about the matter! WARNING: Consumption of alcohol is a major factor in dancing like an asshole. WARNING: Consumption of alcohol may lead you to believe that ex-lovers are really dying for you to telephone them at three in the morning. WARNING: Consumption of alcohol may actually CAUSE pregnancy.

Victoria took a quick look around. "I missed a lot of jokes last week. My computer went down on me."

Tara pounced, "How was that?"

"What?"

"What was it like having a computer go down on you?"

"Like you're always telling us, it only seems kinky the first time." Of course, Tara says that kind of thing all the time, but I never expected it from Victoria. "By the way, Leigh, your skin sure does look good."

"You think so? Thanks. I've been drinking and dialing. Yep, about a month ago I was watching something on a home shopping channel. Before I knew it I was dialing. A few days later I was the proud owner of a few hundred dollars worth of skin care products."

Now Tara looked around to see if anyone was listening in. "That's sort of what happened to me when I ordered the eavesdropping devices. I hadn't been drinking, but I was worked up over … over what had happened."

"Ugh," Victoria and I groaned at the same time.

"All I ask is that you keep an open mind."

"They're hearing aids." The plates were placed in front of us, and we went to town on the food. Just in time, I remembered my manners and thanked the waitress.

I started a more businesslike topic. "Victoria, I balanced our checking account. Hon, you haven't cashed any of your paychecks in quite a while. You haven't lost them, have you?" I knew this couldn't be the answer.

"I don't know how to explain the money," she mumbled with her head down. "Yesterday I decided I wanted to spend the money on my son and his wife and their babies when they get here."

"Was that what you meant after Shorty said they couldn't afford to have kids, and you said they could?"

"Exactly."

Tara pointed at me with her fork. "Success is a bastard."

"Don't you mean, 'Victory has a hundred fathers, but defeat is an orphan'?" Victoria asked.

Tara shook her head. "No, actually I think I meant success is a bitch. That's why Victoria has so much money she can't explain. Where is this Savannah person? We are too busy to put up with no-shows."

I took a drink of tea then looked at my watch for about the umpteenth time. "I have a bad feeling about this, and it's not the ten vitamins I took."

"I think she just chickened out," Victoria offered. "A no-show is the universe's way of weeding out deniers."

"Maybe she decided her suspicions were unfounded. That would be a good thing, right?" After saying this Tara started laughing so hard at her own joke she had to put her face in her hands. "Sorry, I tried."

"I have an idea. My laptop is in my car. I'll log on and see if she left us an e-mail. I'll be right back."

I clicked my key fob as I walked across the parking lot, and the car door unlocked. Just as I reached out to open it I felt myself sway back. It happened so fast it took me that long to realize someone was pulling my arm around. I turned and saw a man, a little heavy and average height, wearing a baseball cap pulled low on his forehead. My instincts kicked in. No, literally. I kicked him in the stomach with my right foot. Then I pivoted and kicked him with my left foot, again in the bread basket. He went down like a sack of flour. I would say like the sack of shit that he was, but that would be indelicate. Victoria and Tara saw some of this from the window and ran out to me. The assailant was lying unconscious at my feet. Tara knelt down to him and Victoria put her arm around me.

"He's the guy that shot at us," I said.

"He's having a heart attack." Tara pointed at his hand, still grabbing at his shirt collar, and started administering CPR. I reached for my cell phone.

Victoria stood there looking down at him. "Well, it turns out the way to a man's heart is indeed through his stomach." This from Miss Congeniality? What is the world coming to? "And you don't need to call 911, they're here."

Tara followed Victoria's gaze. "Oh, my sainted aunt."

Detective Kent walked up, shaking his head, talking on his cell phone slash walkie talkie. Then he put it under his chin. "Just leave," he mouthed.

"That's the man that shot at us yesterday," I whispered, "and …"

Victoria wrapped her arm around my shoulder to lead me away. "It's a long story, and she won't go into it right now." Then she turned me around. I noticed she was walking in, let's say, an overly confident way. Were we trying to act like leaving was our idea all along?

"Victoria, where are you taking her? Maybe she wants to press charges. Have you thought about that?"

"Tara, he doesn't want to be seen in public with us."

"How did he just happen to be in the neighborhood? Do you think his wife told him about our close ties to Cracker Barrel?" As I was talking I became lightheaded. "I'll go pay the check. Be right back."

Behind me I could hear Tara saying, "But Leigh, I left money on the table."

I walked straight to the ladies room and into the handicap stall. Then I let myself slide down the wall to the floor but not all the way. The Cracker Barrel restrooms are always clean, but still. I put my hands over my face. Then I pulled them away and looked first at them and then at my legs. What had I done? I had hurt someone, that's what I had done. If I told Victoria or Tara or just about anyone, they would have said it was self-defense, that he had shot at us the day before and maybe he murdered David Taylor. Even if everyone in the world says you did the right thing, there's a truth in your heart that's louder. We have to save our souls every day. I raised myself back up and went out.

"Okay?" Tara asked.

"I'm fine. Ready for our visit to The Peachtree Group?"

I drove east on Lawrenceville-Suwanee Road to Buford Highway, on to Sugarloaf Parkway. This was not the shortest route as the crow flies, but that time of day it was much quicker. We followed the directions from the six-inch screen of the navigation system to The Peachtree Group office address in Lilburn, east of Atlanta.

"Weren't you afraid back there?" Victoria asked from the backseat.

"I don't believe in fear." Out of the corner of my eye I saw Tara give her a quick glance and realized a statement like that did little to reassure people that you had your wits about you. "Okay, I'm afraid of kudzu."

"Oh hell, everybody's afraid of kudzu. Those vines can grow six feet in a night." Tara was subtly monitoring my driving.

I stopped and let another car onto the road, and the driver waved to thank me. Once she was satisfied I wouldn't do anything crazy behind the wheel, she turned to talk to Victoria.

"You crack me up with some of the things you say, for instance what you said back there about the way to a man's heart. It seemed, mmm, out of character, no offense."

"None taken. I remember when I was growing up and even in my twenties, my friends and relatives were always repeating crazy things I said, like that comment. There's no telling how many census takers resigned after interviewing me. Over the years it stopped. I don't know when, but I think I know why." She looked out the window. "Let's talk about what we want to accomplish in our Peachtree Group meeting. This is definitely a different type of interview for us."

Just like that we had changed the subject. Victoria was in a state of transition, and she would bring it up again when she was ready. I, too, wanted to talk about our appointment. "You're right about that. This is new. I want to know if anyone there killed him, but I guess that's aiming a little high for a first meeting. If we want to know who would have reason to kill the man, it seems getting to know about his world is a good place to start."

As we drove the perimeter road around the office park, Tara commented on the size of the black glass building. "It must contain the manufacturing plant, as well as the management offices." The structure was squat, only three or four floors, but it was wider than a football field. From the front we could see it was actually two buildings, one about a quarter of the size of the other. They were connected on the ground floor, and there was a glass walkway connecting the top floors. I followed the signs to the security gate. The approaching guard had the well-scrubbed look of an Eagle Scout.

"Hello, we have an appointment with Mr. Valentine."

Nodding, he went into his hut and checked a computer screen. He returned with a pass to place on our dashboard and directed us to a visitor's parking space. As we walked the paving stone path, Tara and I reapplied lip gloss, and Victoria checked for voice mail on the Tiara business line at her home. This telephone is physically at her house, but the ringer is turned off. We wouldn't want Shorty to hear a phone ringing and go around the house looking for it. During the week we take turns having calls forwarded to each of our phones. We rarely check the land line on weekends. As Mason said to Dixon, "You have to draw the line somewhere." Her call didn't go through, and she looked down at the phone in her hand.

"My phone is off, but when I press the power button, nothing happens. I could have sworn I recharged it last night." This is the same Victoria that had written the program for a computer game and embedded her resignation letter in it when we founded Tiara Investigations, so if she was perplexed, so was I.

Tara gave me a sideways glance saying that reassurance was called for. "You just forgot, that's all. It's not like you're getting close to 'Delta Dawn, what's that flower you have on?'"

The pavers ended at a sidewalk, and we were looking at twin buildings. "Which entrance do we use?"

"Maybe toward that life-sized sculpture of their logo." Tara pointed at the marble monstrosity on the lawn. The letter A in Peachtree Group was a peach, and the logo was about five feet tall.

"Life-sized? Have you ever seen a peach that big?" Then I heard a swish. Maybe it was time to be punished for something, or maybe it was a warning, but right then, the sprinkler system came on. We jumped and ran toward the nearest door.

The guard looked at our splotchy, see-through attire as we approached the security desk. To avoid his beady little eyes, we lined up and signed the visitors book without waiting to be asked. We jostled to avoid being first, but I lost. "We have an appointment with Mr. Valentine." Saying this a second time, I almost believed it myself. Appointment might have been a smidge of an exaggeration. We had asked Beatrice to leave a message before office hours saying that we would be stopping by to see him later that morning. Let's call it a unilateral appointment. He handed us stick-on ID badges and recited directions to the executive office.

We got in the elevator and slowly looked at ourselves in the mirrored door. We were still dressed almost exactly alike. All three of us were wearing the black skirts or pants to our funeral outfits and white blouses. This seemed like a good idea, because we didn't know if we would have time to change in between this meeting and David's memorial service.

I reached to press a button for the executive floor, but it was already lit by the security folks. "We look like IRS agents."

Tara shook her head. "I was thinking Secret Service."

"Only one thing to do," Victoria said, and we put our sunglasses back on.

Two men wearing khakis and holding smart phones joined us. They lifted their eyes off their e-mails long enough to look at us. "Shower?"

"No thanks, we don't even know you." He pressed the button for the next floor. They took off so fast they left skid marks.

"Leigh, why did you do that?"

"Yeah, you know I usually make those comments." Tara had started giggling.

"I didn't like their looks. Those handheld email-getters are the new pocket protectors."

The elevator doors parted on the third floor at a quiet, controlled place. We hesitated and looked out at the thick carpet. Then Tiara Investigations walked toward the tinted double doors.

I couldn't hear my footsteps, and I panicked. My mind should have been on business, but the scenes from the last few days flashed in front of me. I stopped midway down the hall, overcome and undone. Victoria and Tara were waiting for me and exchanging looks. All I could say was, "It's easy to get lost when you can't hear your footsteps."

Saying this out loud was all it took. I got hold of myself and came to the realization that this was about the last few years of my life. From the outside it looked like a transition, when a restoration was what it had been. For years I didn't hear my own footsteps, and so I ended up where I didn't mean to be. I didn't believe in fear? Maybe not of anything exterior, but I was terrified of ever again being that outsider, dear to no one and without the comfort of a home. I would do anything to save our agency.

"That was disorienting." Victoria reached for me. "But Leigh, we're not lost."

"What are we doing? Who do we think we are?"

"We're just trying to help people." Tara reached up and tucked a strand of my hair behind an ear.

When we started walking again I could hear something, a low crackle, but not continuous like fluorescent lighting. The sound was a succession of slight popping noises, and the sounds were in time with our footsteps. I turned and saw that the spots where my feet had touched the carpet glowed faintly and then disappeared. I motioned to Victoria and Tara to look back.

"That's hot. That's plastic beach chair hot."

Being the professionals we were, we resisted the urge to back up, then stop, then start, start, stop, start, sideways, start, backup, walk crossing our legs over each others, stop, start, stop, stand on one foot, stop, for much more than five minutes. Ten minutes, tops.

"You're going to do the talking, right?" I guess my mini-breakdown was the reason behind Tara's question.

"I'm good."

"What are you going to say to Valentine?" Victoria wanted reassurance that I was on my game.

"I'll ask about the status of their contract with David Taylor's company, Flow Network Design. Then I'll say, 'Oh, and by the way, did you murder him?' Just kidding, you guys. Here we are."

"Praise the Lord and pass the ammunition." Tara tried the door.

A receptionist pressed a button, and the doors opened for us. Then I felt, as much as heard, them close, and she semi-welcomed us. Valentine's secretary was called. He would be free shortly, and then we were escorted to the other end of the lobby. I smiled as the executive secretary discreetly checked us out. I was as accustomed to this reaction from women as I was to men holding their stomachs in when I entered a room. We sat down and removed our sunglasses. Looking around I could see two conference rooms and one office besides Valentine's. We could see into this smaller office, and there were stacks of papers on every surface. *Hey, how's that paperless office concept working out for you?*

A dark-haired man in a black suit sat behind the desk with his back to us, talking on the phone. Next to the computer there was a trophy of a cross country skier with a rod or a pole or something long slung over his shoulder. He held the receiver in one hand, and with the other he reached over for the tiny statue. From where I was sitting it looked like he tipped his head to it. Then he tossed it and caught it mid-air. The familiarity of the bronze trophy made me stare until Victoria spoke and brought me out of it. I knew I had seen one of those before.

I noticed something else. "Look at the way he's dressed. He's wearing a black suit. They knew about Taylor's death before they came to work this morning."

"It was in the *Atlanta Journal Constitution* obituary section yesterday," Tara whispered in response.

"What are you, eighty? Do you read that section? You know who reads that section?" I went back to looking at the guy in the office to our right. "I wish I could hear what he's saying on the phone."

Tara cleared her throat, and we looked at her. She looked straight ahead rather than at either of us and tapped her earlobe.

"We are not getting hearing aids."

"Sound amplifiers."

"I can see Randall Valentine through the side of the glass and he's wearing black, too." Sister Victoria Eagle Eye was on the other end of the sofa and could see into the next office. "It's suspicious."

"Our little business plan took a detour to murder. That's what feels strange to you," Tara said.

I was afraid the receptionist was going to hear, and I needed to call this to a screeching halt. "I agree with Victoria, this place has got murder juju on it, but let's talk about it later."

With that I picked up a copy of The Peachtree Group's annual report which sported the logo with the peach substituted for the letter A. The company was only two years old. I had assumed it was more established, though I wasn't sure why I thought that. The slick publication told a familiar story. High technology firms were incubators for ideas from research wunderkinds, but what good is research without development? Then there was testing and evaluation. While no phase was more important than another, it was the "D" part of RDT&E that was most costly.

"Connecting and protecting the world, what a load of crap."

"I would use the term hyperbole." Victoria was looking over my shoulder.

"I would say twaddle, what with me being eighty."

"Hey, Tara, can I ask you something?" This from Victoria.

"Oh, sure, Victoria, why not? Go ahead."

"How do you feel about Lawrence Welk?"

"Which do you have in your car, a tissue box or stuffed animals?" I wanted to know.

"Okay," Tara refused to look at us. She picked up a magazine and pretended to read it.

"How many miles do you drive with your left turn signal on?"

"Do you yell at squirrels?" I couldn't help myself even though I just hate it when we start laughing while we're on a case. I went back to reading about the company being involved in high-end computing and biometrics.

Tara put her magazine down. "This place feels cold."

I reached over and rubbed her arm like I was trying to start a fire. "Oh, sweetie, you forgot your shawl. I agree it does feel cold. It's the modern interior design."

"If I'd wanted modern, I would have been born later."
Tara looked at her diamond watch. "We've been sitting here
ten minutes. Who does he think he is?"

That reminded me of something. "Actually, who does he
think we are? What did Bea say in her message? Do you think
she told him we're detectives?"

Victoria leaned in and kept her voice low. "I suggested
she describe us as friends."

"If someone here was the guy from Friday night that ran
down the street, he'll know we're detectives." I really wished
this hadn't occurred to Tara right at that moment.

"Or stalkers since we were sitting in front of a house."
Then I saw Santa Claus approaching.

"Ladies?" We had been summoned, so we followed old
Saint Nick, I mean Randall Valentine, down a side hallway.

"Your office is shaped like home plate," I said to break
the ice.

As if seeing them for the first time, he turned away from
me and scanned each of the five walls, two glass and three
cherry paneling. I looked with him. From the window that
would be facing third base, I could see two men and one
woman crossing the glass walkway one floor above us.

"So it is." Rather than sitting behind the massive oak
desk, he moved to a Louis XIV chair and motioned for us to
sit on an eggplant, linen sofa. "Soooo." He drew out the
word, which I believe translates to "get cracking."

So I did. "You're aware that David Taylor was killed on
Friday evening?"

"Yes, it's quite a loss. He was a friend as well as a small
business owner who was making a meaningful contribution
to the war on terror. His software is being used in
Afghanistan, as we speak, and was used heavily in Iraq."

"I thought you said 'the war on terror'." I couldn't stop
myself.

"I beg your pardon." He leaned in. He leaned in! *Hey, fella, don't you know eye contact is just a figure of speech? I thought. You're not supposed to try to touch me with your eyes.*

"The war on terror and the war in Iraq are two different things." I said this because of my abhorrence of the war. I saw the beginnings of a smile. Not a happy smile, but rather an I-just-heard-the-craziest-thing smile.

Victoria stepped in. "Since Mr. Taylor was a one-man operation, Mrs. Taylor will be going through his current contracts. Did he have any outstanding commitments with The Peachtree Group?"

Randall Valentine pried his eyes off me. "Just supporting already delivered products and developing upgrades."

Of course, I had absolutely no response to that. We needed to keep this going, and I had no idea how to do it. This time Tara stepped up to the figurative plate. "Now that we've settled that, we have another matter to talk about. The three of us are always on the lookout for a lucrative investment. Could you give us more information on your company?"

"We have a Board of Funders. These are investors at the five million dollar level." Tara didn't blink, so he continued. "In order to become a funder, my COO informs me, an investor must have a security clearance. If you would care to return in the morning I'll give you an overview of The Peachtree Group's history and goals. If you feel this opportunity is right for you, and you care to pursue it, we'll give you a packet to take to your financial advisors."

I don't know if his attitude change was because he saw the diamond bracelet on her arm, which was carrying a two thousand dollar handbag, or what, but this was going remarkably well, even for us. His last line sounded paternalistic but if it got us back into the building, what the hey.

Nine

Continuation of statement by Leigh Reed. The size of the First
Baptist Church made it appear at first glance that the service
was not well attended. Tiara's job would have been easier if
that was the fact. The majestic sanctuary was three-quarters
filled for David Taylor's funeral. We parked in the middle of
the rear parking lot but walked in separately so that it would
not look odd for us to sit apart. Unfortunately, we looked like
middle-aged triplets dressed in black suits, black hose and
black heels.

Since it was a work day we figured some people would
attend only the service and not the luncheon. That being the
case, the service was our only chance to get a look at some of
the mourners.

We eavesdropped on neighbors, his relatives, her
relatives, his business acquaintances, and their friends, half
white and half African American. Fifteen minutes into the
service Victoria caught my eye and nodded toward the two
men dressed in dark suits in the pew in front of her.   The
man with Randall Valentine was shorter, younger and Asian.
He was the guy tossing the trophy in the side office. Even if I
had not already known who the CEO was, I would have
guessed who signed whose paycheck by his deferential
manner. Victoria was mouthing something, but I couldn't
make it out. Then she started pointing at the younger man.
Next, from a few pews back Tara started pointing at him and
then me.

Had we been paying attention to the minister, we would
have heard him asking if anyone wanted to say a few words
about the deceased. Said minister was, however, paying

attention, and seeing two white ladies near the back waving their arms and pointing, called on the closer of the two. I could hardly breathe. Victoria, shaking, lifted herself up.

"Did anyone here know Eve Wood?" her trembling lips asked. Most of the congregation looked puzzled, then they slowly started to shake their heads no. At first I thought she was going to give a eulogy, but then I could tell she was calling for help from the rest of Tiara. That had to be it. After all, it would have been highly inappropriate to tell these good people how she knew the deceased. *Oh, his wife hired us to follow him.*

She didn't want to go on but she had to while I hatched a plan to help her. Tara was looking up at her patiently, expectantly waiting to hear more about this Eve Wood individual.

"Well, neither did Adam till he tried." Half the church was mortified, and half started chuckling, and then everyone was really laughing. "That's what David Taylor would have wanted us to do, laugh and remember him that way."

Finally, an idea came to me, and when it did I felt like a St. Bernard with whiskey in a little cask tied to my collar. I began sobbing loudly. Tara realized what was up and pulled Victoria with her over to me. They put their arms around me and comforted me as we ambled out of the church.

Victoria whispered, "Leigh, we were pointing at you because that's him. That's Kerry Lee."

We made our way to the back of the parking lot to Tara's Hummer and stood around waiting for the funeral to be over, when we would follow the other cars to the Taylor house. While everyone likes to think his or her funeral will be the social event of the year, here there were rows and rows of cars.

Victoria was visibly shaken but trying to stay professional. "I wonder how many of these people are here for Beatrice. Most of the people looked closer to her age than David's and Kelly's."

"From the conversations I listened in on, I would have to say a lot of these people are her friends." People began filing out of the church. "Tara, when you are behind the wheel it looks like Barbie's been deployed."

She knew I was trying to lighten the mood for Victoria's benefit. "What's the difference in this and what soldiers drive?"

"Well, having ridden in an Army High Mobility Multipurpose Wheeled Vehicle and now a civilian Hummer, I would have to say the main difference is Humvees are rarely strawberry red. And when you see one coming, you don't think it's a huge rolling machine wearing braces." It wasn't working. It was going to take more than joking around to un-upset Vic.

"I will never again suggest changing the password."

Tara patted her back. "Oh, come on. How about, *if loving you is wrong, I don't want to be followed.*"

Victoria still wasn't ready to relax. "Tara, how does this thing drive?"

"Try it," Tara tossed her the keys, and Victoria climbed, I mean climbed, up behind the steering wheel.

"Hurry and get in the procession." I hoisted myself up.

Tara got in back. "I think this guy's going to let you in, hon."

Victoria entered the line of cars a little jerkily, but we were in and on our way. "Let's talk business. That'll be the best remedy for my nerves."

I obliged. "Kerry Lee is a man, so David Taylor wasn't leaving the house to see a mistress on Friday night."

"Mistress?" Tara either hadn't heard or wasn't ready to talk business. "Why is there a word for a woman having an affair, but not one for a man? You can't call him a mister."

Victoria considered this. "And why is there a word for a man whose wife is fooling around and not one for a woman whose husband is having an affair."

"There is?" Tara asked.

"Cuckold."

"Cuckold. Mistress. Hmm, the words sound nice."

"Ladies," I called out, "If we are through building our word power, can we discuss Kerry Lee? What was his reaction when he saw us? Did he remember us from Friday night?"

Victoria was relaxing as she got comfortable with the car. "Tara, do you think he was the man you saw?"

"He's the right size."

We heard a perky little chime. "Victoria, would you press the button to the left of the radio?"

"Ms. Brown?"

"Yes."

"This is Derek from the dealership. I'm returning your phone call. Howyadoin?"

"Fine. I called you this morning because I have a quick question. Are my windows bulletproof?"

"I ... don't think so."

"Then would you find out how I would go about getting them changed? Thank you."

"Yes, m'am. I'll call you back." Tara motioned for me to press the button again, and Derek was gone.

"Leigh, you should complain to your husband about this."

"Tara, I don't think ... Victoria! Where are you going?" She had pulled away from the rest of the funeral procession and off the highway.

"We have to drive through here."

"This is a weigh station. It's for trucks."

"Well, isn't that what this is? Sort of?"

Tara looked in the side mirror. "It gets worse."

I slowly turned around in the back seat, though Lord knows I didn't want to. The remainder of the funeral procession had followed us off of I-985. That was when Detective Kent pulled up beside us. He slowed just long enough for us to see the disgust on his face before moving up to the state trooper on duty at the weigh station. He said something to him from the open window and then got out of his car. Then he waved everyone back onto the highway.

"You're sure I wasn't supposed to go through there?"

I looked in the rear view mirror and saw Detective Kent shaking his head. "Oh, I'm pretty sure."

"This really isn't a truck?"

"Oh, I'm pretty sure. Do you think it's too conspicuous?"

"Are you kidding?" With this Victoria started laughing out loud. "Could we discuss buying scooters?"

"Where would we put Stephie, Mr. Benz and Abby?" I could tell Tara liked hearing Vic laugh.

"Seriously, how often do we need them? We would get Vespas."

"I don't know. I can't see Leigh on a scooter."

"Why not?"

"Since you've got that whole Grace Kelly thing going on."

"I do not."

"Yes, you do," they said in unison.

Vic merged back into the intestate traffic. "Listen to yourself. Your voice is cultured. You practically channel her."

"My only requirement for a scooter is that my ass not look like it needs its own zip code. There. Did that sound cultured?'

Since we had pretty much lost the procession, Tara said the Taylor address to the GPS unit. "Can we discuss night vision goggles?"

"We would need a head mount, and I have no idea how to get either."

"Do they make bifocal night vision goggles?"

"No idea. Let's talk about the case."

"Leigh, this morning, uh, at Cracker Barrel, uh …?"

Tara finished for her, "You mean, when she opened a big ol' can of whoop ass on that guy?"

"Yeah. Were you able to do that because of our kick boxing DVD, or was it your gymnastics training?"

"Gymnastics? I've never trained in gymnastics." I was more than a little surprised.

"Sure you have. That was your talent, wasn't it? Wait, are you blanking on another aspect of the pageant?" Victoria asked.

"That was modern dance."

"That was dancing?" Tara was incredulous.

"Maybe audiences were a little less than keen on my efforts, but that's what it was, or at least was intended to be."

"Hmm."

"Hmm."

"Victoria, you're the dancer. How many years did you study ballet?"

"By the time we were in the pageant, sixteen years. Yep, these kids of today could go to school on my moves."

"And they could go to pre-school on mine."

By the time we arrived at the house, I had miraculously recovered from my outburst at the funeral. We tried to sit near Mr. Lee, but he changed seats just as we sat down. Then we tried again, and again he moved. A coincidence, I'm sure.

The three of us turned our backs to the room to strategize, and I noticed photos on the mantel of Mr. and Mrs. Taylor. In two of the photos they were dressed alike. Victoria read my mind, "He doesn't look like a philanderer, does he?"

"Let's find Kelly."

She was sitting with her mother on the sofa in the living room. Her mother was perched on the edge as if protecting her daughter in a fierce, powerful way. We had planned to ask for a few words alone with Kelly for another go at information gathering, but we thought better of it after seeing Mommy Dearest. They noticed us and walked over.

"We were looking at the photos of the two of you. Were you in the Alps?"

"Oh, no. Neither David nor myself has ever traveled outside the country."

"We're going to be leaving now. We'll give you a call tomorrow." Kelly thanked us for coming and told us good-bye.

Her mother gave Victoria a hug. "By the way, that fried okra appetizer was fabulous. You rarely see okra served as an appetizer in the South."

"I know! Randall Valentine's wife brought it. They're from New York. 'Nuff said?"

The she and Tara hugged. "Bless their hearts."

Bea reached out to shake my hand, but as she took it she leaned in to kiss me on the cheek and whisper, "That photo's ridiculous, isn't it? Everybody knows black couples don't dress alike."

Instead of leaving we walked through the hallway and up the stairs. Tara picked up a glass of wine and Victoria took it out of her hand and put it right back down. We were hoping David's home office was upstairs, but it could have just as easily been in the basement. I glanced around to see if anyone was watching. Beatrice was. She winked at me and I gave her a half nod.

"She's literally watching our backs."

Tara and Victoria saw it too and uh huh-ed in agreement.

All the doors down the long hallway were open. It's only in movies that they're closed and you have to open them one by one until you see something that gives you a jolt. Bingo. It was in a converted bedroom at the end of the hall. Tara sat down in the desk chair and started rummaging through the wide middle drawer. It was orderly but held nothing of interest to us. Ditto the top side drawer which Victoria and I were exploring. We found typical geek paraphernalia: yellow highlighters, pencils, rulers and a calculator.

Tara opened the bottom drawer of files and scanned the labels. "Hello. Check out these two folders in the back." She had reached past the expense report folders and the tax receipt folder, as exciting as those probably were. Both back files were labeled CHINA, and I mean the country, not the dishes. "China? Oh, good. Now we're international detectives."

"That's baby-pool-water-by-afternoon hot." Tara opened up the first file on the desk. Then her eyes hooded over as she considered it further. "Wait, you're not serious."

"Don't worry, I was just kidding."

The first few pages were background on satellites in the form of newspaper clippings and technical articles downloaded from various websites. From his underlines and yellow highlights on the articles, David Taylor had gotten the message that satellites would be to the twenty-first century what oil had been to the twentieth. A satellite can gather all the intelligence in the world, but if it can't communicate the information to a human, it's of no value. Then the idea was taken a step further by raising the possibility of integrating satellite data with feed from a UAV. From there he went into interference of the signal by one with the other. We looked for, I don't know, something that had to do with the Chinese government. There was no sales pitch, proposal or anything else to or from their government.

Tara drummed her fingernails on the page. "Why isn't anything written in Chinese? Something in here should be in two languages. Maybe a contract or product specs, just something should be."

"Good question," Victoria and I said together. We continued to scan through the pages.

David had downloaded and printed an unclassified USSTRATCOM, U.S. Strategic Command publication. The corner of the second page had been folded over to make an arrow to a paragraph. *Information superiority can have a force multiplying effect if, and only if, you add in control of space. The flow of information must be unhampered and uninterruptible.*

"Why was he interested in that?" I wondered aloud.

We scanned journal articles and white papers with more general background information on satellites. One of the margin notes read "G.W.O.T." His handwriting was squared off, masculine.

"Hmm," said Tara, "*Gone with the Wind*. I have to say I never expected that."

I whispered, "It's global war on terror."

"That would make more sense."

We read that several thousand satellites, operative and inoperative, orbited the Earth. The United States owns about eighty percent of the communications and surveillance satellites.

The next file, still labeled CHINA, contained articles on explosives, including IEDs, or improvised explosive devices, the roadside bombs used so often in Iraq and Afghanistan. They are responsible for about half the American casualties in Iraq and about thirty percent in Afghanistan. For a minute I forgot I didn't believe in fear as that term hit my gut and burned all the way to my brain. A vision of my husband in his uniform flashed in my head. The three of us stood at the desk reading as fast as we could.

"We have got to get one of those little cameras that photograph documents. I still want private eye hardware." I was only half joking. Truth be told, I felt like the words on the page had pushed me off a cliff, and I was trying to stop the free fall.

"Eeu-wee, that would be waitress-saying-these-plates-are-hot hot." Tara's nervous laugh betrayed her, but the joke had done the trick. I was back. Had she known?

"Want me to shop for those?"

"No-o-o!" Victoria and I said at the same time.

Clippings from *Army Times*, *Stars and Stripes* and other like publications were included. All the articles were about the search and sometimes the capture of insurgents that build or detonate roadside bombs.

"Assuming he had a contract with the Chinese government, what was the application? What was he working on?" I thought Vic was asking no one in particular, but then she looked at me. "Does the Chinese military have Backpack UAVs?"

"Um, I would assume so. They have the third largest military in the world."

They both looked at me wide eyed, and it wasn't just the white liner we wear in the inner corners of our eyes.

"But let's keep it in perspective; the United States spends more on the military than the next nine largest countries combined."

"Puh-leeze," Victoria said.

"I'm just sayin'. If you add in the supplemental budgets to pay for the wars in Afghanistan and Iraq, we spend more on defense than the rest of the world."

Tara flipped to the next page. "What else was David Taylor into? Working for the Chinese government is big time, right? And now we know that he had a client other than The Peachtree Group. Is that how he was paying for this house?"

Victoria gathered the papers to tidy up the folder, but she saw something and stopped. "What's this?" She pointed to something written on the inside cover of the folder. It was another acronym. David had written F2T2EA.

"It's the Kill chain, Find, Fix, Track, Target, Engage, Assess."

"I want to go over these files again." Victoria gave them to Tara and turned around.

That was when we heard a floor board squeak. We turned and saw the door move slightly. Someone must have looked in on us. I mouthed, "Still out there."

While Tara helped Victoria put the folders in her back waistband, I slipped closer to the door. "If we're going to make our three o'clock tee time, we have to get going. We can't play golf dressed like this."

The folders were in place, and Tara gave Vic a pat on the back. "No, that would be criminal."

In the hallway we found Kerry Lee and walked past him. On television that would have made him start crying and confess, but he just looked at us. Obviously, he didn't give a hoot if we saw him or not.

Our foray into psychological ops warfare having failed, we went back downstairs with Victoria leading the way. "Do you think he'll tell Kelly what he saw us doing?" She was whispering because by this time we were winding through clusters of guests.

"Beatrice will cover for us." I surprised myself with how quickly I had started trusting her and hoped I wasn't making a mistake.

We went home to change and then met up at Hartfield Hills Golf Course. Posted along the winding, climbing road to the clubhouse were about five signs cautioning NO COOLERS. By the time we reached the parking lot, we had taken the hint and figured a blender attached to the battery of the golf cart was more than likely out of the question. We play there anyway.

With our three cars parked next to each other and three back hatches open, we changed shoes and unloaded bags. I pointed over my shoulder. "The City of Hartfield Hills is building a seventy-acre recreation complex over there. It'll include a stadium to hold ten thousand people."

"Your little town is growing up." Victoria patted my shoulder. "I know you're proud."

"Don't laugh, I am." You learn a lot by going away and coming back. "The town was founded in 1939. Since my rule has always been never to live in a town younger than yourself, this works out just fine."

Then it was back to business. I felt like I didn't understand all I knew about David Taylor's murder and figured they were thinking the same thing. We used our push carts, instead of renting two golf carts, so we could talk. While Tara and Victoria were in the ladies room, I made notes about the case on my score card. When they returned, I walked quickly to the first tee box. In some of my golf shirts my stomach shows when I swing so I liked to get the first hole over with and get away from other golfers. "This morning at The Peachtree Group when we got off the elevator our footsteps glowed for a few seconds after each step, and I heard a faint crackling noise. Have you ever come across anything like that?"

Next Victoria teed off. "I did a little research on that while I was home changing clothes. We were tracked."

Tara took her place at the red tee. "What's that supposed to mean?"

"It's the latest in biometrics. Other biometric techniques are fingerprint readers, iris scanners, face imaging devices, and voice readers. They all use an individual's physical characteristics for identification. The tracking system writes and saves a profile of you and your movement in the area."

A bit extreme for most businesses, I thought. "Is this with an electrical charge? Like a body composition monitor?"

"No, that could be dangerous to anyone with a pacemaker. Trackers employ a number of different measuring instruments, like heat sensors and even a scale."

Victoria and I were on the green and Tara was on the skirt. "A scale? You mean they know how much I weigh? Uh-oh." She took her putter and her pitching wedge out of her bag and waited for one of them to say *pick me, pick me*. She replaced the pitching wedge. "Did you notice Beatrice had no intention of letting her daughter know she got together with us last night?"

"Maybe she thinks the investigation is going to be just more stress for Kelly." I kneeled behind my ball and imagined it rolling into the cup.

"I don't know. It sounds controlling to me. I mean, how good a mother do you want?" Victoria had putted in.

After Tara putted in and we were replacing the flag, a golf cart driven by a course ranger pulled up.

"Your fourth is here." Out crawled Detective Kent in golf attire. He looked so much like an ad out of *Golf Digest*, I looked for price tags hanging off.

"Hello, ladies." He got his clubs out and we walked to the second hole. "Are you any good at this?"

"We usually break a hundred, but that's for nine holes. That's okay, isn't it?" Tara's smile and raised eyebrows accompanied this smart-alecky reply.

He teed off the white tee, and the ball shot a couple of stories high. Unfortunately for him it dropped about three yards past our red tee, the ladies tee. "I'll take another."

"That's consistent," I whispered to Victoria and Tara.

"Taking another?" Victoria whispered back.

"Yeah, and cheating."

As we walked to the fairway the detective said, "I'm not much of a golfer."

"No?" I'm sorry, but he was begging for that.

Then we heard the first few bars of "Hey, Good Lookin'," and Tara looked around for marshals as she rummaged through her golf bag for her cell phone. Tiara Investigations' calls had been transferred to her phone.

"Actually, it's mine." The Detective had his open phone in hand and obviously didn't give a rat's ass about course rules. He turned his head away and chuckled. "Later, a little later."

I remember thinking, *what the hell?* When I saw the look of foreboding on Vic's face, I moved over to stand next to her.

"Same song on his phone as Tara? Can't be good," she whispered.

Detective Kent hung up and looked at Tara, "Buffett?"

"Chesney," she answered.

"Black."

"Jackson."

"Keith."

"Strait," they said in tandem.

The two of them laughed, and Victoria and I chuckled. All we were missing was the guffaw. So they could both name all the singers of the song, big deal.

What the hell, indeed.

"How are you doing with the case?" He put the phone in his pocket, and we were walking again.

When we got to Victoria's ball, she appeared to be looking through her bag for the best club to use, but seeing her tightly pursed lips, I knew better. "Case? What case?"

"Have you figured out who killed David Taylor yet? I mean, it's been almost three whole days."

I looked at his shit-eating grin. "I thought the police always warned private detectives to stay out of cases."

"The angle I'm pursuing is the about-to-be-jilted wife, and I take it you three do not agree with that."

"No, that dog won't hunt."

"So what do you have?"

Victoria approached her ball. "Not much. We have learned a little about his business, and everything seems to be on the up and up. He was a subcontractor for a manufacturer of products for DOD."

Kent stopped in his two-timing tracks. He raised his sunglasses and looked at us. "The Department of Defense? As in, defense contracts?"

I saw the look on Victoria's face and put my hand on her arm. It was too little, too late, and she lit into him. "Wait. You're the police. You don't know what kind of work he does? What have *you* been doing for three whole days?"

"We know he's the owner of a computer systems company. We don't have the manpower to go ..."

"Staffing. You don't have the staffing," I corrected.

Kent ran his hand over his head, and no longer was every hair in place. "For the love of ... we use our *manpower* to go down roads that have the greatest likelihood of leading to something." Then he turned to Victoria. "You said he works on defense contracts. If this murder investigation leads that way, I'll have to turn this over to the FBI or to Homeland Security, and I would hate to do that. I would *really* hate that. If it's related to his business, you find out and let me know." Here he stopped and looked at me. "Remember, your business license is at stake. What did I have on that hole, four?"

"Six," we said together.

He looked at me. "The thug that attacked you is named James Goody. He has a history of doing that kind of thing for hire, and that was probably the case this morning."

"And Sunday. Did you hear about that?" I was still staring at his hair.

"I read the report. You sure that was him?"

"Yes, I told you this morning it was."

"You might have been hysterical."

I gripped a club (a three wood, I believe it was) and lowered my head, but before I could take even one step toward him I felt Victoria's hand on my arm and Tara's on my back. I knew I wasn't going to do anything but rant a little. My one foray into aggression this morning was still gnawing at me.

"Okay, look, he's in the hospital. He's not going anywhere."

"Who hired him?" Victoria returned to the cart path, and we walked to Tara's ball.

"He's not talking."

"What's the matter, Detective? Can't you make him talk?" cooed Tara.

Kent looked down at her. He and I and the horse we came in on wondered if she was taunting or flirting. "He's in intensive care." Then back to me, "In your line of work, it could be any of the husbands you've gone after."

I looked down at the club I was twirling in my hand. "Hmm. It's probably just a coincidence that it started after David Taylor's murder."

"Hmm," repeated Detective Kent. He looked into the distance, "For the love of Pete." He pocketed his golf ball and said, "Good luck, ladies. Enjoy your game. I'll try to get Goody's whereabouts for Friday evening." With that he shouldered his bag and walked back to the club house. Then he turned around. "Your statements are ready to be signed. Come by this afternoon."

I was headed to my ball but stopped. "You didn't bring them?"

"Why couldn't you have brought them to us?" He paused when Tara spoke but still didn't turn around.

"I mean, really, wouldn't that have made more sense?" Victoria asked as we watched him saunter off in his little golf outfit.

I said as low as I could, "You look like your mother dressed you."

"You look like your daddy dressed you." I may have blushed, and I tugged on my shirt.

"Bless his heart," we said in unison. Then I made a thirty foot putt.

Under our rules that feat allowed Victoria to pick up her ball. "I don't know what his problem is, but I bet it's hard to pronounce. Leigh, do you want me to ask Frank to let us know when that guy is discharged?"

"Still Frank?"

"Yep."

"No, don't tell Frank, the surgeon once known as Shorty."

"Are you sure?" Tara picked up her ball also.

"I'm sure. First of all, I think that would be hard to do without telling him why you want to know, and second, we have round-the-clock police protection."

"It seems like he's always around." Victoria pushed her cart toward the next hole.

Tara followed her. "Like a fat kid on cake. Don't you think it's cute how he won't use God's name in vain?"

"Yeah, cute. He'll cheat on his wife, but he won't use God's name in vain." Victoria turned and looked toward the club house. "How did he know we were here playing golf?"

Tara and I shrugged our shoulders.

"Do we know any more about David Taylor's business?"

"We know he developed interoperability software for The Peachtree Group's Backpack UAVs, and I found a lot of the same information, with a few modifications, in the China files."

"Was he working on Chinese Backpack UAVs?"

"Actually, I can't tell what he developed for them. It could be an application for Backpack UAVs or ..." She began again, but still in a lowered tone, "Remember, most of the information was about a satellite system. I don't know yet, but it's possible it had to do with that."

We pulled out our drivers, and I walked up to the tee. "The Chinese tested an anti-satellite weapon in 2007. They shot down an old weather satellite. They were criticized by the US and several other countries for doing it." By the time my body uncoiled from the swing, my ball was bouncing on the fairway.

"How do you know all that?" Tara replaced me at the tee.

"We were stationed in Europe at the time."

After Victoria's drive we were walking again and headed for her ball, the one closest.

"Let me see, what else? They're believed to be working on a number of anti-satellite systems. One is a ground-based laser system to disable satellites. Another is a radio frequency weapon that targets satellites in orbit."

We were at Victoria's ball. "According to that second file in his home office, his software was for communications interoperability, like at The Peachtree Group. There was something about the Chinese contract that concerned him, but it wasn't in there."

"How do you know what he was feeling about the contract, or possible contract?" Tara shielded her eyes from the sun and waited for Vic's answer.

"His doodling became x's and question marks. Some almost tore through the paper."

"The Chinese have been adamant in their opposition to the weaponization of space, so the anti-satellite test seemed out of character. Until then the US and Russia were the only nations to shoot down an object in space. That might be what his panties were in a wad about." I continued talking once we were walking toward Tara's ball. "Without knowing what he was working on for the Chinese government, it'll be almost impossible to tell. And it *would* be the government, not a primary contractor. Remember, Beijing doesn't use military contractors the way we do."

I was walking the cart path toward my ball and realized they weren't following. "What? I never said I spent the last ten years knitting." Man, oh man, was that ever the truth.

Victoria was still chewing on the problem. "It seems implausible that his China project had anything to do with satellites. First, a one-person company contracting on space operations projects? I don't think so. Next, a radio wave is a radio wave, but because of conditions in space that business has little in common with the way a backpack UAV works."

Tara had picked up her ball and followed me to the putting green. "Even so, since the call that brought him out of his house was from The Peachtree Group, we're working on the assumption that his killing was work related. Maybe not related to China, satellites, or any of that, but related to The Peachtree Group."

Victoria walked to her ball on the other side. "We've seen his home office. Let's go to his other office."

"It'll have to be tomorrow. It's a three dog night." I told them about the frantic text message I'd received on the way over. It was from a client we had taken on the week before. "Let's go sign the statements, and then I'll pick you ladies up at six to go turn someone getting lucky into someone getting unlucky. Oh, Victoria, can you join us tonight?" I remembered the dinner her husband had mentioned.

"Mr. Benz and I will see you at six," was all she said. *Clunk.* She had sunk her putt.

Ten

Continuation of statement by Leigh Reed. It seemed our client's hubby had left the office early, supposedly to attend a Braves game. Just think, the guy had always thought he was so lucky to be married to someone who followed Atlanta baseball. The way our client put it was, "You know the expression, 'Go Braves?' Well, they went. The Braves are playing in Boston tonight."

Around five o'clock I called Tara to say I was leaving the house. "I'll be wearing black jeans. What are you going to wear? I don't want us dressing alike again."

"I'll wear my jean dress with an empire waist."

"Oh, good cop, bad cop?"

'No, good cop, fat cop. We have really eaten a lot these last few days. If I don't cut back I'm going to have to go back to wearing one of those body shapers, aka girdle."

"I hated those things. I felt like I should be wearing a First Alert bracelet that says in case of accident call for Jaws of Life immediately."

"I need a few minutes. Can you pick Victoria up first?"

"Sure, I'll call her."

I changed into a white tee-shirt, tucked into my jeans and belted, with tobacco brown leather flats. The man's tee-shirt was too thin, so I was wearing two of them and a double-strand pearl bracelet.

Once I had Abby hooked up in her seat belt, I put in a new CD by Celso Fonseca Feriado. Victoria and her dog were waiting at the end of her driveway. She didn't know how I would be dressed, so she didn't want her husband to see me. When Shorty came home to change for the dinner, she told him we were taking the dogs for a walk on the Greenway. Would I look like I was about to walk my dog, or would I be clad in suburban-nonthreatening-housewife-at-the-mall duds? Also, she knew I would be taking the turn on two wheels.

Maybe it was the power of suggestion, but there was something luxurious about Mr. Benz. Vic had a backpack hanging off her shoulder. "So-o-o, we're off to see the Braves play in Boston."

We turned into Tara's driveway and waited for her to come out. "Where is she?" Victoria asked.

With Tara nothing is simple. "She's having a date with her Jacuzzi."

"So we are waiting for her to take a bubble bath?"

"No, hon, she's not taking a bubble bath."

"You seem to think I know what you're talking about."

"Let me put it this way. She's having sex with her Jacuzzi. Also known as self-love."

"Oh-h-h, now I get it. Leigh, sometimes you and Tara mistake me for someone I once was," she said slowly. "That's why Tiara means so much to me. You'll never know how much this is helping me."

"Oh, I know, all right."

"Sometimes you two make me feel like a married spinster."

Tara came out of the house with sort of a glow about her. "Sorry I'm late." She and Stephie climbed in, joining Mr. Benz and Abby.

"You're late, and you can't blame it on one of those erections lasting three or more hours sending you to the hospital. By the way, who are they saying should go to the emergency room, the woman or the man? Victoria, ask Shorty about that."

Tara put on her seatbelt and settled in. "Victoria, you're here!"

"Yeah, I wish I could say I put my foot down and told him he shouldn't have committed me to an engagement without asking, but that's not what happened. He got a call from the hospital and went in to work. He'll make it to the dinner in time for dessert. We did have a few minutes together before he left. I tried to tell him all the ways I had made myself powerless in our marriage and in life, like gaining all that weight and not having my own money, even though I was working. He's seen changes in me this last year, and I think he was happy when I started talking."

"Okay, how much of this talking do you plan to do? Are you going to tell him about Tiara Investigations?" I took my eyes off the road to check the navigation system and glanced over at Victoria.

"Hell, no. By the way, Leigh, do you remember why we didn't tell our husbands about Tiara when we started?"

"We just didn't want to."

"Oh, yeah. Well, I still don't want to hear his opinion of it or get any advice on it. And I want to see how he follows up on this talk. I want it to be the start of a new way for us to be. I realized how angry I am at him. I mean, all the time. I'm angry with him for disappointing me. When we were dating and falling in love, I thought he was perfect. Sometime over the years he disappointed me, and all along I felt disappointed with myself."

"Now that's just crazy talk." I glanced at the GPS thingy and continued. "If there's anyone in the whole world that should not be disappointed in herself, it's you."

"And my job disappointed me. I thought I wasn't cut out for it. Again, I thought it was me, but it was the corporate environment that wasn't cut out for me. This is so much better."

"I'm so happy for you. I have a good feeling about your talk with Shorty." Tara rubbed our friend's shoulder from the back seat.

"For us, this was progress. He can't have a normal conversation. He has to process information and then come back and pick it up again. I'll see if he does that."

I looked over at her smiling, happy face and she caught me. "I saw that look. I know I sound like Pollyanna, but I promise to keep my eyes wide open. For once the state of my marriage is not the most important part of my life. At work I was passed over by younger employees with more flash and less knowledge. That started the downward slide of my confidence level. Add to that the way Shorty talks to me. And menopause. I've thought a lot this year about what I would be like if I ever got my pride back, and now I'm starting to get glimpses of it."

"You love him, don't you?" In our line of work we'd learned love can't be assumed in any marriage.

"I told him I would rather withhold sex from him than anyone in the world."

"It's good to know someone that well, isn't it? My husband knows my secrets better than I do. Oh wait, I'm lying! Except for what I do for a living, how much money I've banked this year, and that somebody's trying to kill me. Other than those things, he knows everything there is to know about me." I was laughing right along with them, but on the inside I was feeling a little funny about how natural this had become.

Tara touched Victoria's shoulder and waited for her to turn around. Looking her in the eye she said, "Just tell him, 'Don't worry about my hair, and don't worry about my lipstick. Just kiss me.'"

"I would sound like a country western song. Even though I didn't know what Leigh was talking about when she said you were having sex with your Jacuzzi, I have picked up some language from you. Shorty wanted to have sex tonight. I told him it would just be mercy sex. He said that he didn't know what that was, but he wouldn't turn it down. Then I said, 'you know, a charity ball.' He said, 'What?' I told him it was the same as duty booty. That's when he asked where I learned language like that. I told him from friends, and he said 'I bet I know which ones'."

"Your mid-term will be next week, so bone up. Pardon the pun." After Tara said this I started humming Elgar's "March No. 1 in D," commonly known as "Pomp and Circumstance."

I didn't mention that Victoria had called her husband Shorty, instead of Frank, because I didn't want us to go any further into this. I asked Tara to call our subject's office and see if he was still there.

"That wasn't tonight's follow-ee, was it?" I pulled into a parking lot until we decided where we were going.

"No, that'd be too easy. His secretary said he had gone to the Y. So since we can't follow him from the office, I guess it's on to Plan B."

Victoria read over my notes on the case. "My first guess, I mean deduction, is that if he does indeed work out, he'll meet his friend, euphemistically speaking, afterward. That has to be the YMCA on Sugarloaf Parkway, the one closest to his office. There are only two hotels in that area. But then they might go to her home."

"I asked the wife what type of restaurant he would most likely choose. A steakhouse, seafood? She said they're vegans." We had the make, model, color and tag number of his car and his food preference, so we were off. I pulled into traffic, and we circled back to Sugarloaf Parkway to head southeast.

"By the way, Tara, you look great."

"I've gained three pounds, and I want to nip it in the bud. I just don't want to have to wear a body shaper again."

"I do remember going to a wedding, afraid if I squeezed my knees together I would squirt out the top and hit the ceiling. However, I thanked the Lord for them." Victoria had her laptop open and logged the case on our Google Doc.

Tara reached in her handbag and pulled out a magazine. "I was just looking at a chart to see what my ideal weight is."

"Look me up. I'm six feet four," I said. "I don't worry about it anymore. I thought we decided the problem wasn't obesity, it was hunger. I don't feel empty or unsatisfied anymore. Aren't you enjoying our work?"

Tara looked out the window before answering. "I would if I wasn't nervous so much of the time. If the tough get going when the going gets tough, where do the rest of us go?"

"Then let's work on that. We can't all be like Leigh, but you and I can do better."

"I think people have the courage they need when they need it."

"Did you know you would need it this soon after we changed our business plan on Saturday to include catching David Taylor's killer?" Tara closed the magazine.

"No, I have to say I did not know I would need it the very next day."

"Then there was that guy this morning attacking you right in the Cracker Barrel parking lot. I can't stop thinking about that."

"Tara, I've thought about it, too. How did he know he would find us at Cracker Barrel?"

"Have we been going there too often? Maybe we should go to other restaurants," Victoria suggested.

"Is someone telling him where we intend to go?" I put on my sunglasses to show I was ready to get to work.

We struck out locating the F-250 Ford at the Holiday Inn and sat there talking. I made a suggestion, "Let's go on to the other hotel and then to the restaurants around there that sell alcohol. That's usually a productive avenue."

Victoria nodded. "We all know you cannot have an affair without alcohol. It's the same old story, drinking makes some people see double and feel single."

"You can bet the barn and the Buick on it." I happened to glance in the rear view mirror. "Waaait, that's them pulling in behind us."

I put the car in gear and drove around the building. When we came back around they were getting out of the truck. We parked and waited a minute. She was smiling like she had not a care in the world. He, however, looked around before he leaned in to kiss her. I got out the digital camera and handed it to Victoria. *Click. Click.*

Instead of going into the hotel, they crossed the parking lot walking toward the McDonalds next door. Victoria followed their movement in the side mirror. "Where is he going? Remember, he's a vegan."

"Uh oh." This had taken Tara's mind off her nerves. "This is getting good."

I opened the sunroof for the dogs, and then we piled out. We hung back, scrutinizing the menu until they had their food and were sitting down. This is something we learned the hard way. If we sat down first, the couple might sit in a completely different section of the restaurant.

Sitting close to one another in a circular booth and more than likely playing footsie, they were eating, you guessed it, double-decker hamburgers. There was a large window behind them, and through it you could see an indoor playground filled with about a thousand brightly colored balls. We walked by like we were on our way to the bathroom but stopped.

I turned to them, "Excuse me, that's my grandson playing out there. Can I just take a quick photo? No need to move. You're fine just where you are." *Click. Click.* The young lady looked up at me. Her open face was unassuming, and I wondered if she knew he was married.

"Huh? What?" Obviously he hadn't heard me, and I took advantage of the delay. Slowly a light came on in his head, and he realized being in a photograph might not be the best idea. He turned and saw there were no children in the play area.

His friend was repeating, "She said her grandson is playing ..." How long was it going to take for him to figure out what was happening? Then he looked at me and jumped up. I may have been smirking. Okay, I was smirking. I'm sorry but when you see a dumb person thinking so hard you're afraid he's going to hurt himself, you want to help. You know he'll probably get there sooner or later, but you get bored to tears watching and waiting. He leaned over the booth as if to charge me.

Tara stepped in between us and looked up at him. "Whoa, big boy."

I leaned over her shoulder, "Actually that'd be ..."

"Oh, right. Anyway, you better sit back down on your bun. She almost killed a real man this morning."

I started to deny this but realized it was basically true. We were leaving before we overstayed our welcome when Victoria turned back around. "Just go home. Just go." She pointed her finger at them. If I'm lying, I'm dying. She was actually wagging her finger at the guy.

We were glad we had parked in the hotel parking lot so there would be little chance of them getting our tag number.

"Do you think they'll take my advice and go home?" Victoria craned her neck, trying to see if they were still sitting there.

I hurried her to the car in case he followed us. "I don't know, but I doubt the meal will be all that happy now."

Tara was practically trotting. "When you're in the mood for one hundred percent beef, it's hard to stop until you get it."

"He wasn't letting his meat loaf," Victoria said and giggled.

"Victoria! Are we in junior high?" I yelled this as we jumped into the car. Once I had the doors locked, we relaxed.

Vic looked at her watch to get the time for billing. "I think our work here is done and in an hour and change. Cooking on the front burner, I'd say."

"Why couldn't Detective Kent see us tonight?" Tara asked.

Victoria turned around in her seat. "Untrained, ill equipped and incompetent? Bull puppy! Want to go to Cracker Barrel for a dessert to celebrate?"

I pulled onto Sugarloaf Parkway. "It's a little late for me to be eating." It'd been a long day and I was, for once, in the mood to go home.

"Me, too, but I'll go with you and sit if you're hungry."

Victoria gave a half laugh. "I'm not really hungry. Isn't it amazing the lengths you'll go to get out of having sex?"

Tara slipped off her sandals. "Hey, I thought things were better between you and Shorty."

"Not that much better. Puh-leez."

After a minute or so I said, "I'd rather not tell Detective Kent about Kelly being pregnant."

"He might already know. I mean, he's not here, is he?" We knew Victoria was kidding, but we did look around the car before taking up our conversation.

"Why not tell him?" Tara nudged one dog or another off her lap.

"He's not exactly what you would call enlightened, and I think he might try to say her hormones made her do it. My woman's instinct says she didn't kill her husband."

"Mine, too." Victoria had logged off and was closing down her laptop. "If he's so sure, why hasn't she been charged?"

"Do you think she'll be an okay mother?"

Victoria and I looked at Tara. "Are you asking if she'll pass on this dependency gene?"

Victoria sort of hummed while she got her thoughts together. "She's dependent on her mother, another woman. I don't know, but it just seems like that's okay. Or maybe just better. At least the baby will have a strong grandmother."

"Amen." Tara pulled her legs up on the seat and enjoyed our success.

Victoria reached into her backpack and pulled out cotton clothes, both pants and tops.

"Are those scrubs?"

"Cool. We haven't used a disguise in a long time. Which case are these for?" Tara inspected hers.

"Are we wearing wigs? Remember the first time we tried those? " How could we forget?

Using disguises is harder than you might think. I bought a wig identical to Tara's hair color and style. She bought one like Victoria's hair and Victoria bought one like mine. Like I keep saying, we had a lot to learn.

"I was thinking we would go by the hospital to interview our friend from this morning. These should get us by the police officer stationed at his room."

"Wait a minute. Is this a trick to get me to apologize to him?"

"No, hon. Lord, no. I would just like to know who that guy was. What was his motive? Were these attacks related to David Taylor's murder?"

I stifled a yawn. "David Taylor's murderer would assume we saw him, which would be a motive for the attacks on us. And that we have photos. Come to think of it, anyone would assume that."

Tara handed the scrubs back to Victoria. "I'm an autumn." Vic exchanged these for another color. "What do we say when we see him?"

"His reaction to seeing us should tell us a lot." I turned into Tara's driveway.

"I have an idea for finding out more about The Peachtree Group. We need to be carrying large handbags tomorrow when we go to hear their pitch for investing in the company," Victoria said as Tara got out of the car.

I lowered the window, and Tara talked to us while Stephie jumped out and ran to the porch. "Have you noticed that no one seems to have known David Taylor? The people at the memorial service respected his intelligence and admired him, but that was about as far as it went. I know I said all this before our first Peachtree Group meeting, but I want to give it another try tomorrow. Maybe we can find an employee that worked with him."

Victoria leaned over me toward the window. "I would like to know more about the company's financial footing. If I can see what projects the employees are working on and what kind of hardware they use, I'll have a better idea of the company's profitability."

"And I would like to know more about the Backpack UAVs they produce," I said. "It's boots on the ground time, folks."

"Good night, ladies," Tara turned to go in her house, swishing the scrubs behind her.

"Wonder what made me think of this?" Victoria asked herself mostly.

Before I knew it Abby and I had dropped Vic off and were in the garage. "How ya doin, girl? Water?"

She mouthed my hand as if to say, "I need to find a spot! Now!"

We went out onto the deck off my kitchen and she scurried down the steps to the backyard to find just the perfect place. My floral gardener's smock was hanging on one of the three antique door knobs lined up on the wall by the door to the family room, and I put it on over my clothes.

I looked up at the night sky, breathed and tried to see a path through the constellations like I did when I was a little girl. My father, a physics professor at Georgia Tech, had taught me to read the night sky like a map. We dark-adapted our eyes and carried red-filtered flashlights to keep that night vision.

We would stand together, and he would say, "Begin with the Big Dipper."

I would recite with him, "Arc to Arcturus, Spike to Spica then leap to Leo." My favorite star was the North Star, which is directly over your head at the North Pole but on the horizon if you're at the Equator. The nearer a star is to us the more it appears to move. Even in science sometimes things are not what they seem.

My father would say, "We are on the Earth."

I would respond, "In our solar system."

Then he would say, "In the Milky Way Galaxy."

To which I would respond, "In the Local Group of galaxies."

He would add on, "In the Virgo Supercluster."

And I would finish with, "In the Universe."

Sometimes I would start the phrases. The one who said "universe" had to say the ending, "To the Universe you are small, but to me you are big." Then one day, he was gone.

Why was I all of a sudden digging up these bones? I wanted clarity on my feelings about attacking James Goody, whoever he was, sure, but I didn't want to make this more complicated than it was. I would have to talk to Tara and Victoria about all that.

I returned to the flower arrangement I had started. I added rosemary for remembrance and lavender for devotion to it. Then I trimmed the three box trees on the deck. They were in different topiary shapes and planted in large, but simple, Terracotta pots. I hadn't made much progress, at least not enough to tell, when the telephone rang, and Abby and I went inside to the kitchen desk.

"Leigh, this is Paul Armistead. I apologize for calling so late, but I really need to talk to you."

"No problem." *Oh, how sweet, he probably wants to surprise Tara with a gift. Hmmm, what would she like?*

"I think Tara is in danger."

"No-o-o-o!" *You think?*

"I found a threatening note on her floor Saturday afternoon. It said for her to stay out of Cracker Barrel. Now, Cracker Barrel is that restaurant chain that advertises home cooking."

"Oh?"

"I kept hoping she would confide in me about this, but she hasn't, so I'm going to call the police."

"Oh, I wouldn't do that! I mean, not just yet."

"Then what do you think I should do?"

Other than minding your own business? "How about Victoria and I keeping an eye on her?"

"Would you? That would really ease my mind. You three do spend a lot of time together. And call me if you need me."

If we need a big, strong man? "Sure thing."

Eleven

Continuation of statement by Leigh Reed. Early Tuesday morning we were sitting in my car in front of the Cracker Barrel, meeting with one furious Braves fan. "That lying sack of shit! He's not even good in bed. He's hard of hearing. I used to talk dirty while we were having sex, but I had to repeat everything three times. 'Oh, yeah, harder, harder. Oh, yeah, harder, harder. Oh, yeah, harder, harder.' How much do you think I got out of that?"

She opened the door to get out of the car but stopped. "And something else, our friends don't like him. There's nothing worse than having a husband that makes people feel sorry for you. My marriage inspires pity!" She walked away, but after just a couple of steps she turned around again. We three jerked up like we were at attention.

"By the way, I like your uniforms."

Shit, we had done it again. We were all wearing winter white pantsuits. Off came the jackets, revealing different color silk blouses. Mine was black and white striped, Tara's a hot pink, and Victoria's beige.

I watched her walk away. "Whatever. Anybody want ice tea to go?"

"Sure." This from both colleagues.

"How mad do you have to be to reveal information about your sex life to strangers?" Victoria held the door open.

Once inside Tara turned around. "I think it made her feel better. You know what I hate? I hate it when the client asks us for advice for preventing this. We're not marriage counselors."

I nodded in agreement, "I don't have any advice to give."

"Neither do I. Most women are too busy to follow their hubbies around, and they shouldn't have to, anyway," Vic said.

"No, they shouldn't, not when you can have a GPS unit installed on his car," I was reaching for my ringing cell phone in my handbag, but I missed the call. "As for advice, there's always the tried and true, 'spend all his money and make him beg for sex.'"

We had the time, so we enjoyed the tea there instead of in the car. I took the opportunity to return that call I had missed.

"H-a-a-a-l-o-w," poured out of a toddler's mouth.

I hung up.

Victoria put a ten dollar bill on the table. "Did hubby answer?"

"Nah, a kid. I don't want to do business with anyone that lets a kid answer the phone. I really hate that. It's like biting down on a piece of aluminum foil with a filling."

"You are going to be some auntie to my grandchildren." Victoria shook her head at the thought.

"Are they going to be allowed to answer the phone?"

Then it was back to my house so Victoria and Tara could leave their cars there. I drove to The Peachtree Group for our second meeting with Randall Valentine. As requested, Tara was hauling a large handbag, Victoria had her Prada backpack, and I had my Louis Vuitton backpack.

"Victoria, why didn't you say anything about me being an auntie to the twins?"

"Oh, hon. I thought you had gotten quiet. You like kids, Leigh doesn't. I don't have to worry about you. You really will be a wonderful aunt."

"Thanks. I'm overly sensitive this morning, and I've been having one hot flash after another. Leigh, you still don't like kids?"

"The problem I see is people over-raising their kids." That was something you could not accuse my mother of, and for a second I wondered what it would have been like.

"That's my only true regret in life, not having kids. We tried, but it never happened for us. I'm sure I would have over-raised them, to use Leigh's term, like crazy."

I needed to lighten the mood. "Oh, Tara, Paul called me last night around eleven."

"What did he want?"

"It wasn't to give me the time and temperature. He found the note with the *stay out of Cracker Barrel* warning."

"You couldn't have told me that before? We were just there."

Victoria shook her head. "You remember we wrote the note, don't you?"

"Oh-h-h, that note. He found our note. What'd you tell him?"

"I told him Victoria and I would keep our eyes on you."

"That's so sweet," she cooed.

"No problem, we're happy to do it," Victoria answered dryly.

"I meant, he was sweet to be worried."

"Yes, he was. I wonder if my husband ever worries about me."

"You're not the kind of woman men worry about," Victoria said.

"I guess you're right." I filed that away. "I wonder if the kid at the security gate will have our names."

Fifteen minutes later we were with Randall Valentine, CEO. "Ladies." Was he being sarcastic? Valentine tilted his head.

"Gentlemen." I tilted mine.

"Nice to see you. You're all looking lovely this morning." As he said this I happened to look over at Tara. She had perspiration above her upper lip. Then I saw the pink neck. She was having a hot flash.

Randall Valentine followed my gaze, "I believe you're blushing, Tara. It's not often you see a woman blush these days. Charming. Just charming."

Victoria and I bore our eyes into her. *Leave it alone! Just go along with it!* We knew we were fighting a losing battle. We had lost control of her. She had gone over to the light side.

"It's a hot flash." *Why, Tara why?*

"Can we get you anything? Coffee? Bottled water? Oh, I forgot. If you're native Atlantans you'll probably want Coca-Cola, right?" He shoved his hands into his pockets and rocked back on his heels and started chuckling. Too late, he realized that we weren't. The three of us gave him a dead stare. That stone-faced routine is a little something we like to do to pompous people. He cleared his throat and led us to a pretty darn impressive conference room. Kerry Lee, CEO Junior, was already there and stood when we entered. The table had a dark mahogany finish and inlaid marble top. The chairs matched the mahogany of the table and had rose wool upholstered seats and backs. The perimeter of the room was elevated about a foot, sort of like stadium seating. Chairs for underlings were up there. If I had an underling, that's where I'd park him.

Tara started in right away. She's great with money and investing. "I have a couple of questions off the top of my head. How many funders do you have so far? And what will the total number be?"

We sank down into chairs by which all other chairs must be measured. It was all I could do not to go, "Ahhh." At the end of the table three fancy leather binders sat.

"Those are important questions since they do determine distribution of profits. We currently have five, and not all of them are individuals. We will stop at ten." He fawned over

Tara, looked at Victoria and scowled at me. What were we, the three bears?

Tara tilted her head. "Fifty million isn't what I would call a staggering amount of money."

"Kerry, do you want to take that one?"

"Sure. First of all, we're very lean, which is a function of both our youth and our management philosophy. We don't have the overhead of companies that have been around longer. For instance, we don't have high salaries for longer tenure employees, that kind of thing. And we have our traditional businesses, mostly defense contracts, which are our bread and butter."

Valentine took control again. "We have a short video to give you more background." The video was projected on a bank of four monitors, two by two. We swiveled in our chairs to face the back of the room. I admit that here I got bored, and my mind wandered, but there didn't seem to be much of substance being said.

When it ended Mr. Lee pressed the button on the table to return to overhead lighting. "That's hot." Victoria and I slowly turned our heads ninety degrees to look at Tara. She cleared her throat. "I love videos."

Valentine looked down, not smiling, as she spoke. As he raised his gaze he took the opportunity to check out my legs. I uncrossed them and turned back to face the conference table.

"What are we being asked to invest in, other than freedom's future?" Victoria's question meant he had to get his eyes front and center.

"The Peachtree Group is a surveillance technology firm. Our success as a manufacturer of Backpack UAVs has positioned us to successfully compete with many larger companies. That same success, however, has labeled us as a Backpack UAV manufacturer, only. We intend to diversify while staying true to our core which is," pause for effect, "situational awareness."

"What other products do you want to develop?" I had learned they manufactured the physical UAV, not just the software.

"Software and hardware for components for video links used on any size UAV is one example. Drones to be used by police departments is another."

"Who supplies materials for the hardware?" This was from Victoria, and Valentine had to swivel to face her, but before he spoke he was interrupted.

"We have a number of sources, domestic and abroad." It was Kerry Lee, and a touch of annoyance had crept into his voice, just a tad.

"How much control do you have over the flow of significant parts? Are any of these sole sources? Do you have backup sources?" I gave Victoria a telepathic, *you go, girl*. She had been in upper level management in a multi-national corporation when she left the corporate life, but she should have been running the whole dadgum place.

"We have a good bit of information that should answer all your questions. Should we have it couriered?" This time Valentine addressed me.

"We'll just take it. Thank you." My answer clued Tara and Victoria to get ready to leave, and we stood. "Can we talk to our financial advisors about this and call you in a few days?"

Half a beat later Valentine stood. I'd swear on a stack of Bibles he was looking at my butt. I either saw or sensed a hint of a grin from Kerry Lee. Then he handed the binders to us one at a time. There was so much ceremony in the way he did it, for a second there I felt like I had graduated from some place.

"Certainly, I'll look forward to hearing from you." Then he gave me a double take. What the hell? Had he recognized me? Did he know my history, or had he met me at a dinner with my husband? Or maybe he had finally noticed I have a face.

Kerry Lee walked us out. Once in the corridor Tara sniffed the air. "Is that coffee I smell? The employee lounge must be around here."

"No, the employee lounge is in the east wing. Over here we have private kitchens. Would you care for a cup?"

"No, thanks, I was just commenting."

As soon as we left the tinted double doors of the executive office area Tara glanced back. "Well, that went well," she laughed and shook her head.

"Really?" Victoria's face lit up.

I leaned against her. "Yeah, hon. A lot of men don't mind getting their asses kicked by girls." She had no idea how good she was.

"Sure. Just a myth. Don't worry about it." Tara stifled a laugh.

I walked between the two of them, and we hooked arms. "We learned a lot. If The Peachtree Group was on a strong footing, Valentine and Lee would not have gotten defensive with Vic's questions. We did good."

Victoria stuffed all three binders in her bag. "Time for the real reason we're here. Are we ready to see more of this place?"

"Are you sure this will work?" Tara looked up and down the hallway as she spoke.

"Let's hope so," Victoria answered.

Tara checked out the hall a second time. "Remember, Detective Kent said to call him if we learned anything."

"Then remember yesterday we learned our cell phones don't work in here," Victoria corrected. "We have to be careful."

"There's the stairwell." I pointed to the exit sign.

I took a dumbbell out of my bag. As we walked toward the stairway, I handed the five pound weight off to Victoria, who handed it to Tara, who handed it back to me. Then we repeated the sequence.

"Wait. We don't want to get to the top floor and then not be able to get out of there. Let's be sure these doors aren't locked to keep hoi polloi from entering the executive floor." I went out and let the door close behind me. Could I get back in? No, I couldn't. I resisted the temptation to look up to see if there were any security cameras, because if there were, my face would be seen.

"It won't open. Let me out." Then I waited. When there was no response I tried tapping the door.

"Open the door!" For about a half hour, or maybe just a good minute, nothing happened. My heart rate was going up, and my stomach felt warm. I desperately wanted to look around. With both hands I started flat palm slapping the door.

Finally, Tara opened the door. "Did it lock? Why didn't you say something?"

"I was enjoying myself in there. Yes, it locked. And these doors must be soundproof. It looks like we'll have to take the elevator."

We pressed both the up and down buttons. We were going up to the bridge that would take us to the other building, but if Randall Valentine or Kerry Lee walked up we wanted that down button lit up.

By the time the doors opened on the top floor I had a five pound bag of sugar out of my backpack and I'd lined Victoria's Prada with a plastic garbage bag. I got behind her, and as we walked I slowly poured the sugar. While I did that she and Tara passed a ten-pound weight back and forth.

"Victoria, tell me again you're pretty sure that this will work."

"This should fool the biometric sensors."

When we reached the walkway, I pulled two light blue, queen-size bed sheets out of my bag. Holding them up we walked through the glassed in walkway, hoping the double thickness hid us rather than silhouetting us. We wanted to be just another patch of sky. At the end we put both sheets away. As soon as we took the hallway to the left we would be in a bustle of people, and there would be no more tricks, only a fib or two or three. After we passed the room divider, I saw the windows were blacked out. This meant the area housed workers with security clearances working on sensitive projects. Or a bathroom. How long we would be welcome there was anybody's guess. We walked along the side of the room like we knew what we were doing—for about two seconds. Frick and Frack, the two geeks constantly reading their mobile devices, approached and stood blocking us. "Can we help … you?" The hesitation and then the softening of their tone came when they saw our ID badges. The three of us looked down and read our own badges: EXECUTIVE OFFICE.

I looked at Frick then Frack. "We're here from the auditing firm, uh, of Frick and Partners. Where's the break room?"

"Down the hall," said one.

"On your left," said the other.

"Thank you."

They turned to re-enter the field of cubicles, and above the half walls we could see that all eyes were on them. Frick, or maybe it was Frack, mouthed "Auditors!" Lucky for us he was so unnerved by our encounter that he let his breath out when he did this, and we could hear him.

Four employees stood around the combination cappuccino and coffee maker, two men that looked to be in their mid-thirties and two younger women. None looked ready for a *GQ* or *Vogue* photo shoot, but they didn't look like minimum wage workers either.

"Hi." Victoria said this in her cheeriest voice, and I've never had the heart to tell her she didn't have to put on an act. She could never be mistaken for anything other than a nice and normal person.

"Uh, hi," one of the men said as we approached the machine.

"Don't worry, we're just here for the coffee." Tara chuckled.

Note to self: compliment Tara on being such a good chuckler.

My turn. "Actually, I would like to ask you something. We're friends with the wife of one of your consultants, and we heard something happened to him. His name is David Taylor. Did any of you know him?"

Both women nodded. "He was murdered," one of them said almost whispering. She was African American, slim and about medium height.

"That's what we heard. He was nice and so smart. There's no telling what he was working on here." Tara was doing so well, I stole a quick look at Victoria, and we let her run with it.

"We were told not to discuss him. I would like to, but I couldn't if I wanted to. They," here she nodded toward the other wing, "would know." At this point she looked to the floor, and we knew she was referring to the tracking system. That got me to thinking, how long would it take for the system to report that there were unknown individuals in the building?

"No, they won't," Tara said. Oops. I held my breath, then she recovered with, "The biometric sensors are overridden for us. Let's sit down. You don't tell we were taking a break, and we won't say anything either." The woman refilled her cup and joined Tara while the others said their good-byes and took their cups back to their desks.

I leaned over to Victoria. "We should split up."

We sauntered out of the room, and before we went our separate ways she said, "What about that Tara solving a problem we hadn't thought about?"

"You mean these people reporting that we were here?"

"Yep."

I continued down the hall, and she backtracked to walk through the cubicles, eavesdropping, I assumed. In the very next room I hit the jackpot. It was the size of one of Tara's walk-in closets, and along the back was a glass case. Several canvas bags and boxes were lined up, and peach colored cards with the year of inception written in gold stood by each. I saw only Backpack UAVs, just different models. The Peachtree Group logo was sewn on the flaps, their signature peach for the A.

"David was proud of those, well, sort of." I jumped. "Sorry, I didn't mean to startle you." It was Frick, or maybe Frack.

"I didn't mean to be startled either." I had no idea what I meant by that.

The clock was ticking, and if he had something I could use, I needed to hear it in a hurry and get the hell out of there. "Why sort of proud?"

"There was a glitch, and that was distressing to him." He looked at his shoes and then back to me, "I think it's so sad he died without finding a solution."

"Did he tell you what the problem was?"

"No, he was too professional for that. He may have told the Executive Office, but only them." Was it my imagination, or was there a sneer when he said that?

"Well, I better get back to work." I walked passed him, tickled pink at the information.

Tara was walking my way, and when she got to me we turned around and headed out looking for Victoria. She saw us and joined us at the entrance to the connecting bridge. We stepped into the niche discreetly hiding the restrooms and a stairwell door.

"Do we have to go back through the bridge to get out of here?" Tara moaned.

"Here's an exit door, but fat lot of good it's doing us. Damn thing's alarmed."

"Let's switch our weight around and go." Victoria turned around for me to pull the sheets out of her backpack, and Tara went behind me to get the weight out of mine.

"Do you think deaf people are ever startled? I was just wondering."

"Shhhh." I looked around Victoria to see why she was shushing me. Kerry Lee was headed our way. I didn't know whether to shit or go blind.

I mouthed this news to Tara. Her little feet started doing a cartoon run but she wasn't going anywhere, so I turned her to face the ladies room. She tried the door but it was locked. That didn't stop her from trying the knob over and over again. I tried the gents. No luck.

All of a sudden we heard moans, jeers and ejaculations (not the sexual kind) from cubicle-land. "What's going on?" someone yelled.

"Not again!"

"Is my work backed up or did I just lose an hour's worth?"

We heard Frick or Frack say, "It's okay, everybody. You know the drill. When there's a suspected security breach, our computers are shut down." His derision earned him my esteem. "I would advise you to cover your ears before the alarm goes off."

"What caused this?" a voice farther from us asked.

"They do it, manually."

An alarm was about to sound? If it was possible for three people to meet eyes, we were doing it. Holding our breath we faced the exit door. "Wait," I hissed. "The door downstairs will be locked."

Tara wiggled out of the huddle. "Not if there's a fire." She had pulled her sleeve down over her hand and reached around the wall to a red fire alarm. We heard a blast of noise from the offices. Tara pulled the fire alarm and added to it. I threw the exit door open, and the volume rose again. We ran down the stairs. A few seconds later we were rewarded with air, sunshine, adrenaline and a little calorie burn.

Twelve

Continuation of statement by Leigh Reed. We were back in my car and on Highway 78 as fast as our kitten heels could take us. "So what did we get out of that?"

Tara fussed with her hair and make-up. "Randall Valentine is defensive, and Kerry Lee is suspicious."

Victoria sat in the backseat going over the literature The Peachtree Group had bestowed upon us, occasionally brushing sugar off the page. "Understandably so, I think. They are not on the best financial footing."

"From what I saw in the display room, they seem to have all their eggs in the Backpack UAV basket. But then again, the offices are pretty fancy. You think that's smoke and mirrors?"

"Could be. That makes David Taylor a rainmaker for them, doesn't it?" Victoria was going to town with a yellow highlighter.

"Yes, but the phone call did come from their office," Tara reminded us. "I learned more about him. Susanna told me that he was a rule book guy all the way. The strict security didn't bother him. Actually the regular employees accepted it with a better attitude because it was okay by David."

"That's consistent with what someone told me. He also said there was a glitch in David's product, and it really weighed on him."

"Hmm." We thought about this while I drove just over the speed limit.

"What about us?" Tara patted my shoulder. "We lied, we penetrated their defenses, we escaped. No, wait, that would be when we follow husbands."

Victoria looked up from her reading material and gazed out the window. "Did he say anything else about that glitch? I used their wireless network to see what kind of security they have. I can stop their production line if I need to, like if the malfunction is on an important component."

"Uh-h-h, Victoria, sweetie, I think that may be a little over our pay grade. I mean, shutting down production of a defense contractor during a war?"

"But we can't report it to the Army. They would do background checks on us and find out who your husband is."

"True. Anyway, let's jump off that bridge when we come to it."

Victoria was adjusting and readjusting her glasses. "Maybe we could be anonymous informers to the FBI. I mean, if they can break away from that vital and dangerous DVD piracy work they do."

Tara took a deep breath. "Those people were so nice. I'd hate to have them lose their jobs, but I know we might have to do it."

"Victoria, you just might get your wish to find out more about the malfunction when we go to David Taylor's office."

"I intend to spend some quality time with his computer."

The Tiara line had been transferred to my cell phone, and it had been vibrating like crazy while we were in the meeting, but only one message had been left. I retrieved it.

"It's a text message from Savannah Westmoreland, and she wants us to go to the Mall of Georgia this afternoon. She has reason to believe her husband will be at Nordstrom with his girlfriend."

"What the hell? Did she say why she stood us up Monday morning? And we don't even know what the husband looks like." Tara was getting worked up.

"Actually, we do." I showed them my telephone screen. She had sent me a photo of the wanderer.

"Let me see that." Tara grabbed my phone. "Ordinarily I love a man in a uniform, but come on. Her husband works at T.G.I. Friday's, and he can afford to take his mistress to Nordstrom?"

"When we finish at the hospital and Taylor's office, let's go to the Friday's across from the mall for lunch and see if he works there. After all, we are detectives. Speaking of uniforms where can we change into our scrubs?" There was no e-mail from my husband this morning, and I was happy for so many excuses to stay busy rather than returning to an empty house. I didn't care if it did have six bedrooms.

"There's a fast food place down the street from the hospital."

"Sweetie, are you okay with this?" I was concerned about someone recognizing Victoria.

"It's hot," was her reply. Tara looked at her like a proud mentor. We drove back toward the other end of Gwinnett County.

Within the hour we were in the medical field, at least in a fashion manner of speaking. The only unauthentic part of our get-ups was that we had poked holes in our shoe covers to accommodate our heels. That was in case we needed to run like hell. Or as we like to say in the medical field, first do no harm.

"This is great. I've always wanted to be the one in a uniform, and here I am. I love myself." Tara was grinning ear to ear.

I was stowing our handbags in the trunk and took Tara's from her. "Weren't you in Girl Scouts?"

"What do you think?"

"I worked at Six Flags Over Georgia when I was in high school," Victoria said.

"Did it give you this being-in-uniform high?" Tara wanted to know.

"You know it."

We entered, pretending to discuss the medical files we carried. I was trying to be inconspicuous. Tara doesn't know the meaning of the word. "Hmm, this is an interesting symptom. I don't believe we can cure him. He's a dead man."

"Are we doctors or nurses?" I whispered.

Victoria had learned the room number and led us that way. "I don't know. Don't worry about it. If we were either, we would know which one we were."

"Excuse me, doctor." A man the size of a door stepped into our path, and we stopped, like we had a choice. "We play for the Falcons, and my buddy here is in for a follow-up on his torn meniscus. Can you come in and have a look at his leg?"

"Yes! Yes, I can!" Tara blew past Mr. Hunky Football Player and into the room.

I took her by her shoulders. "We're on our way to operate on someone who probably won't make it. We'll get someone for your friend."

Our next stop was the cardiac unit and the room of my attacker. Sure enough, there was a police officer at the door. We nodded at her and walked in. My attacker looked small but mean with a stubbly beard, gray skin, sunken cheeks and a full head of gray hair. For the life of me, I couldn't feel angry. I saw a human being with very few choices who might now be at the end of the line.

He woke up and saw us hovering over him. He smiled as he looked first at Tara and then Victoria. When he got to me his eyes widened, and his mouth opened to an O.

"What are you doing here?" he croaked. Then he did a double take at Tara. "You the one I swapped spit with? Thanks." Some thanks this was for the CPR she'd administered.

"Don't mention it."

I leaned over to his ear, "What did I ever do to you?" He looked up at the ceiling and stuck out his lower lip like he was pouting. What kind of criminal does that? "Who hired you?"

"It's not worth my life to tell you that."

"Give us something, and I won't testify against you."

"You won't testify? You kiddin'? Look who's in the hospital bed. You could get ten, twenty years for what you did to me."

"You started it!"

"Maybe. Okay, I'll tell you somthin'. How about this? Don't worry, ladies. Old detectives never die. If I wanted you dead, you would be." I kept eye contact with him, because I knew Tara and Victoria would be grinning at this exchange, and I didn't want them to get me tickled.

"So you were just trying to scare us? You did make it easy for me to see that you were tailing me on Sunday."

"You did what I wanted you to. You called these two. That way I could give the message to the whole trio at the same time. I'm trying to do you a favor. Leave what you know nothing about alone. One person's already been …"

Victoria moved up to the bed. "Killed by you?"

"Not by me! Now get out."

As we turned to leave, he called to us. "Hey, how old are you anyway?"

"How old are you?" Tara shot back.

Victoria pretended to make a note on a chart and headed for the door. She ignored him. "You all look a little long in the tooth to me."

I was headed out, but I backed up a step. "We're closer to Medicare than to jail bait." Then there was a loud bang.

"Awwh!" he yelled.

"Did you kick his bed?" Tara asked me.

"Maybe."

"Old detectives never die," he said again.

We returned to the hamburger joint and changed back into our suits. Then we got three half-sweet, half-unsweet teas to go. Sitting in the parking lot we remembered what we do for a living and started trying to analyze Mr. Goody's comment. "His parting remark was a take-off on 'old generals never die.' Do you think he was referring to my husband?"

Tara was neatly folding her scrubs. "That little squirt had better think twice before messing with him."

She handed the scrubs to Victoria. "Just keep them. We might use them again. He can't get to your husband anyway. I think he was talking about us."

"It's pretty clear now that his sorry attempts are related to David Taylor's murder."

Tara tied her straw wrapper in a bow. "How do you figure that?"

I tore off one end of my own wrapper and blew it at her. "Simple, we only know one murdered person."

Tara opened her laptop and looked up David Taylor's office address. "Push has come to shove."

"Well, what's our next move?" I started the car and waited for instructions.

"We need to figure out how to get into David Taylor's office and snoop around. If we call Kelly, I bet she'll take us over there." Victoria was dialing before she finished her sentence.

~

Beatrice said Kelly would be busy that afternoon, but if we would come now she would give us the key to David's office and the directions.

From Kelly's house we drove south on Peachtree Industrial Boulevard to Peachtree Corners at the same end of

Gwinnett County. I looked in the rearview mirror, and who did I see but Detective Kent.

"I was about to start missing him." Victoria was tapping away, updating our record on the case.

We read off the street numbers until we came to the cluster that included David Taylor's place of business. A small brass sign on the door told us we had found Flow Network Design. The office was small, in a medium size building, but we guessed with a large rent since it was near The Forum, a chic outdoor mall. It was close to his house in Duluth, and that plus the upscale address may have made it appealing to the late Mr. T. There was a reception area, a private office and a bathroom. We doubted the outer office had ever been used. The walls were bare, and there was not so much as a throw pillow in the way of decorative accessories.

"I would love to get my hands on this place." Mail had been dropped through the slot, and I helped myself to it.

"You and me both." Tara sat at the receptionist's desk and played with the fifty or so buttons on the telephone.

"Let's decorate it. He's dead, he won't know." I was a little surprised at Vic saying this, because she doesn't enjoy decorating the way Tara and I do.

"Really? Okay," Tara said.

"No, not really! I was being sarcastic." Victoria went back to David's office and started pulling files out of his desk drawers.

"Damn."

The mail consisted of a phone bill and three sale flyers. Back in the day, this would have meant he didn't have much going on, but today it just meant all his correspondence was done with e-mails. I took a seat in one of the two jade leather upholstered chairs. "Look through that Rolodex and see if any of them are written in Chinese."

A couple of minutes later Tara had finished. "Almost all of the cards are blank, and there's nothing written in Chinese."

Just then the door opened, and a man backed in. I looked at Tara, and we raised our eyebrows. "Excuse me." He jumped and turned around at the same time. He was tall and skinny. He looked to be in his late twenties and had acne like you wouldn't believe.

"Who are you?" he demanded. Then he heard Victoria opening and closing desk drawers in the back office. "And who's back there?"

"*She* is Mr. Taylor's partner." Tara pointed over her shoulder by flicking her wrist. She was trying to give the impression of being a super-efficient secretary, but instead looked like a real smarty pants.

"I'm his partner."

"No, you're not. He didn't have a partner," I countered.

"Then who is back there if he didn't have a partner?" Okay, he had me there.

Tara stepped in. "I'm his receptionist. Don't you remember me? Since you're his partner you see me sitting here Monday through Friday." I mimed to her to keep up the who's on first routine, and I took my handbag to the window. Detective Kent was outside, and I signaled him with my makeup mirror. It took him a few seconds, first, to realize he hadn't been blinded by a laser, and second, to figure out where it was coming from. Finally he started walking toward us. Victoria saw him from the window in the office and came out to see what was up.

Detective Kent presented his badge to our new friend, who promptly reported, "I think these ladies are breaking and entering."

"May I see your ID?"

"They say *she* is Mr. Taylor's partner." He pointed to Vic and tried to do it the way Tara had. "Well, there is only one office here, and one and one equal two. You do the math."

"Actually, you already did. You came up with two," I interjected helpfully.

Detective Kent stood in the doorway and made a call on his cell phone. In one motion he hung up from the call, took the handcuffs out of his back pocket, and before I knew it, had them on the guy's wrists. "It turns out Mr. Anniston makes a habit of breaking into homes and offices after an obituary is in the paper. I've called a car to take him to the station."

"We're ready to lock up now." When Victoria turned, I noticed her Prada looked a little heavy on her shoulder.

We left Detective Kent with his prisoner and went on our way. As I walked by he nodded. I don't know how I knew, but I knew that meant, "I'll let you know if he's connected to anything else."

We stopped by my house to let Abby out, and less than an hour later we were heading down Highway 20 toward the Mall of Georgia, Victoria driving this time. "I'm going to cut through here to avoid some of this traffic."

We passed a row of modest houses, which is a euphemism for paid for, with well-tended front yards. When we stopped at the intersection of West Broad and Temple Avenue, I pointed out a plot of land backing up to Home Spun Restaurant. The city had bought the parcel to add to Hartfield Hills's little downtown area. "There'll be shops and several restaurants here when they finish." I pointed to my left. "This was the NuAir plant. It had been here since 1944." Cattycorner to where we were sitting was City Hall and the police station. A familiar car pulled up behind us.

Tara gave a laugh. "How does Detective Kent do that?"

"Let's wave," Victoria said. We all did, but he didn't see us. That was when we noticed he had a passenger. By that time we were back on Highway 20. I started to get out my opera glasses when they turned in to the Holiday Inn parking lot.

"You have got to be kidding." Tara and I were both thrown to one side of the car when Victoria turned into the next driveway, hell bent for leather. Then she had to backtrack to the hotel. I didn't like the look in her eyes. We parked, and she got out with Tara and me on her heels. She marched right up to the desk to the only female clerk on duty.

"I would like to check in, and I would like the room next to the couple that just registered."

Tara winked at the woman, and money changed hands. Not the lady's first rodeo.

"Whadaya know? It happens to be available."

We went to the elevator. I felt like I was in a bad movie and couldn't figure out the plot. "Should we ask Victoria what's going on or just let this play out?"

Tara looked calm but curious. "She looks like she feels good, really good." I shrugged my shoulders. I guess we had decided to wait and see how it played out.

We let ourselves into Room 206 and jumped on the bed. Next we put our ears to the wall to try to hear Detective Kent and his date. Soon we heard a female voice saying, "Wait, wait, I can't breathe."

Tara sat back and got a nail file out of her handbag. "They're having sex with asphyxiation."

"Ooooh, it hurts." Her again.

"Now that's anal sex," Tara ho-hummed and narrated, looking up from her nails. Victoria and I looked at her. "I'm honestly impressed."

"Don't stop. Don't stop!"

"Now, I'm impressed." Tara put her shoes back on.

"I do not understand that guy." Victoria slapped the bed with both hands and stood. "And I never will. You know why?"

There was no time to answer, because she kept going. "He has no morals. And you know what? I don't want to understand a man like that. Let's get lunch." She headed to the door. Obviously, whatever had gotten into her had been exorcized.

"Wouldn't it be something if this girlfriend had a parrot? Seriously, do parrots repeat what their owners say during sex?" I asked.

Tara considered the question. "You mean, like Polly want a blow job?"

Victoria dropped the room key at the desk. "Tara, can I ask you something? At what age did you lose your virginity?"

"Hon, I am so bad I never had virginity."

Thirteen

Continuation of statement by Leigh Reed. The waiter at T.G.I. Friday's asked Tara for her order without taking his eyes off his pad.

"I-eeee. I'll have a margarita on the rocks."

Victoria and I almost gave ourselves whiplash when we jerked to look at her. "Three salads and three waters with lemon, please." I took my eyes off Tara, but when I turned to the waiter, I was looking at the business end of a penis. His unzipped fly caused me to jerk my head back down to study the menu even though I had just ordered. Victoria looked to her right because I was hanging onto my menu while he was trying to take it from my hands. That's when she saw mini-me. I gave the menu to him, and he, or should I say they, thank the Lord, left.

"Should we tell him his cucumber has left the salad?" Tara was still staring at him as he walked away.

"Just say, 'someone tore down the wall, and your Pink Floyd is hanging out,' or 'you've got Windows on your laptop.'" Victoria giggled and put her glasses back on.

"Elvis Junior has left the building. Let me borrow those. Damn my eyesight."

"Sailor Ned's trying to take a little shore leave. Ensign Hanes is reporting a hull breach on the lower deck, sir!" This had definitely gotten my mind off murder. "And your soldier ain't so unknown anymore."

"You need to bring your tray table to the upright and locked posit ..." Victoria couldn't finish her sentence.

Tara was dabbing her eyes with a napkin. "Our next guest is someone who needs no introduction. Paging Mr. Johnson, paging Mr. Johnson."

Victoria's cell phone rang. "It's my daughter." She flipped it open and put the speaker phone on. That's just how proud she is of Alexandra, just starting her residency at University of Chicago Hospital, and how happy she was to get the call.

"Hi, sweetie. I'm having lunch with Leigh and Tara."

"Hi, Mom and her BFFs. Aidan and I can't decide what to get you for your birthday. Anything special you have your eye on?"

"Oh, Alexandra, you don't have to get me anything for my birthday. Your brother's news was the best gift ever."

"Uggh."

"No, I'm not pressuring you to have kids. And if you insist, I would like an MP3 player."

"I'm on it. Want us to load it with music before we give it to you? All you have to do is give us some suggestions."

"No, I'll do it myself. Thanks, honey."

She hung up. "No way I'm telling those two the music I want."

A waiter trainee brought our drinks. Tara was disappointed. "Why not let them do that for you?"

"Because I would never hear the end of it if I told them to download 'Johnny Angel' plus everything Donna Summer ever recorded."

"Wait, 'Johnny Angel' happens to be the best song ever written." I was about caffeine-d out and was glad for the water.

Tara had her makeup bag out and was repairing her eyes. "Right, who doesn't know that? But still, it's probably best to keep it to yourself."

Someone from the kitchen brought our salads. "Anything else for you ladies?"

Unintentionally, but in unison, we cleared our throats, "No."

"We might want dessert." I don't think I need to tell you who said that. Oh, good Lord.

We started eating and got down to business. I took two brochures out of my handbag. "I picked these up at David's office. They're Flow Network Design company brochures. His service mark was Information Controls. A double meaning there, I like that." I began to read. "If information is important to the civilian economy, it is vital to national security. Dominant battlefield awareness (DBA) is pivotal for the United States in achieving and maintaining information superiority."

Victoria picked up the second brochure. "Here's something interesting. The second brochure is exactly the same, except 'for the United States' is missing, and the last line says that 'information superiority will help you achieve that.' You being China?"

Tara was pushing her salad around. "Are there any other differences?"

We opened up both on the table and read together. Both publications described software applications that would provide "the capability to collect, process, and disseminate an uninterrupted flow of information while exploiting or denying an adversary's ability to do the same."

I pointed to my brochure in the center of the table. "So this brochure is for American clients, and that one is for international clients like China, I assume. Taylor seemed to be going to a lot of trouble to get business from someone he had concerns about."

"I guess that came later. I mean, who knows when he started having those worries?" Tara picked up the US market brochure. "When was this printed?"

Victoria turned the one that he used for international marketing over. "This was printed in May, just five months ago."

"That tells us he was looking for additional clients. Maybe he didn't want to be wholly dependent on The Peachtree Group."

"Kelly says he started being gone at night and being secretive a few months ago," Tara said, "and why is it printed in English? Why not in Chinese?"

"That's a good question." I pointed my fork at Tara.

Victoria took two USB drives out of her handbag. "I made copies of the program and passwords of the product he sold The Peachtree Group, and I'm ninety-nine percent sure this one is for the Chinese project."

"Why not one hundred percent?"

"He spells it CINA."

"Okay. Let's go take a look-see." I made eye contact—I was careful about this—with the waiter, and he headed our way.

"My home computer is in a network with Shorty's office computer. Leigh, to be on the safe side, can we use your computer?"

"Sure, it can probably handle it. We have a large one for my husband's work projects. The military likes even their unclassified documents to be massive."

"We're ready for the check," Tara said, looking our waiter up and down, but mostly down. Same waiter, same problem, depending on your point of view. Tara stared at the check, trying to figure out the amount for the tip. We waited. She had gone into some kind of trance. The waiter had walked off, and I think in her mind, Tara had gone with him.

I tried mental telepathy. *Carry the one,* I thought. *Carry the one. Come on girl you can do it. Just carry that one.* Finally, it worked.

"Big tip?" Victoria asked.

"Fair to middling."

"Wait." Victoria stood up and then sat back down. "What did we come in here for? Oh, yeah, we're supposed to be looking for Savannah Westmoreland's husband."

We fanned out over the restaurant, and I found him tending bar. I relayed this to Tara. "I'm on it."

"We'll wait near the door." Victoria and I shuffled that way.

"One for the ditch," Tara said to the bartender. She finally got her margarita, but in about five minutes she was heading our way.

"His name isn't Westmoreland, and he's never been married."

Victoria clicked the car doors open. "We've been set up."

Tara was taking short, quick steps. "You think? Sorry, but I can't help it. I'm being sarcastic because I don't like having my time wasted."

"I know what you mean. If Mrs. Westmoreland stands us up a third time, I'm going to start to lose faith in her." I take a back seat to no one when it comes to sarcasm. "I want to know who's behind this. Obviously, someone wants us at the Mall of Georgia, so I say we go there. It's a public place, so we should be safe."

Vic drove us across Highway 20 to the Mall of Georgia, and we sat in the car watching the courtyard and eating after-lunch candy bars. "What are we looking for?"

"We're looking for whoever is looking for us." The candy bar was good, but I wished I had more water.

The day was sunny and not too hot. Victoria opened the sunroof. "So, Detective Kent hasn't been slowed down by his wife catching him."

"Everybody's got the right to love." Tara was staring out the window.

"What about his marriage commitment?" Victoria reached into the glove compartment and pulled out the camera. And opera glasses.

"You're right. I think I'm just mad at his wife for being disloyal to us. After all, we were trying to help her." Tara took the glasses from Vic. "She made us killer catchers."

"How do you figure that, Tara?" Victoria was reviewing the stored photos.

"If we hadn't taken her case, Detective Kent wouldn't know who we are, and then he wouldn't have gotten us involved in ..."

"Hold on. We were sitting in front of David Taylor's house. We would have had to tell him why." Victoria had gotten to all the photos of Abby and turned the camera off.

"And if my aunt had balls, she'd be my uncle," I said.

"Huh?"

"Huh?"

"I mean, it is what it is. Now we have to deal with it."

For a minute or so, no one spoke. "Can I ask you two something?" Neither answered, because we were way past that point in our friendship and because it wouldn't have stopped me anyway. "How can you stand being married to, or dating, a doctor? I mean, I used to think I couldn't be married to a proctologist, because of where his hands had been all day. Then I added gynecologists. Then dentists. Then I ruled them all out. They're all touching used skin all day."

"Used skin?" Victoria wadded up her candy wrapper.

"Speaking of marriages, what's it like being married to someone gone so much?"

"If my husband was one of those losers we follow around ..."

"And invariably catch," Victoria interjected.

"... it wouldn't have lasted. It was not my lot to fall in love with someone that works a nine-to-five job."

"Hoo-hoooo!"

"What the hell was that?" Tara shrieked. The call had come from a gentleman in the outdoor courtyard of the mall. He was trying to get someone's attention, or possibly he was calling a well-trained bird.

I started a rant. "I hate it when people do that. Walk over to the person. Don't whistle, send up a flair, or shoot a gun."

"Send a text message." Victoria's suggestion was less violent.

"Holy shit." We looked at Tara and then at the hoo-hooer. He was African American, dressed in jeans with a turquoise belt buckle the size of a pancake, and he was carrying a man purse. He could have been gay; I couldn't get a clear reading on my gay-dar from that distance. The hoo-hooee ran up to him, and he kissed her on both cheeks. The three of us stared, speechless. It wasn't the two-cheek kiss in Buford, Georgia thing, it was who she was. As I live and breathe, it was Kelly Taylor.

Tara was first to get hold of herself. "Like the song says, 'Save a horse, ride a cowboy.'"

"It's only been a few days since her husband died." Victoria was really disappointed in that young lady.

"Who's that she's kissing?" Victoria had the camera at the ready. "I can't believe she's with someone this soon. Aren't you shocked?"

"I am." Not hearing anything from Tara, I looked back at her. She was cool as a cucumber. "Tara? Tara?"

"I'm shocked, too."

"Botox?"

"Yeah."

"I've put up with a lot to get my wrinkles. I figure I earned them fair and square so I'm keeping them." Victoria was waiting for a clear shot.

"We need to know who that is." I was trying to find an appropriate place for my candy wrapper. "Let's go."

"What about the Savannah Westmoreland case?" Victoria hadn't made a move to get out of the car.

"There is no Savannah Westmoreland. Someone wanted us to come here and see what we saw." This was said as I opened the car door.

They followed me across the parking lot to the courtyard. The mall was hosting a Salute to Disco. Note to file: never, ever wear a white pant suit to a Salute to Disco. Ever. Before I knew what was happening, the crowd starting dancing around us. Tara, of course, starting dancing. Victoria and I froze.

"Just tell me, do they still do The Bump?" I didn't know what to do since I don't know how to dance. At one time I did, or I thought I did, but since my husband doesn't dance, I've lost my moves. If lip-syncing was invented for people who can't sing, why won't someone invent leg-syncing for people who can't dance? I was just wondering. I started moving in time to the music. Front kick, back kick stance, back kick, front leg turning kick. The beat to the Bee Gees song was slow, so it wasn't hard to do. Tara and Victoria looked at me and immediately recognized my dancing for what it was, the moves on the kickboxing video. They looked at each other and shrugged their shoulders. What the hell. They joined me, and we were quite the hit.

"How deep is your love?" came from the large speakers on the edges of the courtyard.

Tara leaned in to us, "If we're talking about that waiter, pretty darn deep."

We were doing the same steps, but Vic did them better. "Thanks. Now I'll never be able to listen to that song again without ..."

Unfortunately, just then Kelly turned to see why the crowd was clapping and singing. She pulled her companion's arm, and they both took off running through the courtyard and through a side door of the mall.

"Where does that lead?" I pushed through the circle of people and ran.

"Nordstrom's loading dock," was Tara's answer.

"Remind me to ask how you know that." Victoria had caught up, and we three were running side by side.

We stopped in our tracks. We found ourselves in the dark, literally and figuratively. "How are we going to find them now?"

"Shhh." I'd heard a rustle and needed to figure out where it was coming from. I headed off to my right, Tara and Victoria on my heels. We found the two in a corner between rows of shelves stacked with naked mannequins, letters made of Styrofoam and cans of paint.

"Kelly, why did you run?" I offered my hand to help her up. She declined.

"I didn't want to see you; I have nothing to say to you. I can't believe you couldn't have prevented David's murder if you had tried harder." Her voice was high and breathless.

"There's only one person responsible for David's death, and that's the murderer." Then I turned to her friend. "I'm Leigh," hoping that would prompt him giving his name in return. It didn't, but Kelly gave it.

"This is my brother, Michael." We three looked at the two of them. They looked like twins. We felt like idiots. All we could do was apologize and slink off.

Tara turned around, "By the way, congratulations."

"For what?" Michael asked her.

Kelly gave Tara a pout before turning to her brother. "I asked you to meet me because I have something to tell you."

We didn't need to hear this, so we headed for the nearest exit. This took us into the Nordstrom stock room. We looked around to get our bearings. Tara closed the door behind us.

"Kind of a chilly reception, huh? Obviously, she's not Savannah Westmoreland."

"That means we still don't know who she is. On the bright side, it's a good thing Mr. Goody said we wouldn't die." I was remembering his strange comment.

"I could have done without the 'old' part," Victoria added in.

"Ooooh," Tara slapped her head. "Maybe he is really Savannah Westmoreland. Get it? 'Old soldiers never die, they just fade away.'"

"That was MacArthur that said that," I corrected her.

"Shit."

I spotted an exit and headed that way. "Yeah, and I think that was what Truman said."

"Well, what did he mean by it?" Victoria had taken the camera out of her pocket, I guess to power it off.

"Maybe he knows as little about history as Tara, and he knows the person that hired him was using Westmoreland as an alias."

"So, are we going to die or not?" When Tara turned, she bumped Victoria, and the camera went skidding across the concrete floor.

I dove and stopped its slide, then I looked at it like I had never seen it before. "It occurs to me that we shouldn't store photos on this camera. What if we lost it, or it was stolen? There's a lot of sensitive information here."

With that we went into our handshake, not needing to say a word. We had risen to a level of professionalism.

I saw an elevator on the far wall. "Let's see where this takes us." It took us to the store's upper level. We had entered the elevator in the back, and we exited it via the front door.

Tara pointed to a sign. "Look, there's a semi-annual shoe sale going on." We turned to get on a passenger elevator to go to the lower level, but a small boy ran between us and got in first. His mother was trailing, and we stepped aside.

"Asher, can you press the button? Go ahead, sweetie, press this button. You can do it," she cooed.

Asher mistakenly thought he was being cute by holding his little finger just in front of one button and then another. I reached over and pressed the button for the lower level. "We can't spend too much time shopping, okay?"

Three pairs of shoes each later, we were walking through the mall. I had bought espadrilles like Victoria's.

"Oh, can we stop in here? I wanted to buy one of those *What to Expect When You're Expecting* books." Victoria had stopped in the entrance of The Story Store. "I think they carry it."

The three of us entered and approached a sales person. The noise was deafening. It seemed they were about to begin toddler story time. Victoria had to raise her voice to be heard, "Excuse me. Do you have ..." the rest was drowned out. I headed for the door, but another sales person stopped me.

"Did you bring a little one to hear the story?"

"No."

"What age is your child?"

"I don't have children," I said as the noise rose to a level not meant for the human ear. "I don't even like children!" I shouted. Just then, as if a switch had been flipped, the entire store was quiet—or in children's book store vernacular, quiet as a mouse. Every eye in the place was on me.

Tara took my arm. "I'll just be taking her away now. We're, uh, leaving."

Victoria understandably pretended she didn't know us, and a few minutes later she joined us in front of Starbucks, a bag from The Story Store in hand. I treated us to shaken iced teas to calm my shaken nerves.

Tara found a bench in the mall area just outside. "You know why Starbucks' drinks cost so much? It's so you won't drive off with the cup on your car roof."

"Right, it's for our own good." Victoria seemed to be thinking about something else, and I hoped it wasn't the scene I had made in the book store. "I wish we had stolen more than just those two files from David's home office. If we had some of his administrative files, we could see if there were any bills to a company in China or money transfers from a bank there."

I was pleased as punch not to talk about the incident. "Victoria, do you want to ask Kelly if we can come back and look at them? You and she seem to have bonded."

"After her less-than-positive reaction to seeing us just now? Did we look bonded?"

Tara had downed her tea and was chewing on ice. "Remember, she doesn't exactly know we saw the files the first time."

"Let's see what's on these two disks first. This is strange, but I feel like I'm finally getting to know him."

"Really? Because I don't feel I know him at all."

"Neither do I," Tara agreed with me.

"Looking through his files at home and in his office and rummaging around on his computer, I felt like I did. For instance, sometimes he spells China, CINA. That was his shorthand, and I saw it."

I heard a buzz, and something hit my left foot. "I'm so sorry!" The young man wore khakis and a blue polo shirt with a Sharper Image insignia over the pocket. He was carrying the controller for the model sports car which had just t-boned my foot. "I'm practicing driving this thing so I can demonstrate it to customers. I had no idea it could go that fast. Are you okay?"

While he was talking, I thought about the radio signals that control those toys, similar to how Backpack UAVs work, much the same as David Taylor's communications programs.

"Leigh?" Victoria and Tara were calling my name.

"Uh, yeah, I'm fine. Ready to go?"

We exited the mall near the courtyard. "The work Taylor was doing for the Chinese must not have gotten very far. After all he hasn't been to China. Shhhh, Detective Kent."

"Where?" Victoria was looking around.

"There." I was trying to point with my head, but he was dead ahead, and it looked like I was nodding or head-butting the air.

"I don't see him," Tara said.

"Uhhh, noon, I mean, twelve o'clock."

"He's not here now?" Tara looked back at me, honestly puzzled.

At that point I grabbed their arms and slowed them down enough for him to walk ahead far enough so I could whisper. "See? Let's go."

We ran around the courtyard shops and came out beside Barnes & Noble. He was crossing the street to the parking lot.

"Where's my car?" Victoria moaned. Indeed, we were looking out at a battalion—no, make that a brigade—of SUVs.

"It's someplace over there." Tara pointed at a section to our left. We walked over to three silver Lexus SUVs in a row.

Victoria pressed Unlock on her key fob, and the lights on the middle car flashed. "If we had been running from someone, that would have been a problem."

"Aaah, this happens to me all the time. Someone steals my car and leaves it someplace else in the lot." Tara climbed in the backseat with her package.

I threw my new possessions in with her and got in the front. "Vic, you're the one that won't let me have a bumper sticker. That would help. Maybe we should get matching bumper stickers, like, WE ♥ MARRIAGE."

"Or the overly earnest, I LOVE MY WIFE. Have you seen those?" Tara asked.

"How about, WE ♥ DIVORCE?" Victoria said.

Fourteen

Continuation of statement by Leigh Reed. Victoria sat down at the desk in my upstairs home office and her supernatural fingers went to work. "See, the program is linking to a webcam."

"Whoa, that's going to make me sick." Tara and I had pulled up chairs behind Victoria, and she swayed. On the screen we saw a slow motion movie of a road and a few mud-walled houses. The screen was bathed in green light.

"This is a live feed. The camera is on a UAV in either Iraq or Afghanistan, and it's around midnight there. The camera's using a night vision lens." Disparate memories were flooding back: the dry riverbeds called wadis, rooftop gatherings, and so, so many stars. I had the feeling I needed just one more clue, and I would know what I was seeing. A man clad in a white tunic walked along the road. There was a whir in the background, and he picked up his pace. He stooped to the ground and began frantically digging. We lowered closer to him as he gingerly, almost lovingly, placed a container about the size of a cigar box in the ground. He turned and looked over his shoulder at us, and his expression changed from surprise to shock to anger, then finally to resignation or defiance, one or the other. There was an explosion, he was thrown forward and lay there, we presumed dead. It took a moment to reorient ourselves. He was lying on his side, and we saw this image sideways, and then the screen went black.

"I think you should exit the program."

"UAVs have guns on them?" Tara's head had jerked back with the explosion.

"Some are armed with missiles. The Predator is flown by computer from Nellis Air Force base outside Las Vegas. We were given a tour of the facility, actually tents, and I saw the screens. But that can't be a Predator, unless the lens zoomed in to a high degree. I think that camera was much closer to what it was filming. Besides, David Taylor only worked on Backpack UAVs right?"

"As far as we know." Victoria was still clicking away on the keyboard.

Then something else occurred to me. "That guy was burying an IED but didn't look up in the sky when he heard something behind him. So it wasn't the Predator. It flies high up."

"He was burying an IED?" Tara's hand was trembling on the back of Vic's chair.

"I think so. We didn't see what was in the box, but that's a pretty good ..."

"Something's wrong." In one sudden move Victoria reached down and disconnected the disk from the universal port. Then she took off her glasses and studied them.

"Yeah, for one thing, we shouldn't be seeing that. And as far as I know, Backpack UAVs aren't armed. You have UCAVs, Unmanned Combat Aerial Vehicles, but they ..."

"There's something else. This is the disk I downloaded the Chinese program onto." Victoria looked over her shoulder at Tara and then me. "Are you two thinking what I'm thinking?"

"I doubt it."

"I'm pretty sure I'm not." Tara leaned in to face Victoria. "It may come as a surprise to you how little I know about computers and the Internet, but it doesn't to me."

"This is the program the Chinese have, but it opened with the American password."

"Shit," Tara added succinctly.

"Let's look at the other one." It was not a particularly creative suggestion, but it was all I had. We loaded that program. It opened, and we were viewing a different scene, still in the dark, still in the Middle East, but this time the camera was looking down into a courtyard.

"So that last UAV was destroyed?"

"I think so," Victoria said.

"Holy shit." Tara was right, an upgrade was needed.

"Does this mean the Chinese government can see what American UAVs see? I mean, if they have the pass code, right?"

"The pass code was encrypted. It's possible they could crack it. I did."

"David Taylor was also working on software for satellites. Remember all the background information on satellites in the China files? Satellites communicate with the ground on different frequencies than Backpack UAVs. It's not possible for one program to work on the other." An image from the afternoon went through my mind. "The Backpack UAVs operate a lot like that remote-controlled model car at the mall."

"What about the pages on his research into signal interference?" Tara had wrapped her arms around herself and rubbed as if she was cold. "What signals did he think were interfering with UAV communications?"

"I'll work on this more at home. There are a number of hidden files on this disk. I'll try to open them. Then I'll know more. I do know that there was a problem with the China program, or as he calls it CINA, and he was running tests and documenting his analyses."

Tara massaged Victoria's shoulders. "You are so smart."

Victoria patted Tara's hands, "It's not how smart you are, it's how you're smart."

Then Tara said, "There's just one thing I want to know."

"Wait." Victoria stopped her. "Thank you for saying that."

"Saying what?"

"That I'm smart."

"Well, you are."

"I have been made to feel guilty about my intelligence and sometimes disliked. Just like I think sometimes Leigh feels guilty about being strong, even though it saved her on Monday morning and probably on Sunday, too, when she was able to handle that boat."

I knew she was right. "Let's agree that all there is to feel guilty about is having power and not using it."

"Agreed."

"Agreed."

"Tara, what were you about to ask?"

"If Backpack UAVs don't have guns ..."

"Missiles."

"... missiles on them, what killed that guy?"

"Victoria, can we look at it again? Is it saved on there?"

"'Fraid not, it's real time."

I rubbed the back of my hand back and forth over my forehead. "There could be newer Backpack UAVs that are armed, but the operator would have lazed and then fired. We never saw that. I'm going to assume it was the IED he was trying to bury that exploded and killed him."

"Leigh, what's the matter?" Now Tara looked at me.

"At our meeting with The Peachtree Group this morning they said they're expanding their business to include software for other-size UAVs."

"We're getting closer to that bridge, aren't we?" Victoria was referring to the point where we would have to turn all this over to the government.

"I do believe in fear."

Victoria patted my arm, "We are going to take care of this."

"Yes, we will," Tara added, "but I think we've all had enough of the computer for one day."

She was right, and I smiled at her. "Victoria, I want to give you the digital camera program disk so you can load it onto your computer, and I'll give you the camera, too. When you're finished with it, pass it along to Tara."

Then like an itch that has to be scratched, Victoria was back on the subject of the murder. "Do you really think someone from The Peachtree Group could have killed David Taylor? That Kerry Lee acts suspicious, but what do we know?"

"I'll bet you a pretty he's up to no good. Remember the way he was lurking around us Monday?" Tara stood and stretched.

"My aunts use 'pretty' to mean a toy. They all say, 'I'll bet you a pretty'." I pushed my chair back to its place in the corner. "But seriously, does The Peachtree Group have any skin in the game?"

"What motive would Kerry Lee or Valentine have?" Victoria was using the correct detective terminology. "Where does this chair go?"

"We're trying to save our company. Maybe they're trying to save theirs." I pushed Tara's chair to the side of the desk.

"They were making money off him, right? That is, unless they have other engineers working on the same project," Tara offered. "Do they?"

"Let's go back and see." Victoria interlaced her fingers and raised her arms over her head for a good stretch.

"I'll call them and say we want to finalize the investment." While I waited for his administrative assistant either to put the call through or make up something, I picked up my Pelikan fountain pen and started doodling on a notepad of stationery from France that had a green toile pattern. I was thinking, *so beautiful.*

He did take my call, wonder of wonders. "Is this lovely Leigh?"

"Uhhh. My friends and I have been going over the information from this morning. Could we stop by to see you? We have just a couple more questions."

"Could you and I meet alone?" The delicate point bent with the pressure I had applied.

"Alone?" I said and wrote at the same time.

Tara took my pen out of my hand before I hurt myself, bobbing her head yes.

"Sure."

"Say, the Buckhead Ritz-Carlton in about an hour?"

"Sure." I hung up the phone. "There is no way I'm meeting him alone."

"Let him think he's meeting you alone. We'll be in the nearest ladies room." Victoria was doing her level best to calm me down.

"It's a public place. Which car are we taking?"

"I'll drive," I said.

"I'll take Abby out while you change clothes. Be sure to wear one of your good girl gone bad outfits."

"I have to get something out of my car." Victoria said over her shoulder on her way downstairs.

After Abby did her business Tara went to move her car so I could back out. I threw my pantsuit in a heap in the middle of my closet and pulled out a tangerine silk pencil skirt with its matching sleeveless top. I slid my feet into taupe Charles David heels. This was turning into too long a day for a headband, and I took mine off. I twisted my hair into a chignon and went downstairs.

From the garage door I stood and watched the Hummer backing down my driveway. My mind went back into that hole where I was when I saw the IED explode. I thought about un-armoured Humvees and up-armored Humvees. I thought about my husband talking about "staying left of the boom."

"Leigh? Leigh!" Tara called to me, and I shook my head to try to clear it. "Don't you want to pull your car out?"

Embarrassed, I ran and jumped into my car. A few minutes later we were headed south to Buckhead, so named because the main intersection resembles deer antlers. Atlanta has numerous prestigious addresses, but there's only one Buckhead. This area of multi-million-dollar homes is the grande dame of Atlanta real estate.

"Leigh, what happened back there? What were you thinking about?" Tara asked.

"I was thinking about IEDs. The percentage of US deaths they cause has gone down, but it's still high. Now some are able to penetrate Bradley tanks."

"It was hard for us to look at, so it must have been doubly hard for you," Victoria said.

I pinched the bridge of my nose. "Let's talk business. What do we know so far?"

"It's time to think outside the Botox. We know someone wants us to leave this alone. Not enough to want us dead, just enough to scare us. I figure if a criminal lives to be as old as James Goody, he must be pretty good at his job. I believed him when he said if he had wanted us dead, we would be." Tara had thought this through, and her words tumbled out.

I pulled into the HOV lane. "He claimed he didn't kill David Taylor. That may or may not be true, but if he did, why would he not kill us, too?"

"I think he wanted to see if scaring us would be enough. Either way he's the scum of the earth." Tara's bottom lip was trembling.

Victoria noticed this, too. "Then there's the fact that if he killed one of us, he'd have to kill all three of us. Maybe he doesn't want to go that far."

"Okay, the solidarity, while really sweet, does not make me feel any better. We're still talking about getting ourselves killed!"

Victoria's last tactic was a mistake, and I took over. "It's amazing how much the Atlanta skyline has changed." As we drove south on I-85 we saw Atlanta's tallest buildings.

Tara looked out the window. "Remember when none of the buildings had tops?"

I nodded. "They were post-modern."

"I think it's because of John Portman." Tara was referring to the architect of several of Atlanta's tallest buildings.

"You're probably right." Then I thought about it. "The Sun Trust building has a top on it, and it was built in 1992."

"An aberration. Am I the only one that cares how Atlanta buildings look? I hate John Portman for doing this to us. Atlanta is an international city, and what our skyline looks like is important." She took a breath. Only slightly calmer, she said, "Did you know the Westin Peachtree Plaza is the tallest hotel in the world?"

"Tara? What's the matter?"

"What do you mean?"

"I don't believe you hate John Portman. Have you ever met the man?"

"Is he even still alive?" I felt something touch my right leg. It was Victoria slowly taking my CD case from the floor to the passenger seat. She slowly unzipped it and flipped through the titles.

"You're nervous, aren't you?"

"Hell, yeah, I'm nervous. My motto has always been, 'If there's a coward's way out, take it.' The man we're going to meet might be a murderer. Have either of you stopped to think about that?"

"We'll be in a public place." Victoria inserted a CD, and the car was filled with the music of Yanni.

"Tara, it's okay, sweetie. I mean, it's not like it's John Portman we're meeting." I couldn't help myself, and that got us all laughing. Oh, no, what had I done? I had started the laughter, and it was up to me to stop it. "Victoria, would you hand me the CD case?"

I found exactly what I was looking for, and a second later Bobby Goldsboro was crooning "Honey." We enjoyed a real good buzz kill.

Even Tara had to laugh. "When you said we would work on my nervousness, I never thought you intended this. Where does this gallows humor we have come from? Is it because we are in the pain business?"

"Actually, I was going for flip. Maybe it's a defense mechanism."

"Considering what Leigh's husband does for a living and that my husband has patients die on the operating table, we need it. We don't want death to be too real."

"But those are anonymous people. We saw a real person die."

"I think it's like whistling when you walk by a graveyard. Would it make you feel better if we kept our sick jokes to ourselves?" I asked.

"No. We shouldn't censor ourselves, and I don't want anyone walking on eggshells around me. I'll just be glad when we know who killed David Taylor, and he or she is behind bars."

"I thought you wanted to work on a case more challenging than what we've had. You said it was hot."

"Finding a murderer will make the saints pray and the sinners repent. It's harder than I thought it would be."

"Amen."

"Amen."

Half an hour later I was in line for valet parking. We wanted to get there well before him so he would not see all of us getting out of the car and so we could pick out the best table for our purposes.

A teenager wearing a uniform of white shirt and white shorts opened the back door, and Tara pivoted and swung her legs out. "How are you ladies?"

"Why, what have you heard?" Yup, Tara was a little on edge. Her response had a paralyzing effect on the young man.

Victoria opened her own door. "We're fine."

A co-worker opened my door, and I joined my partners at the entrance. "Why do you think he is in such a hurry to meet with us?"

"If you recall, he's in a hurry to meet with *you*. He does seem anxious, doesn't he?" Victoria said.

"Hmm, like he wants to find out how much we know?"

Tara nodded. "Yeah. That's probably it."

Victoria and I nodded in agreement.

"Oh, come on, I was being sarcastic. Men like that keep us in business. He likes you."

"Ooooh," Victoria and I said together.

Our first stop was the ladies room, because we three have to go every five minutes and because we wanted to check out the cell phone reception. It was okay.

"I'll go get a table facing the door."

The lounge was dimly lit and elegantly furnished, and we were too late. Randall Valentine was already there. I wanted to accuse him of murder in the worst way. And he was facing the door. There's evil and then there's evil.

I stretched out my hand and smiled. "Hello, Mr. Valentine."

He stood and took my hand and squeezed it, when a handshake would have sufficed. "Please call me Randall."

"Randall."

"So glad you could make it on such short notice."

We ordered wine from the wine list. I asked for a glass of Cabernet Sauvignon, and he said he would have the same.

"How many employees do you have?" His head jerked a little with how quickly I got down to business.

"Around a hundred, I guess. I don't really keep up with that kind of thing. My man, Kerry Lee, handles all that."

"About how many engineers are there?"

"Now that I know. There are six on staff and a handful of consultants."

"Like David Taylor?"

"Exactly," his mouth said, but his brain was watching two pairs of legs in miniskirts walk by.

Funny, I thought, *except for the skirt length those are the outfits Tara and Victoria are wearing. And those women have long, thick hair flowing down both of their backs … oh, shit.* All of a sudden I knew what was in the bag Victoria put in my car: wigs. One was red and the other blonde. They sat down at the table behind ours. Tara gave me a little wave, and Victoria started tugging at her skirt.

A waiter was at their table in about two seconds flat. *If there's a God in heaven, they won't order margaritas.*

"Two margaritas, on the rocks, no salt." I wondered if I had just become a Buddhist.

I turned my attention back to Randall Valentine. "Is there anyone else that can complete David's project?"

"He had completed it."

Well, I thought, *my work is done here.* The Peachtree Group no longer needed David Taylor, and someone or ones from there went to the top of the suspect list. Just then he received a call on his cell phone. It was set on vibrate, but I saw the light in his suit jacket pocket.

"I had better take this." He stood up and took a couple of steps toward the door.

"Hello. Hello?" Then he hung up and returned to the table. I had been trying to make eye contact with Victoria, but she was busy with her portable computer in her lap. Tara couldn't take a chance turning around.

"Randall, I couldn't help but notice your building's security system. Quite elaborate."

"Yeah, Kerry Lee is into all that. Leigh, since we know each other better now, I'm Randy."

Tara snorted her drink out her nose and started coughing. It would take Victoria a sec to get the appropriateness of the nickname.

"Randy, what does Mr. Lee use all that high-tech gadgetry for?"

"He wants to track how often the contractors are in the office."

"To see how much work they're doing?"

"That's what he said when he had it installed, but I think the real reason is he suspected them of coming in after hours. That system was expensive, and now it's on the blink. He said you and your friends disappeared when you left after the presentation this morning. Ha!" For a split second I thought he was checking for my reaction. Was that why he suggested the meeting?

The waiter placed our wine glasses in front of us. Valentine picked his up and reached over for a toast. "Leigh, a beautiful name for a beautiful woman. Do you think we could ..." and his cell phone rang again. "I had better get this." Once again he rose and walked toward the door.

"Hello. Hello? Are you there, Margaret?" Again, he hung up and returned to the table, but this time I was ready. I had stood up.

I reached out to shake his hand. "I really appreciate this. I feel like I understand your company better now. I won't take up any more of your time. Really, thanks again." I was walking, and unfortunately, he was following.

"I was just about to ask if we could have ..." and his cell phone rang. We had reached the hallway, and I ducked into the ladies room but not before I heard him yell into the phone, "What *is* it, Margaret?"

I stayed put, because I knew as soon as the coast was clear Victoria and Tara would join me.

"Did you see that? I was literally saved by the bell. Get it?"

"Actually, you were saved by the brain." Tara pointed her thumb back at Victoria as they came in.

"What did you do?"

"I got his home number and routed a couple of calls through there to his cell. He thought his wife was calling both times."

"You mean all three times."

"I only did it twice."

We put our arms around each other and laughed until their wigs fell off their heads. Finally, we composed ourselves enough to get to the car and head back to my house.

Victoria unrolled her skirt to a more modest length. "I feel more comfortable like this."

"That's just fine. Remember, it's not what you wear, it's how you take it off."

"Thank you, Goethe," I said, and with that we climbed into the car. "Victoria, what are you smiling about?"

"That was fun. It really was."

"We didn't get caught." Tara laughed in relief, no longer nervous. "And what if we had? What could he do to us?"

Victoria was fluffing her hair back into shape. "I usually exaggerate in my mind what the punishment will be if I break a rule. That's made me afraid to take chances all my life."

"What rules do you ever break?" I was just about rubbing the skin off my hands with hand sanitizer.

"You know how the gelatin box says you shouldn't add pineapple or kiwi? I thought something bad would happen if you did, like poisoning."

"Like you would drop dead?" Tara was carefully folding the wig. "Why, oh why couldn't she have used strawberries or bananas? She was so young and beautiful."

I carried this on, "What a shame her brilliant career was cut short. It didn't have to happen. She had a perfectly good can of mandarin oranges in the cupboard."

"Excuse me, but I like to follow rules."

"Honey, I don't think there are any rules where we are now," I said.

"Well, I'm more comfortable when there are rules."

"Then you make them up so you can follow them. How does that sound?" Tara suggested.

"I like it."

"I like productive afternoons. We learned what we needed to know. The Peachtree Group no longer needs David Taylor. His project was finished, and he was just a guy with inconvenient information. I think someone there has a motive."

"We don't know the whole story. We don't know what he was doing for the Chinese," Victoria reasoned.

"It was Kerry Lee's call that brought him out of the house the night he was murdered." Tara was reapplying lipstick. "So if it was anyone at The Peachtree Group, wouldn't it be him?"

"I suppose someone else could have used his phone, but for the purposes of discussion let's assume Lee made the call." I did some calculation. "There was time enough between the call and the shooting for him to drive from the office to the Taylor house."

"We're back to three suspects, James Goody, Kelly Taylor and Kerry Lee," Tara said.

"We don't know for sure that James Goody is connected to the case. Oh, no!" I screamed and jerked the steering wheel to the left. I had run over a squirrel. "I'm so sorry." About ten seconds later we saw a hand come out of the window of the Ford Escort behind us and attach the flashing light to the roof of the car. I pulled to the side of the road and lowered my window. "Oh, come on, it was a squirrel!" We watched Detective Kent through the rearview mirror saunter up to us.

"Bullwinkle is going to be very upset," Victoria said from the passenger seat.

"I just hope he doesn't press charges," Tara said.

"Ladies." Kent nodded and looked at us one at a time. "Out giving someone a bad day, I presume. Everything okay? I saw you swerve and thought I'd better check on you."

"I ran over a squirrel." And I didn't believe a word he was saying. "What a coincidence that you happened to be driving by."

"I had hoped your run of bad luck was over."

"The squirrel is the one with bad luck now." Whatever he wanted, I wished he would spit it out.

"James Goody had a bad day, too. It started out well enough. He was visited by three very attractive docs that no one seemed to know." Here he looked at Victoria. "Then this afternoon, he died."

"How? From the heart attack?" I asked.

"That's been known to happen now, hasn't it?"

I heard someone say, "Nobody likes a smart ass." Too late, I realized it was me.

"Or maybe something not so straightforward, we don't know yet. Did he say anything about who hired him or about being in danger?"

"When we asked him who he was working for, he said it wasn't worth his life to tell." He was looking at Tara in the back seat. I was obviously boring the guy, so I trailed off. She wasn't flirting with him, she wasn't even smiling. She was examining him the way a researcher would an interesting, hitherto unknown specimen.

"Did you find out where he was on Friday night?" This was a cute little vignette, but it was not as important as the, what was it again? Oh, yeah, the *murder.*

"He was in Birmingham until at least midnight on Saturday night."

"Can we go now, Detective?" I was going to have to break up whatever was going on.

He looked back at me, "Uh, you know to be careful, right?"

"Right."

"Have a nice evening." He walked back to his car.

"What do you think is the real reason he follows us?" We were on our way, and Tara had rejoined us.

"At first it was to find a reason to have our license revoked. Then it was because the victim was a consultant for a defense contractor, and he didn't want to lose control of the case. Do you think the reason has changed again?"

They were considering the question. Tara's brow had nary a crease. "Maybe he thinks he's protecting us."

"No, thanks!" Victoria yelled as she started laughing. "When there's trouble, I'll just stand right behind Leigh."

"James Goody died, and he's still on us like a mosquito on lip gloss. So it's not him he's protecting us from. It's whoever hired him." Tara was getting nervous.

I was about to give a smartass girl power answer, natch, but just then another possibility occurred to me. "Or using us? Maybe he's finally figuring out how good we are. Not that he's ready to nominate us for businesswomen of the year, but I bet his estimation of us has gone up."

Victoria pursed her lips, and I knew she was about to come out with one of her quips. "Up is the only way his opinion of us could go, or have you forgotten, 'untrained, ill equipped and incompetent'?"

We all three moaned. Nope, no one had forgotten.

Soon we were back home. I got out of the car and stretched like a cat. "I haven't jogged since Saturday. It's still light out. Do y'all have workout clothes with you?"

They both had the items needed for a run in gym bags in their cars. Fifteen minutes later we were pounding pavement.

"I think the most important question right now is, does this, let's call it programming problem, apply only to Backpack UAVs? I mean, if another government can get access to Predator transmissions, it's much more serious. Victoria, can you find out?"

"I'll do my best."

"Mark my words, if anyone can, she can. Who-hoo!" Tara raised her fist.

"She's our wo-man!" I patted Victoria's back. I knew we were asking a lot of her, especially since she was dealing with some personal issues. Tara sensed it, too.

I brought up a subject other than work. "I want us all to train for the Atlanta Women's Triathlon. How does that sound?" I had hoped they would be just as enthusiastic about the idea as I was, but the looks on their faces and the silence didn't exactly say they were in.

Victoria was first to speak. "I'm not a very strong swimmer. Do they have a biathlon so we can run and bike?"

"That's a duathlon."

For the next half hour we talked about buying bikes and maybe hiring a swimming coach. When we completed the loop back to my house and the cool down, I walked them to their cars. That was when I saw the beige car hidden behind the Hummer. It had US Army written in block letters on the door.

I just turned and sprinted away, as fast as I could go, back the way we had come. First Tara and Victoria caught me by my arms, and then another pair of hands on my shoulders turned me around. I jumped up into my husband's arms, and we kissed. There he was in all his towering, burly glory. The rest of the agency and any thoughts of Tiara Investigations dissolved away while the Major General and I walked back to the house.

From the corner of my eye I saw the driver trying to start a conversation with my co-workers. That was a nonstarter, and he got in the car and left. The General grabbed me up in his arms, and I wrapped my legs around him. It didn't occur to him to lock the door. Yep, he is just that tough.

Fifteen

Continuation of statement by Leigh Reed. There have been times when I've been wearing a dress and we haven't made it upstairs, but that day I had on running shorts, so we did. Right away, I could tell there was something he wanted other than the obvious, which he was in the process of getting. He wanted to know where I had been the last few nights.

"Shopping, spa-ing, doing the M.O.G."

"That had better be the Mall of Georgia," because doing the M.O.G. was a slogan American soldiers used, meaning being deployed in Mogadishu, Somalia.

"Yes, and playing golf." I was doing fine until the last one. *Golf at night?*

"Is. There. Someone. Else."

"No." I slapped him. That's when things got wild. Naaahh, I made that up. Sometime during the night we got up, and I made nachos.

"Do you have any meat to put on this?"

"Sorry." I hesitated before I answered, just enjoying his sonorous voice.

"It's okay. Hey, I haven't had avocado in a long time. Remember when I proposed to you?"

"I remember every word." That weekend had been the most romantic of my life. We had rented a sailboat and sailed on the Intercoastal Waterway and the Kiawah River. He had proposed at midnight. It was a clear night, and his tan glowed in the moonlight. He is so handsome. His prematurely gray hair was set off by his tan, and I can still feel how his finely chiseled cheekbones felt to my fingers.

Remembering his face, my breath caught, just like it had that night. I had answered, "Everyone asks me to marry them." He was dumbstruck.

"I've dreamed of falling in love like this and proposing, and that's what you say to me? Aren't I any different from the others who have proposed to you?"

"Yes."

"What's your answer?"

"That's my answer. Yes."

"Well, maybe I don't want to marry you now."

"Oh, please …"

"I'm thinking."

"Look, if you'll marry me I will speak French to you and close my eyes when we slow dance and wear cowboy boots. Now that is my final offer."

He picked me up and swung me around, the boat rocking like crazy. "We're getting married!" he had yelled.

"We're getting married!" I had said, imitating him.

"We're okay now, right?" I had closed my eyes, remembering, and I jerked back to the present, because it was a serious question.

"Oh, yeah." I meant it, and he knew I meant it.

"You really scared me when you told me you were leaving on the next thing smokin'."

I reached up and wrapped my arms around his neck and laid my head on his chest. "I had to do it."

"I understand. I think. But you have to understand, you keep me from being a machine."

"I needed a home."

"Wherever you are is my home. Is it this house that has made you less restless and happier this year?"

I closed my eyes, caught in midair between two worlds. "Having friends again has made all the difference."

"A-l-l-l-l the difference." Have you ever noticed there are some people who can mimic you and not be annoying? "It's good to be back where people talk like me. I was thinking the other day about how with a Southern accent you can make anything rhyme. Like, 'she was standing there wearing nothing but a tile and a smile.' A Northerner would say 'a towel and a smile'. Loses something, doesn't it?"

I knew he didn't talk to anyone else this easily, and I loved him for that. I wanted never to hurt him again.

"Let's look at the stars." He opened the door to the deck. He didn't go out, he just reached a hand out for me to join him. "Whoa! Are you sure everything is okay?"

"Yes."

"Then how do you explain this tropical jungle? And this is something you have in common with your mother, but her front and back yards are filled with flowers. Whereas our front yard looks like everyone else's. This back here is a little over the top, don't you think?"

"It just looks like that because you've been looking at a desert for too long."

"It's what you do when you're extremely happy or extremely worried. So, which is it?" I didn't have a ready answer. He closed the door. "Remember when you threw that bike? I couldn't believe you would be so violent with a piece of athletic equipment."

I did remember. I had put my bike on the back of our Land Rover, and I couldn't get it tight enough on the rack to feel secure. I had already taken off my belt and used it as a tie on and I asked him for his. "This is part of my uniform!" he had exclaimed.

"Tell you what, we'll salute it. Would that make you happy?" And when I said the word *happy*, I broke down. I detached the bike and threw it. Then I walked away.

"Oh, yeah. I definitely remember that." I hesitated, unsure how much old stuff I wanted to excavate, and he waited for me. I loved it when he did that. "I had had a dream the night before that disturbed me. I didn't remember all the details, just that I wasn't in it. I had a dream, and I wasn't in it."

He rubbed the back of my head. Then he ran his fingers through my hair and pushed it back from my face. "Your hair was about this long when we were dating."

"Uh-huh."

"Then you cut it short. Why?"

"I guess I thought that was what a wife did. You know, how a wife was supposed to look."

"Maybe that's how other wives look, I really don't know, but you're not like other wives."

You have no idea, I thought. And just like that I unintentionally broke the spell. I went somewhere else, and he felt it. "Ready to go back to bed?" What was I doing? Was I choosing the agency over my marriage? No, I felt certain I could have both, but in what should have been a rare time of intimacy with my husband, I was being more loyal to Tara and Victoria than to him. Why did I have to figure this out at this stage of my life?

He took my hand, and we walked upstairs, Abby lumbering behind us. Somebody, don't know who, once said, "Nothing makes us so lonely as our secrets." Amen.

Then we slept, curled together like puppies. The newspaper was still downstairs. I never did find out what happened in the world that day. As I drifted off I thought about his comment about other wives. I was just doing the best I could, and so were they.

On Wednesday morning one of his cell phones rang, and I rolled over while he answered it. He was wide awake and up in a half-second, out in the hallway. After what could only have been a few minutes, my own cell phone rang. It was two minutes after seven, so I answered, "Good morning, Victoria," without checking the screen.

I got up with every intention of closing the door all the way rather than listening in, I swear on a stack of Bibles. "I've been getting more information on what David Taylor was up to before he was killed."

"UAVs," said The General into his phone. I knew I had heard the word in stereo. I just knew it. After all, I am a detective.

"Leigh, are you there?"

"Yeah, I'm here."

"I was able to access the hidden files on that disk. They were three layers deep. They're videos of IED explosions. Tara asked what killed the man yesterday when we were logged on. Well, it was the IED he was burying."

"It looked like he was startled when he saw the Backpack UAV. Did he accidentally detonate it himself?"

"There are over twenty cases of the same thing on this disc, so I doubt that would happen on all of them."

"You're right, that's unlikely. Was there anything in there about China?"

"Not that I've found."

"So we still don't know what this has to do with China, if anything. Didn't you say sometimes he wrote CINA instead? Does that mean anything?"

"He named the hard copies, the folder on his computer and the removable disk China. It's got to have something to do with the Chinese, but I'll try to find out if CINA means anything other than he was writing fast. I called to ask you what radio frequency a Backpack UAV uses."

"Are you asking if the frequency used by a Backpack UAV could detonate an IED?"

"Yes." Victoria was still whispering.

"No idea."

"What's that in the background?"

"My husband is talking about UAVs on his cell. He's talking about data transmission, too."

I held the phone up for her to hear him saying, "I was about to tell you I'm on my private phone, but I see we've moved to a low-side mission. Just a sec, I'll need to increase my situational awareness." His joking tone was downright delicious, and it wasn't easy, but I got hold of myself and moved away from the crack in the door.

"Great. What's he saying now?"

"Nothing, he's not talking. Wait, now he is. Something about, 'Just a second and I'll ask my wife.' My wife! Holy shit." I jumped back into bed and pushed my cell phone under the covers.

"Sweetheart, are you awake?"

"Un-huh."

"General Kosloski's wife wants to have lunch with you. Do you have her number?" He was rolling his eyes.

"I don't think so. Can he e-mail it to you?"

He went back into the hall. I pulled Victoria out from under the duvet, in a manner of speaking. "I've got to go. I'll find out what I can."

"See what you can …" Her voice was cutting in and out. "Wait, that's Tara calling. I'll conference her in."

"Hi, Tara. I was going to ask Victoria if she had heard from you. Victoria, why are you whispering?"

"If I wake Shorty up, he might want sex."

"So?" Tara asked.

"So that would waste a good two or three minutes."

Tara started singing "Sixty Minute Man," substituting the words "sixty second man." I recognized the tune and joined in. Victoria either didn't appreciate us serenading her, or she was afraid she would start laughing and huffed into the phone.

"Vic, tell Tara what you told me about the IED detonating when the Backpack UAV approached."

After being quickly brought into the loop, Tara hmmm-d. "Sort of like a premature ejaculation?"

"Call me later. Bye." Victoria hung up.

"Bye."

"Bye."

I realized that while I loved my husband so much it hurt, I could not say with any certainty that my marriage was the most important relationship in my life. Nor could Victoria about hers or Tara about her whatever with Paul. I felt as torn and twisted as our covers, which I slid back down into a few minutes later when my husband came back in the room.

Sixteen

Continuation of statement by Leigh Reed. When I woke up for the second time, he was looking at me. "Let's go for a massage." He was referring to the couples massage they give at the High Hill Day Spa. All I could think was, *what if someone says something to him about Tiara Investigations?*

"I doubt they can fit us in on such short notice."

"For a regular like yourself? Give it a try."

"Wouldn't you rather go sailing?"

"Not as much as I would like a massage."

Being no fool, I made the appointment. Then I called Tara and told her to let Ronald know he was not to say a word about our little business.

I showered and dashed downstairs, drawn by the smell of his special recipe French toast. He looked around and smiled. That made me so happy. In your twenties you could stay up most of the night and the next day have wet hair and no makeup on and still look good. It's much harder to pull off in your late forties.

He put the spatula down and walked over to me. With his arms wrapped around my hips he moaned in my ear. "You look good, but are you okay?"

"What do you mean?"

"Well, you've lost a lot of weight."

"Oh, that's from horseback riding."

"You got this fit from riding General?"

"Riding him? No. It was from the sad look on his face when he saw me coming toward him. It was like, 'If there's a God in heaven, she's not coming over here.'"

"Want me to go kill him?"

"Actually, I rode him Sunday, and he wasn't nearly so cruel."

"I love to see you ride and jump. I don't know how you do the things you do on that horse. I wish there was time to watch you this trip."

I was so busy catching myself before I said, 'I wish I had more time for General' that it didn't occur to me to suggest that as an alternative to the massage. "The secret is knowing where your center of gravity is. Just like you do with race car driving, white water rafting, and a lot of sports." There was so much I wanted to say, and there was never enough time.

"You're my center of gravity." This stopped my rambling. "Here's something for you." Keeping me circled in his arms, he reached into the black nylon satchel he had brought in the afternoon before. He took some photographs out and spread them on the granite counter top of the kitchen island. The first was a photograph of him standing, unsmiling, with one foot on a small box. My heart stopped when I saw the peach-shaped A in the logo and the words The Peachtree Group. I guess I gaped too long. "I thought you wanted newer photographs of me. You don't like those?"

If this was his way of letting me know he knew about Tiara Investigations, it was out of character. He's not like that. If he wants to know something, he asks, like last night when he wanted to know if I had sat under the apple tree with anyone else but him. But I still couldn't speak. I reached out and touched the photograph, which he took to be a question. "That's a Backpack UAV, Unmanned Aerial Vehicle. UAVs are the long pole in the tent in this war. We've come a long way since spy planes."

"This isn't arsenal rationalization?"

"Oh, hell no," he answered as he reached for the stack of pictures. He pointed to a Predator in the background. "It has about a fifty-foot wingspan. We have about forty different configurations. They travel at a range of speeds, carry different payloads, and have varying mission profiles— altitude, range, duration, and so forth. The operators of the early Predator used in Kosovo didn't have the ability to determine the UAVs location, so they couldn't tell what the hell they were filming. The Pioneer Air Vehicle was used in the first Gulf War. Its range exceeded six hours, and its video sensors gave pretty accurate surveillance and reconnaissance data, but that's nothing compared to what we can do today. I used the Predator in Yemen in 2002. That's how I got Abu Ali al-Harithi. It's armed with two armor-piercing Hellfire missiles, as more and more drones are these days."

He wrapped his arms back around me. "Remember when we went to Nellis last year?"

"Sure. The pilots of the Predator control them from there."

"Well, this orb is where the camera is housed." He pressed me against the counter edge.

I was thinking about Victoria's question about the radio frequency a Backpack UAV uses compared to one that could detonate an IED. I wanted to know, but I couldn't ask. I wouldn't ask. He told me about Abu Ali al-Harithi when it happened. No one knows that I know. He had taken me into his confidence. There's been a price on my husband's head in the Middle East for years because when he and his team go out at night, someone ends up dead, and they all go back and sleep like babies. It wouldn't help matters if that bit of information on Harithi was public knowledge.

I picked up the photograph and pointed to the red and white scarf tied around his neck. "You're still wearing a shemagh? This time of year?"

As I spoke he took some of his weight off me. "Yeah. They're not just for mosquitos and flies anymore. They help with the smell of dead bodies."

I involuntarily dropped the photo at his harsh words. "Can I make a suggestion? Why don't you just not kill anyone? Then you won't have to worry about the odor."

He stepped back. "I'm sorry."

I changed the subject back to UAVs. "Do you use backpack UAVs?"

"Yeah." He tapped the photograph. "Whether we've used the hellfire missiles on a drone or called in the A-10s, sometimes we send in the backpack version for confirmation of the kill or to see if we had any civilian casualties. With CAS, uh, do you remember what …?" and he trailed off.

That *do you remember* stung. "Close air support, sure."

"My guys have a Backpack UAV you download a mission plan into. The operator on the ground can update the plan using RF… "

"Radio frequency."

"Yes, radio frequency signals, and it can keep going even if it loses the signal!"

"You sound excited, or what passes for excitement for you," I said to my stoic but sexy husband.

That was quite enough, and I knew I needed to back away. "We have an appointment."

"Waaait a minute. Your peace people aren't down on UAVs, are you? Come on. It's the Backpack UAV that can keep us from walking into a trap. They increase our situational awareness. Usually the mission is manned by …"

"Staffed."

"Manned."

"Staffed."

He inhaled and then huffed. "Staffed by soldiers that specialize in communications. Intelligence depends on a system of systems. The program isn't perfect, you're never going to have complete intelligence during a war …"

"The fog of war," I interjected, clumsily, embarrassingly trying to show I could still fit into his world.

"Exactly. Some I use are launched with a bungee. We've found weapons caches with them. The security forces use them. Sweetheart, puh-leez. Tell your peace-nik posse, or whatever they are, that UAVs, excuse me, unstaffed aerial vehicles are not nukes or anything."

"Just tell me this. Why are they called Backpack UAVs? At that size how could they be anything but unmanned?"

"Don't you mean unstaffed?" Then he looked down at the photo, up at me and then back down to the photo. Both our smiles started at the same second, and then we were kissing.

"We need to hurry. I'll dry my hair and be right down."

I heard a groan, "They couldn't be manned, could they?"

When I came back downstairs he put the newspaper down and waited at the garage door. Abby was right under foot.

"Abby, stay." He reached down and scratched the top of her head.

"You'll be the man of the house until I get back." I blew her a kiss.

His head jerked just a little and as he opened the door for me, and I saw his jaw grind.

Seventeen

Continuation of statement by Leigh Reed. We were shown into a room with two massage tables at High Hill Spa. The air was saturated with that complicated spa smell produced by mingling herbs, oils and essences. Ordinarily, I love that smell. I shrugged off my terry cloth robe and climbed onto a table. The General watched as I scooted under the blanket, then rolled onto a table. Ronald and Dwayne, the masseurs, joined us just a few minutes later. Ronald walked over to me and winked with his back to my husband. That calmed my fears that someone would mention Tiara Investigations. We had the first half hour of bliss. Then the masseurs left the room for us to turn over.

My husband got up from his massage table and leaned over me, stroking my back and kissing my neck. "Happy anniversary."

I smiled. He wasn't always with me for our anniversary, but he always remembered. "I have to say you've seemed happier this last year than you have for a long time. Is it all right if I retire? " Then he had to get back on his table, because either Ronald or Dwayne knocked to come back in.

"Retire? Happy anniversary to me."

"And to me." He smiled and nodded.

Then it hit me. I hadn't gotten him a gift or a card. Oops. I had forgotten to roll over while the guys were out of the room. Double oops. And what would happen to Tiara Investigations if he was home all the time?

I rolled over, keeping as much modesty as I could. I saw The General's eyebrows hood over, his eyes and his jaw tighten.

When the massages were over, we were left alone to put on our robes before returning to the dressing rooms. At least those were our instructions. When I got up from the massage table, my husband picked me up in his arms. Then he sat on the chaise lounge in the corner of the room with me on his lap, both of us were completely covered in massage oil. He pulled me down and down and down. At one point there was a knock on the door. He jumped up, and I whispered in his ear, "Nail me, don't mail me." After that we started giggling and decided it was time to get dressed and re-enter that other world. As we put on our robes we could not stop smiling at one another. The smiles said, "I know you, and you know me."

Before we left the room he took my face in his hands, "I've been in a war zone for six years, but you are going to be the death of me yet."

I floated down the hall to the dressing room, thinking how lucky I was to be married to him, then how lucky I was not to have gotten caught. This was what I was thinking as I walked past the pedicure room. The barbershop-like client chairs were facing the floor-to-ceiling windows that looked out on the rear courtyard, which was crowded with urns of fall flowers. I stopped dead in my tracks. I was looking at the back of Detective Kent's head. I recognized it easily, having seen so much of it in the last week. I hadn't pegged him as the pedicure type. Then I saw who his pedicurist was, and surprise escalated to stun. It was Tara. She saw me, and while her eyes were mostly on Kent's feet her expression said, "Just keep walking," and I did.

While I was dressing there was a quick series of knocks on the door, "Three dog night." I let Tara in. "You're grinning like you're running for mayor."

"I just got lucky," I bragged. "When did you go on the payroll here?"

"It was all I could think to do."

Then there was a gentle, almost inaudible tap on the door. "Did you know Eve Wood? Let me in."

We opened the door just wide enough for Victoria to join us. She held an eight by ten photo up for us to see.

I took the photo from her. "What am I looking for?" I had to remind myself to keep my voice down.

Victoria pointed to someone in the background looking at Kelly Taylor and her brother, Michael.

"That's Detective Kent, isn't it?"

Victoria nodded.

Tara took the photograph and held it away. "That's hot. That's metal-anything-left-in-the-sun-hot. That explains a lot."

Ordinarily I can follow Tara, but that time I had no idea what she was talking about. "What does it explain?"

Victoria put her hand on my arm. "Allow me. He must have left the hotel pretty soon after us, meaning he's not a snuggler. Which explains how he has time to follow us." Ohhhh.

Tara beamed at her apprentice. "By the way and for what it's worth, Ronald was telling me that Detective Kent takes all his girlfriends to Buford Dam."

Victoria put the photos back in her handbag. "Gives a whole new meaning to 'shoot the hooch,' doesn't it?" Then she giggled. "Shooting the hooch" means rafting down a section of the Chattahoochee in north Atlanta.

I resumed dressing. "Hon, that's one of those comments that sounds like it means something, but it doesn't."

"You had sex with Shorty!" Tara gave her a high five.

"Ms. Reed? Do you need anything?" the attendant asked.

"I'm fine, thanks." Then in a whisper, "I've got to get out of here. I'll call you this afternoon after my husband leaves."

"We should have our eavesdropping devices pretty soon, or have you forgotten?"

"No, Tara, I haven't, but aren't they really just hearing aids?"

Victoria was getting exasperated. "Can we talk about business before you go?"

"Are you okay?" Tara and I asked at the same time.

"I'm fed up with Detective Kent. This is how I felt when I found out some little bastard at school was bullying Aidan."

"When was this?" Even I was appalled, and you know how I feel about kids.

"When he was six."

"And the little bastard was six?" Tara stared, because of how she feels about kids.

"Okay, glad we cleared that up, but I don't see what that has to do with Detective Pedicure, out there. Do you feel bullied?"

"He's trying to bully Tiara Investigations." I guess she had heard herself calling a six-year-old a bastard, because she changed the subject. "Anyway, last night I figured out how to open those hidden folders. David Taylor was tracking how often a Backpack UAV recorded an IED exploding. It was quite often."

"A grateful nation thanks you." As I said it, I wondered if my flip answer meant I was choosing my husband over Tiara. I pushed this line of thought away and paid attention to her.

"Too often for it to be a coincidence. Plus, I found out the software was only applicable to Backpack UAVs, not Predators."

"Leigh, explain again, what detonates an IED?"

"Some use passive infrared sensors, like those used to turn on your outside lights with a motion sensor when someone walks by. These are particularly awful, because they don't emit a signal before they detonate. Others use a command wire, and still others use a wireless device to detonate, like a cell phone."

"Are you thinking what I'm thinking?"

This time I really was. "That the Backpack UAVs are detonating the IEDs?"

"Is that possible?" Tara asked. "And wouldn't that be a good thing?"

"Only if you knew it was going to happen. Operators can be very close to a backpack UAV. For instance, if it's being used to see around a wall. I've got to go, let's talk about this as soon as he leaves."

"Wait." Tara stopped us. "What does this have to do with China?"

Victoria and I looked at her. "You always ask the right questions."

"But what's the answer?"

"No idea." I turned to go.

"No idea." Victoria got behind me for the door.

"How can we prevent any more from being shipped?" Tara asked.

"Another salient and significant question. Victoria, good luck with it."

"Wait." This time both spoke, and they grabbed my shoulders.

"Can we talk about this later? My husband is waiting and I have to get out there before he wonders where I am."

Victoria still hadn't moved her feet. "I owe both of you an apology."

"I accept your apology."

"We don't know what she did!" Tara wasn't moving.

"Probably nothing. You know how she is. I gotta go!"

"*She* is standing right here. I want to apologize for taking so long to get to this answer. David Taylor was so smart I didn't want to believe he could make a mistake. That's all I wanted to say. Bye."

I stuck my hand out, and they did the same. We did our signature move and gave air kisses. Finally, one at a time, we slunk out of the dressing room

A minute later I was dragging my husband out the door and trying to keep him from looking back inside. "I think I saw a guy I know in there. He's a police detective. He's good people."

Oh, he's just great, I thought.

"Jerome something."

"Kent." Then I caught myself, but a little too late.

"Oh, you know him?"

"I've met him." I was careful of my tone.

"Let's go before he sees us and tries to start a conversation."

"Foxtrot Alpha," which means that works for me. Okay, that's more or less what it means.

Eighteen

Continuation of statement by Leigh Reed. We had a little alone time before the car came to take him to the air field. I was in the kitchen getting a water bottle out for him. I scrounged around for cookies or anything else he might like for the flight.

"Would you like peanut butter and crackers?" I yelled up the stairs.

"Sure." He joined me and walked to the other side of the kitchen and got a plastic freezer bag out of the drawer by the sink. My breath caught because it meant he didn't feel like a visitor in the house. I felt truly happy. In the cupboard I got out the peanut butter and the kind of crackers he likes with it. I was struggling to open the jar and didn't notice that he was reaching for it until our eyes met.

"I remember when you would have handed me the jar without a second thought."

"I don't think the new way is a bad thing."

He went over to his canvas luggage, stopped in front of it and sighed. He took his wallet out of his pocket and his watch off and put both of those in the freezer bag. These he replaced with those in his luggage.

"Why do you do that?" Until I spoke I hadn't realized I was holding my breath, waiting for a response to my last comment.

He slowly turned to face me. "Because I don't want a single speck of sand to touch you," he looked up at the ceiling, "or here."

"I wrote to Roger Wilson's mother." He looked down and shook his head, but when I walked over and rubbed his back, he shrugged me off. I guessed it was still too raw. It never doesn't hurt. I turned to walk back to the sink, but suddenly his arms were wrapped around me, pulling me back.

"I guess I can't keep every bad thing from you."

"Don't worry. I'm tougher than you are." I punched his arm.

"Is that right?"

"Yeah, you hold your nose when you go underwater."

"You sleep with a night light on," he countered.

"You look both ways before crossing the street." He pulled me to him and kissed my forehead.

Then he let me go to talk about his travel plans for the next few days. "I'll be in Washington, staying on the base at Fort Myers. This afternoon and tomorrow I'll be on the Hill and at briefings in the building," meaning the Pentagon. "On Thursday I'll leave for London to conduct a briefing for allies."

First I snickered. Then I started laughing with tears running down my face. He smiled. "You're thinking about the last time we were in England together, aren't you? I was an Army brat and a city boy, okay? I'm never going to live that down, am I?"

I still couldn't speak. The countryside had been dotted with sheep and cattle. My husband had seen a calf in a pasture and had mistaken it for a pig, and I had said, "Yeah, it's a grazing pig. One of those English grazing pigs." My laughter died away, and I wiped my face with my fingertips. The conditions of my life at the time made this seemingly insignificant moment stick in my mind. I had been relaxed and laughing. My husband, worshipped by many, feared by many more, hadn't known a pig from a calf, and his appendage-slash-wife had. He hadn't caught my sarcasm either. He didn't know that pigs don't graze. What was wrong with that picture? Thinking about those years, I felt any consideration of telling him about Tiara Investigations slip away.

"You will meet me in London, right?"

I jerked my head up. "Of course."

He pulled back and stared at me.

"I said I would be there."

"You pick our hotel."

"How about some place in Mayfair? We haven't stayed there in a while. Or someplace near a good pub. I want to go to a pub every night."

"Well, decide. I'll call you when I land in DC, and you can let me know then."

I smiled, knowing good and well that he would call me before his plane took off.

Too soon, the car was there, but we took our time saying good-bye. The military flight out of Dobbins Air Reserve Base couldn't leave until he got there, so I kissed my husband one more time. His ribbons dug into my cheek, but we wanted to stay like that forever.

Finally, I pushed him away and told him I would see him on Friday.

"I almost forgot. There was a message on the phone. Someone named Paul called to tell you that Tara had explained the note to him. She told him she was on a diet and had written the note to remind herself not to eat at some restaurant until she lost weight. Does that make sense?" I was wishing he hadn't remembered every damn word, because again I was holding my breath.

"Paul Armistead is Tara's boyfriend. He's been worried about her."

"If he worries every time Tara does something bizarre, that poor man is going to be worried all the time."

"Do you ever worry about me?"

"Should I?"

"No, sometimes I think it would be nice, but then I remember I would rather you have your mind on keeping yourself safe than worrying about me, an adult capable of managing my own life."

"Hey," here he raised my chin so I had to look at him, "there's no shame in having someone watch your back."

"You'll really retire and watch my back?"

"Yes, and I'll watch your front, too."

The car was in the driveway, and a lieutenant walked up to me with a big smile. "Did the yellow ribbon fall off your car? Do you want me to get you another, Ma'am?"

"No, thanks. People might think I support this war if I have one on my car."

"You do support the troops, right?" I could tell he wanted to dig a hole and fall in it as soon as he heard himself say this to a general's wife.

"I do not support this war, but I support American troops. One in particular."

"We're there so we can have a more peaceful world."

"A war for peace? By the way, I think it's interesting the ribbons are magnetic."

My husband jumped in the car, "She's gonna blow! Get in the car and drive!" As they pulled out he blew me a kiss and mouthed, "Friday."

I was praying that it would be so and that by then I would not have to be "available." When the car cleared the hill I thought, *whew*. It scared me to think that I was relieved that he was gone so I could get back to my real life. I would go for a jog with Abby and think. I remembered to tuck my cell phone into my waistband in case Victoria or Tara needed to reach me, that's how back in my element I was. Our rule was that when The General was in town, they were not to use the landline.

I didn't take the time to warm up, I ran full out. Abby looked up at me like I was crazy. Simply for me to be his wife was all he had ever asked, and I had done that as long as I could. I packed and moved and waited and walked around foreign cities, and then I started all over again. Finally, it was time for me to have a home. I used money I inherited from my grandmother and bought the house outright. I had researched Atlanta homes on the internet for months. Then I told my husband I was going home. He took leave and found me. I hadn't made it hard. I had kept my cell phone, and when he called I gave him directions to Hartfield Hills and to the house. He had said, "Who lives here?"

"We do."

"Then show me the bedroom." And so I did. Later he said, "This is how I tell where I stand." Just like that, it was settled that we would be okay. I prayed we would stay that way.

Nineteen

Continuation of statement by Leigh Reed. I was jogging back to the cul-de-sac when I saw Kerry Lee sitting in a green Buick Park Avenue, looking like he smelled something bad. I didn't like it. Where was Detective Kent when I needed him? Abby and I ran up the drive to the community swimming pool and clubhouse rather than turning onto my street. The hill is steep, but with adrenaline pumping I didn't feel a thing. I was reaching for my cell phone and speed dialing Tara. She said she would pick Victoria up, and they would put our back-up-emergency-oh-shit plan into effect. No detective agency should be without one of those.

Mr. Lee turned on his engine from time to time, and each time I thought he might be leaving. That would have been fine with me, but he was just running the air conditioner and cooling off.

A half hour later they called back as they were entering the subdivision. I jogged back down the hill to the car. Tara and Victoria parked in a nearby driveway. When I was a few yards away, they jumped out of Tara's car with Stephie and Mr. Benz tumbling out after them, and we surrounded the Buick. The dogs were already yelping.

Mr. Lee was surprised, to say the least, and started the engine to make a speedy exit. Tara tried the passenger side door and joined him in the car. Not wanting company, I guess, he jumped out. He faced forward, and Victoria was behind him. She thought he was about to attack me, so she used her best kick boxing DVD move to kick him in the pants. Tara climbed over the console into the driver's seat in an attempt to get out of the car to help her. The pressure of Tara's thigh on the gear selector caused the car to switch from park to neutral. The car drove right over Mr. Lee's foot. He let out a yelp. Tara, however, looked unperturbed. Botox.

Either Stephie or Mr. Benz squatted and peed on Lee's other foot. I didn't know which dog it was, and it didn't much matter. Stephie looked up at me, and I saw Tara had painted a black beauty mark right on her beard.

I expected just another pain cry from Lee, but what I heard was, "Stop, I'll tell you what you want to know."

I wanted to ask him to repeat it, but I stopped myself in time. "It may be too late, you've made her mad." I gave Tara a quick look and added, "She's been in trouble with the law since the day she was born," quoting the opening song from *The Dukes of Hazzard* and hoping it didn't sound familiar to him.

Victoria stepped up. "We can't always control her when she gets like this, so you better just put your head between your legs and kiss your ass good-bye."

"Please try!" Lee begged.

The car had rolled off his foot, and Tara shifted to park and put the emergency brake on. Victoria gave the dogs the sit command.

"Tell you what, we'll take you to the hospital, and you talk. If you stop talking, we stop the car. As long as you talk, we drive." I thought it was a fair bargain.

"Does she have to be in the car? I want to know."

"No, but she'll be following us, and if we pull over she'll intervene. Understood?" Victoria sounded tough.

"Yes, let's just go."

I opened my front door and let the dogs inside while Victoria situated Lee in the back seat of his car. She drove, and I sat in the back seat with him. As promised Tara followed us in the Hummer. He told quite a tale on the way to Gwinnett County General.

I began to question him, "Did David Taylor do any work on a Chinese satellite program?"

"The Chinese?" he sounded truly surprised, then a light came on. "He wasn't really involved with the Chinese. He called what he was doing the China Program. CINA is the acronym. It stands for corrective, intentional, negative application. Uh, is that your cell phone?"

"Yeah, I'm sorry. Would you excuse me? I need to answer this." I saw it was Tara on my caller ID, as well as in the rear view mirror.

"It's me! Be sure he's telling the truth."

"How?"

"Tell him what my Dad always told me, 'You know you go to hell for lying just like you do for stealing.'"

I looked over at him. "You know you go to hell for lying just like you do for stealing." He just stared at me.

Victoria was concentrating on her driving but spoke up. "Was the signal emitting from the Backpack UAVs detonating the IEDs?"

He grunted in the affirmative.

"Does this CINA program correct it?"

He grunted again.

We were doing pretty good replacing our incorrect assumptions about China, but we knew we should stop while we were ahead and let him talk. "I figured his program caused it, why shouldn't he spend his time correcting it? Then one day out of the blue, Kelly Taylor phoned me."

Victoria and I were stunned. Maybe more experienced private detectives wouldn't admit that, and to our credit, we kept our mouths shut. Had we been that wrong about her?

He had met Kelly at a company dinner, and she called him the next work day. "She knew about the flaw in the program and wanted it kept quiet. Her husband, on the other hand, planned to report it to the Pentagon. She said if The Peachtree Group paid her a substantial amount of money, she could guarantee he wouldn't report it. I didn't know if she was acting on behalf of her husband or shaking us down was her plan. She said her husband's career would be ruined even if his corrective patch worked, and our company would go under. There she may have been right.

"Look, I don't want The Peachtree Group paying settlements and losing the contract, but I'm first and foremost concerned with casualties. The controllers are never far from a Backpack UAV, and when the IED is powerful enough, there are casualties." He had stopped looking at me sometime during the speech, and he kept his eyes on the cloth back of the front seat. "Finally, I decided to meet with Taylor and find out if he was in on it or not. He was shot that night."

"If you didn't kill David Taylor, who did?"

"His grieving widow. I saw her."

We left Mr. Lee at Gwinnett County Medical Center. As I led Victoria away, she was still thanking him profusely for helping us, and Tara was apologizing for the broken bones in his foot. Tara said she would pay his hospital bill, and Victoria left the Tiara phone number for him to call if he needed anything. Anything at all.

"Do you think he was telling the truth?" I had waited until we were in the parking lot to speak.

Victoria rubbed her forehead. "Remember, one of the hidden files on that disk was a chart of when and where IEDs exploded, and there was a Backpack UAV close enough to either film it or be destroyed by it. At first David Taylor thought a satellite signal might be the cause, but when he tried to correlate the explosions with which satellite was passing overhead, there was no match. That much fits."

"I wonder if any other communications network systems have been affected. Victoria, did you see any mention of the Joint Tactical Radio System? JTRS is the acronym, and Jitters is what it's called."

"I don't remember seeing any of those terms."

"It's a radio and data system for all the service branches. How about Blue Force Tracking System, or BFT? Does that sound familiar? It tracks the location of friendly forces."

"Nope."

I shook my head. "We should have figured out this had nothing to do with China. Remember when Kelly Taylor said neither she nor David had ever traveled outside the country? Wouldn't he have gone to China to negotiate the contract?"

"Nothing to do with China?" We forgot Tara wasn't in on what Kerry Lee had said during the car ride over, including accusing Kelly Taylor of murdering her husband, and we caught her up.

"I'm having a hard time believing that she was involved in her husband's business."

"Remember, she took a while to come to the door after the shooting," Victoria said.

Tara clicked the doors open. "It was the guy the dogs were tracking that killed David Taylor!"

"There's just one problem with that theory." I climbed in the backseat.

"What's that?"

"Our dogs have no idea how to track."

"Okay. It was the guy our dogs were chasing to see if he had a chew toy in his pocket. Better?"

I turned around to scan the other cars on the road. "Hey, where is Detective Kent?"

Tara checked the mirrors. "You're right. We haven't seen him since this morning when he got his pedicure."

"We need to tell him all this. Troops are close to Backpack UAVs." I got my cell phone out of my new Delvaux handbag.

"When did you get this?" Tara shrieked.

"My husband gave it to me. Our anniversary was yesterday."

"Oooh!"

"And he wrote 'I wish we were together every time I see your face' on the card." I finished dialing Detective Kent's cell phone, but there was no answer. "Let's go to the station."

Tara turned onto Highway Twenty, heading southeast to the precinct office at the Mall of Georgia. "So the part about David Taylor's product is consistent with what we know, but does it track with what we know about Kelly Taylor?"

I closed my phone. "I fault her for blaming anyone she can for anything that happens to her. But as far as being a murderer, I can't believe anyone raised by Beatrice would go so wrong."

"She seems isolated and lonely but not a traitor to her country or an embezzler," Victoria said.

"Or a husband killer." Tara was clutching the steering wheel so hard her knuckles were white. "Relocating for a hubby's career has made a lot of women do crazy things. I'll give you that. My sister used to pull the Jehovah's Witnesses right in to her living room by their neckties. It'd scare the bejesus out of them. Anyway, Kelly has such a sweet way of looking at the world."

We stopped talking as we traversed the parking lot of the Gwinnett County police station. I looked around for the Ford Escort but it wasn't there.

"He's not here right now," the good-looking young officer at the desk told us. Actually, he was addressing Tara, who was leaning over said desk.

"Did he say where he was going?"

"He was going to check on the local parks, take some paper work over to the Hartfield Hills City Hall and then take care of some personal business."

"Would you ask him to call Leigh when he returns? He has the number."

We sat in the Hummer and discussed our next move. "Leigh, where to?"

"Going to check out the parks? We know which one. Detective Jerome Kent is up to his old tricks."

"What if he's not at Buford Dam? Maybe we should pay Kelly Taylor and Beatrice a visit first," Victoria suggested.

"Good idea," I said. "Let's do that first. I'd like to talk to them."

Tara pulled her cell phone out and dialed the number. After a brief conversation she hung up. "Beatrice answered. Kelly's not there. She went to Buford Dam for a walk."

We looked at each other, and Tara put the Hummer in gear. She laid rubber as we left the police parking lot. I'm not sure that was the best idea of the day, but no one followed us. They probably thought it was one of their officers. To get to the dam we had to drive all the way through Hartfield Hills.

"Victoria, do you still have those mall photos in your bag?"

She rummaged through and handed me the envelope. I looked closer, and I didn't stop looking when I found Kent in the photo as we had that morning. "Here's Kerry Lee watching Kelly and her brother."

Tara speeded up. "You mean Savannah Westmoreland, don't you?"

"But, why …?" Victoria started. "I mean, if he wanted to get away from her, why was he following her?"

We would have to finish the conversation later because we were at Lake Lanier's West Park. I heard voices and sprinted down the trail, trying not to slide on the pine straw. Vic and Tara were right behind me.

The couple stood by the lake. Kelly was facing Detective Kent. He glanced away from her, a look of confusion on his face. While his head was turned, she pulled out a small handgun.

A shot rang out, and Detective Kent's mouth opened in shock. He fell forward toward Kelly, who started screaming. I mean loud, too. That young lady has got some lungs on her. He fell onto her, and she slumped under his weight, dropping her gun.

I ran over and picked it up. It was cool to the touch. I looked over at Victoria and Tara. We saw the hole in his shirt, and we realized at the same time that he had been shot in the back. A fine piece of detective work there.

We heard the rustle of leaves, and Gina Kent walked into the clearing. I realized something else, too. There was no blood. He was wearing a bulletproof vest. I held my finger up to my lips for Gina to keep quiet. He was out cold for the time being, and he never needed to know who shot him. What they say about no good deed going unpunished is true.

She walked up and turned him over with her hiking boot. Then she aimed her gun at his head. I threw down Kelly's gun and shoved Gina. Tara and Victoria were there in a split second, and they sat on her. That was when we heard the cock of a rifle. We looked into the woods to our left and there was Beatrice Englund walking toward us.

"You girls okay? Need any back up?"

"Mom?" Kelly looked confused.

"Baby, you weren't going to kill a policeman, were you?"

"No, this is what I was going to do." Too late I saw she had picked up her gun. She slowly raised it to her temple.

"No, baby, no." Her mother stopped and just stretched her arms to her, the hunting rifle under her arm.

"Kelly, what about your baby?" I asked. She dropped her head and then her arms and shrugged her shoulders.

Beatrice was moving slowly forward. "Why did you want Detective Kent to see you kill yourself?"

Kelly didn't answer.

"You wanted to tell him something, didn't you?" She nodded her head, just barely, but I saw it and pushed on. "You wanted to tell him that Kerry Lee killed David." I could feel Victoria and Tara's eyes on me. I hadn't held out on them. I was just then figuring this all out.

Kelly's little girl voice was hard to hear. "Kerry Lee kept pressuring me to tell him what you three were doing, where you were and what you had learned. I told him I didn't know and that what I did know was that you were trying to help me." She looked her mother in the eye. "I know when people help me, Mom. I tried to tell *him* about Kerry Lee." She tapped Kent with the toe of her pump. "But he just ignored me."

"We've got to get Kerry Lee!" Tara yelled as she got up off Gina.

"Get Kerry Lee? Are you forgetting we are the only ones here not armed?" Victoria's voice of reason reminded us of that most important fact.

Gina Kent got up off the ground, walked around and picked up her handgun. "And I thought I had problems." She was walking off but stopped at the path and turned around. "He's not even worth shooting." She pointed at Detective Kent. Unfortunately, she was pointing with her gun and my heart skipped a beat. But pointing was all she did.

"By the way, thanks for this." She threw a crumpled photograph at her husband unconscious on the ground. "I never would have found this place without it. Now, how do I get out of here?"

"Is that what I think it is?" Tara asked.

"It's one of the photos she took from us." It was of the West Park entrance sign.

By this time Beatrice was at her daughter's side. With one hand she took the gun away from Kelly and handed it behind her back to Tara. Then she put an arm around her daughter. She turned her around and walked back out of the woods with her. She was speaking gently to her and rubbing her back. I couldn't take my eyes off of them.

The idea that Tiara Investigations was the child I never had hit me like a ton of bricks, but I couldn't think about that yet.

We sat down around Detective Kent. I looked down at him. He was out cold. "I wonder how long this is going to last? We need to be sure Kerry Lee doesn't leave the hospital."

Tara handed the gun to Victoria who put it in her jacket pocket. Then she leaned over and lay down on her side, propping herself on her elbow. She pulled his cell phone off his belt as we watched. "Remember this is a walkie talkie, too. There must be a button for that. Here it is. Breaker, breaker."

"Thirty years ago," I said. "Say, come in."

"Come in," she said but more like she was welcoming someone at her front door.

"Is this Detective Kent's radio? Ma'am, put the Detective on the line."

"He's using the bathroom. I have something very important to tell you. It's a message from him."

I whispered, "Send a few officers to Gwinnett General Hospital and guard Kerry Lee. Do not let him leave until you hear from Detective Kent."

"Did you hear that?"

"I still need to talk to the Detective, ma'am."

Said detective stirred, moaned and found himself lying next to Tara eyeball to eyeball. "Well, hello." Then he was out again.

"Thank you, Detective Kent. I'll call the hospital now." Tara replaced the phone on his belt.

Victoria got to her feet. "When did you figure out Kerry Lee killed David?"

"I think all three of us have been feeling like we were overlooking something. By the way, why does overlook mean you didn't see something, but overheard means you did hear something? Just wondering.

"Anyway, remember when we talked about competing in a triathlon? Victoria suggested the biathlon, and I said that she meant duathlon. A biathlon is cross-country skiing and sharp shooting. That reminded me I had seen a biathlon trophy in his office. It dawned on me that David Taylor's killer had to have been an excellent marksman. Remember, it was one shot to the heart."

"Wow," Tara said.

"I remembered seeing that little trophy in his office of a skier with a rifle over his shoulder. I knew then that he had the ability to shoot from a distance. Then he must have made the same mistake we did about the man Kelly was spending time with. He was at the mall making sure Kelly was good and incriminated."

"It was Savannah Westmoreland that got us to the Mall to see them and to Cracker Barrel on Monday morning so you would be attacked!" Victoria enjoyed seeing all the pieces fit together too.

Tara was still lying beside Kent. "He would have seen us on Friday night and thought he could pay someone to scare us off the case. It was Lee that James Goody was referring to. That connects the two of them."

"Let's face it, we violated one of our rules. We trusted a scared person."

"He was scared after Tara ran over his foot."

"He was scared before that. He knew we were getting closer and closer to the truth. He knew we stayed in the building, eluding his security measures and connecting The Peachtree Group to the murder, and he knew we would never go away."

"So what he told you on the way to the hospital was a lie?" Tara propped herself up on her elbow.

"Oh, I think some of it was true, just not the whole story. I think he wanted to stop David from correcting the software so his company could keep the lucrative military contract. Victoria, do you have the flash drive with you?"

"Yes."

"Do you think the insurgents ever knew they had a way to destroy American UAVs?"

"I didn't see any indication they had intentionally attracted a Backpack UAV in order to destroy it."

Tara reached over and rubbed my arm. "That means you don't have to tell your husband about this. He would want to know how you knew, and you would have to tell him about Tiara Investigations."

"We need to tell someone since the defective ones are still out there. But who should we report it to, the FBI?"

"We need to stop The Peachtree Group from shipping any more out." Victoria pushed her glasses up.

We looked at Tara, the attorney in the group. "Let's tell Detective Kent. He can take credit for as much of it as he wants when he turns it over to the FBI. They'll take the matter to the appropriate military investigative office, and they can get the answer to your question about other communications systems being compromised." Amazingly enough, she seemed to have forgotten she had a man lying next to her.

Then Detective Kent moaned again and tried to get up. Unfortunately when he did he rolled over onto Tara. After a roll or two in the pine straw, rather than the hay, they extricated themselves. Victoria helped Tara, and I helped Kent, get up. He moaned and removed his shirt and then looked at his bulletproof vest.

He felt around his torso. "I guess getting knocked out is a small price to pay for this thing saving my life." While he was doing that I leaned down and picked up the photograph and stuffed it in my waistband.

"The bullet hole's in the back." Tara trailed off because he was no longer listening to her. He turned and looked at me because I was standing behind him.

"Oh, no, you didn't ..."

"No! Good Lord, no. I didn't shoot you."

"I don't guess you saw anything?"

"We heard a shot and found you on the ground." The other Tiara detectives jerked their heads in my direction, but other than that they were cool as cucumbers.

Victoria moved to stand in front of him. "We're wasting time talking. We figured out who killed David Taylor. It was Kerry Lee from The Peachtree Group."

"What evidence do you have for that accusation?"

We hadn't put our heads together to decide how much to tell him, so I had to think fast. "We just went through all of that. Somebody ought to invent a jacket that doesn't cause short-term memory loss."

"I'll call for back up and go pick him up. He's probably at his office." Detective Kent winced.

Tara jumped in, "Well, see, I didn't mean to, but I ..."

"He's not there," I interrupted her. "He had an accident, and he's at Gwinnett General."

"I need to call an officer to go and guard him at the hospital."

"You already did," Victoria said. "Hmm, memory loss. You better have your head looked at."

"Wait, if Kerry Lee is in the hospital, who shot me? None of you saw or heard anyone leaving the woods?"

"No."

"Sorry."

"Nope." When Victoria spoke, he turned and glared. I guess he had expected more of her, at least.

"For the love of Pete."

We helped him to his car and waited for him to leave. Victoria could hardly wait for us to talk. "Why didn't you tell him his wife shot him?"

"I have no idea." While I tried to think of the reason, Detective Kent's car peeled out of the parking lot, spraying gravel. "No harm, no foul?"

Tara looked at me and then Victoria, "As Whitney Houston would say, 'ain't it shocking what love can do?' Anywho, I think he knows what his own wife is capable of, and that's why he never stopped suspecting Kelly Taylor."

Okay, so that completes my statement. That's how we saved the world. And how we saved our worlds with a day to spare, a well-spent spa day, that is. Now I have to catch a plane to London. I wonder if they give couples massages there.

Leigh Reed

P.S. Was this office decorated by the Gwinnett County Police? You'll want to do something about that.

Epilogue

I was able to join my husband in London. On Thursday night I sat down in my business class seat and collapsed. I had already planned to use the flight to do some serious life evaluation thinking. I was deceiving my husband, as Victoria was Shorty. How long could we keep up these double lives?

My cell phone rang. Victoria had sent me a photo of Tara sitting on a bright yellow scooter with three or four sales people, more specifically salesmen, around her. The text read, "What color do you want?"

I hugged the phone to my heart. Then I typed in *army green.* I would have it all a little longer.

Meet Author Lane Stone

Lane is a native Atlantan and graduate of Georgia State University. She, her husband, Larry Korb, and the real Abby divide their time between Sugar Hill, Georgia, and Alexandria, Virginia. She's a member of both the Chessie Chapter and the Atlanta Chapter of Sisters in Crime.

Look for the second book in the Tiara Investigations Mystery series, *Domestic Affairs*. And coming soon, *Foreign Affairs.*

If you like a little romance with your suspense, check out *Maltipoos Are Murder* by Jacqui Lane, aka Jacqueline Corcoran and Lane Stone.

www.LaneStoneBooks.com

Made in United States
North Haven, CT
23 March 2022

17448117R00134